UNNATURAL SELECTION

DOUG STEWART

AN EVEN MONEY BOOK
LOS ANGELES

Even Money Press
Los Angeles
Copyright © 2015 by Doug Stewart
Second printing. April 2018.
All rights reserved.
evenmoney.press
ISBN 978-0-9962204-2-2

Front photo: South Massif and the Taurus-Littrow Valley.
Back photo: Footprints in the dust; South Massif.
Photos courtesy of NASA.

BY THE MEANS
OF NATURAL
SELECTION

I have called this principle, by which each slight variation, if useful, is preserved, by the term of Natural Selection, in order to mark its relation to man's power of selection. We have seen that man by selection can certainly produce great results, and can adapt organic beings to his own uses, through the accumulation of slight but useful variations, given to him by the hand of Nature. But Natural Selection, as we shall hereafter see, is a power incessantly ready for action, and is as immeasurably superior to man's feeble efforts, as the works of Nature are to those of Art.

Charles Darwin [*On the Origin of Species by the Means of Natural Selection, Or the Preservation of Favored Races in the Struggle for Life*]

PROLOGUE

"I just met him that one time over at his place."

It was early June, and very hot. By the time they got there from the airport they were exhausted.

"This was up at his place in Portales Canyon?"

"Yeah, the last place he lived before he disappeared. I was there with a friend of his. Jack?"

He shook his head. "Ghana?"

"Before that. So Jack knocked and he said it's open, come on in." He smiled. "I guess he was expecting us."

"Why am I not surprised?"

"So we go in, but it's so dark in there we can't see anything. Not at first, anyway. Then I see him lying on a couch over by the sliding door out to the back deck. He said he'd get up but someone else had priority, and he pointed to this little kitten that was asleep on his legs. Just a little guy all stretched out in the sun."

"I've heard about his cats. Didn't he also have a parrot?"

"An African Grey. Messy, like a child, but smart."

"Because of the distance it looked like they were moving in slow motion. Just slowly drifting across the face of the moon." He was trying to explain to them how it looked. "But that's a quarter of a million miles, so we're talking about thousands of miles an hour."

They stared at him, trying to imagine what that must have looked like.

"Then, when they got closer, we could see these ropey smoke trails."

"Smoke trails?"

"I know, no atmosphere, but that's what they looked like, just hanging there." For a moment he stared out the sliding door at the palo verdes. "I was watching them on the monitors with the scientists. They were tracking everything with their equipment. Incredible magnification. They said it was dust and debris drifting in space. Then some of the smaller craft—by then we could see that's what they were—seemed to corkscrew away like something shoved them aside." He looked over at them with an odd smile. "The scientists said that meant something really big was up there. Perhaps there was even more than one. I guess their instruments were going crazy. Finally, they said the whole mess was headed our way, but by then that was pretty obvious."

"What did you do?"

"Do?" Setting the kitten aside, he sat up straight and laughed for a long time. "When I was a kid people used to make jokes about bomb shelters. I never knew anyone who actually had one, and no one took them very seriously, or at least serious people didn't, but the thought was that it was only a matter of time before the Russians nuked us. Then some of us would survive down in our bomb shelters breathing filtered air and eating canned goods. A few weeks later we'd crawl out and start all over again. At the time it seemed preposterous, but watching those damn things coming our way . . . well, suddenly it no longer seemed so foolish."

The other man shuffled his feet and looked away like he was embarrassed.

"No? So you think it's better to not even try?" He smiled. "That's probably how we thought when we were kids. That it was better to die a glorious, romantic death. Something hopelessly tragic and utterly pointless." He laughed again. "That's such bullshit. When you see it coming—when it's staring you right in the face—believe me, you'll do whatever it takes to stay alive, even if it's just for another five minutes."

2

"And you never reported any of this?" Jack knew he hadn't.

"At the time?"

"Yeah."

"Right. Hello, this is Sam Moss. Looks like we've got something here on the order of about an hour before it all ends in fire and ash." He smiled at them. "Now that *would* have been tragic. Wasting what little time I had on some pointless up-the-chain-of-command warning that no one was ever going to believe. Anyway, the scientists were already going nuts, so I thought, well, let them tell someone."

"Did they?"

"Yeah," he laughed. "Their wives."

"Seriously?"

"I take it you've never worked with scientists."

"So what did you do?"

"I went for a drive."

He stayed with the astronomers for as long as he dared, watching the visuals with them on their monitors as they became more and more agitated. Their reactions were interesting. Some were fascinated, barely able to restrain their excitement as they frantically tried to calculate speeds and how long it would be before whatever it was arrived, while others just sat there dumbfounded. But once they began talking about how they had less than an hour left he was out of there, focused solely on hoarding what little time remained as he bounded down six flights of stairs, not even willing to wait for the elevator, taking the steps two or three at a time, the metal staircase booming and shaking, the security alarm honking when he hit the crash bar at the bottom of the stairwell to open the outside door.

He used his key fob to unlock the car as he sprinted across the parking lot. A moment later he was waving to the guard as he flew past, barely slowing to drive around the small security barrier and out onto the main highway. There he stopped, faced with what he thought was probably his last decision: up to the top of the peak, or down to the desert floor below? Well, down *was* faster.

He was really sailing, his BMW floating, momentarily weightless as it crested each little rise. The first time he looked he was doing 115 miles an hour, 140 when he bottomed out in the next arroyo, then he slowed, 80, 60, until he pulled over on the gravel shoulder and stopped. He patted the cell phone in his pocket. No, this didn't feel like something he wanted to share. Solitude seemed better. More appropriate. He shielded his eyes with his hand and looked to the west. That's where they'd be entering the atmosphere. He turned on the radio and got out of the car, then leaned back against the fender. While it lasted it was going to be one hell of a show. He looked at his watch. Almost time.

"So what happened?"

"It was like the Fourth of July in broad daylight. Didn't you see any of it?"

Everyone was amazed by how few people actually had, but if you hadn't been in the right spot at the right time . . . and even then it didn't last for very long. It was the big stuff that came down first, and that was over pretty quickly, though the smaller stuff continued to rain down for weeks. Of course there were those grainy videos on YouTube, and many photos on the web of bright, streaking objects and smoke trails, but none of that was very informative, and whatever the government knew—and they certainly knew plenty—remained a secret.

"I heard it," Jack said, "but when I looked all I saw were smoke trails."

"Debris. There must have been some sort of aerial combat. None of what we saw actually made it down, or at least not in one piece."

The other man smiled. "Black-ops?" he asked. What bullshit.

Moss turned to stare at him. "Yes, well I suppose there's always the official explanation, for those who prefer that sort of thing."

"It could've been the space station breaking up," Jack said. "It did come down."

"Did it?" Moss smiled at him, wondering why anyone would be so willfully naïve. "I wonder what those guys up there had to say in that last transmission? Before it broke up. Too bad it's so garbled."

The two men looked at each other. It was easy to shrug this conspiracy stuff off when it cropped up on the Web, but hearing it from Moss made them both very uneasy.

"It sounds to me like Moss didn't have much to say."

"Oh?"

"Well, what did he say? That he saw something. *Some thing*. Lots of people said that. Those scientists certainly never said they saw anything like that."

"And that surprises you?"

"So that means you believe him?"

"I'm just telling you what he said. Now, do you want to hear the rest, or not?"

"Go ahead."

"So later that evening he began to loosen up. It was Jack. They went way back. Lots of reminiscing about the good old days and the guys they'd known. Getting up-to-date on old so-and-so and where he was and what he was doing. All this while we're sitting out back on the deck drinking beer and eating the turkey burgers he'd grilled. I was amazed by how well informed he was, what with him being a guy they'd branded a pariah. But that's how these guys are. It's an exclusive club. Once you're in you're never really out, and none of them give a damn for what the government says."

"That certainly hasn't changed."

"And we do?"

"Okay," he said, laughing. "So what did he say?"

"All sorts of things, but somewhere in there he and Jack started talking about this guy X they'd both known in the service."

"I thought they worked for those private contractors? The ones who do all the government's dirty work."

"They do, that's just their way of talking. Though most of them are ex-service in some sense."

"So they both knew this guy X in the service . . ."

"And Jack asked if he'd heard the story about X going down without a trace in a helicopter somewhere in Africa. He said, yeah, he'd heard that, but then he smiled."

"He was fucking with you."

"Of course he was. It's just their little game. But he clearly wanted to tell us. So Jack laughed and said that if what he'd heard wasn't true he'd sure like to know what was."

"Assuming anyone actually knows."

"Oh, he knew. He told Jack the story he'd heard was slightly different. In his, X supposedly died when his emergency reentry vehicle burned up in the atmosphere. Seems X was part of this big battle to save the earth."

"Seriously? Save the earth?" The other man shook his head.

"That he'd been one of the casualties that afternoon when we took on the bad guys."

"I don't suppose he happened to tell you who these bad guys were?"

"No, but he may not have known."

"How convenient. So this guy, X, I suppose this makes him some sort of hero."

"No . . . it makes him missing in action."

"Ah," he said, smiling.

"Exactly."

1

"Why don't you drop that down so I can see your back." She was pointing to his light blue gown, which he let slip off his shoulders as he lowered himself onto the examination table.

"Yes," she said, leaning forward to examine his back, touching the wound. "This *is* nasty. How on earth did this happen?"

"I fell on some broken glass."

She straightened up to look at him. "And landed on your back?"

"Not intentionally. Someone got pushed into me and we both landed on my back."

"You and Mr. Callender?" She'd seen him in the ER waiting to get his own stitches.

"He's the one. Journalist. Seemed like a nice guy, so I thought why not break his fall."

"Very considerate, but you certainly got the worst of it."

She poured hydrogen peroxide in a bowl and soaked some cotton swabs. "Just lean forward." She took her time, carefully cleaning the gash, then prodding a bit looking for glass shards, plucking them out with her forceps when she found some. "Sorry. Did that hurt?"

"What?"

"I asked if that hurt."

"Sure."

She studied his face. Relaxed, alert, pupils perfectly normal, not a touch of the gray pallor people commonly got when they're in shock.

"You're quite the stoic, aren't you?"

He chuckled and smiled at her. Little wrinkles around his eyes. "Actually, I prefer to think of myself as an epicurean."

Her eyes widening with surprise, she glanced at what her assistant had written in the log. She smiled. "It says here your name is . . . Chris Chapstick?"

"It is today."

"Oh?" She stepped back to stare at him. "And tomorrow?"

"I haven't decided yet."

"How about Burt Bees?"

He laughed. "I'll have to give that one a try."

"And this scar?" She was pointing to his shoulder. "Old surgery?"

He looked over his shoulder and smiled at her. "Okay."

She put her log down on the examination table and tapped the end of her pen against her chin. "Okay?"

"Why not? I'm agreeable." Then when she frowned, "Now, now, Doctor, don't sulk," and nodding at his shoulder, "Go ahead, I know you're dying to poke it."

She carefully prodded the scar with her index finger. It felt lumpy. Not caring for that, she picked up her log and wrote something down. "And will it be okay with you if I call this scar tissue?"

"Only if you insist on writing something down."

She smiled as she wrote, wondering why she found him amusing. "Mr. Chapstick, you should learn to trust your doctor," she said, finishing off her sentence with an emphatic little period.

"I should?" He looked genuinely surprised by the notion.

She touched the scar again. She was sure she could feel something down there. No, she really didn't care for that. She patted his shoulder. "If we did an X-ray, do you suppose we'd find something surprising in here?"

He shrugged. "It wouldn't surprise me."

"What wouldn't surprise you?" She leaned forward so she could watch his face. "That we'd find something? Or that it would be surprising?"

"Both."

She sat with a soft thump on the small stool next to the examination table and shook her head. "You know, you've really got me wondering about something."

He raised his eyebrows and glanced back at her. "Oh?"

"Uh-huh. If you ever give a straight answer."

"No," he said, turning to look straight ahead.

"Other than that one."

"One's all I've got."

She stood, flipping her log onto the countertop with obvious frustration. "I can't proceed until this is done, you know."

"Doctor Sybout, I assure you, liability is not going to be an issue, so why don't we just stitch the old guy up and send him on his way. Then bright and early the company will cut you a check and that will be the end of it."

"Yes, just so long as there aren't any more questions, or at least ones you don't want to answer."

"Sorry. I know you take your job seriously, and now here you are saddled with this tiresome smart-ass."

"Yes, and I will continue to be saddled with this tiresome smart-ass until I get some cooperation."

He stared at her a moment before he smiled. It was obvious she really meant it, which was fine with him, that she took her professional obligations seriously, that she would persevere in the face of his annoying refusal to be her good patient.

"All right," he said. "Let's do your questions. Ready? Recent tetanus shot? Had one."

She stood and noted it in her log, happy to be back within the routine confines of her job. "Any allergies to medications you're aware of?" she asked.

"None, except that aspirin upsets my stomach. But I don't suppose that's an allergy."

"Tylenol?"

"Actually, I prefer morphine."

"Please. For a little gash like this?" She gently touched his back.

"I have a very low pain threshold."

"Uh-huh." That hardly seemed likely, judging by the scars she saw on his body. "Any other surgeries?"

"Other than fixing broken bones? Stuff like that?"

"Yes."

"No."

She looked at his scars. "Really?"

"Just some old cuts and scraps. No real surgeries."

"Fine. Are you currently taking any medications?"

"No."

She looked at him over the top of her glasses. "No statins?"

"Lipitor?"

She nodded and made a check mark in her log.

He chuckled. "Looks like you were right to question me."

She looked up. "Men never tell the truth about their medications."

"We don't?"

"Never. So . . . Lipitor, any others you suddenly remember?"

"Is there any other way *to* remember?"

She sighed and looked at him. "You just can't help yourself, can you?"

"Apparently not. Can something like that be medicated?"

She raised her eyebrows and smiled. "I'd love to try."

"There, you see? That's just the sort of thing about doctors that bothers me. I answer one trivial little question . . . and now you'd like to medicate me?"

"Actually, what I'd like to do is anesthetize you."

He laughed and put his hands on his knees, pushing himself up to stand on the floor in front of her, the suddenness of which surprised her as she took a quick step backwards. That she reacted like that was also a surprise.

"This," he said, pointing to the scar on his shoulder, the one she'd been puzzled by, "is a chip like they use to tag wild animals."

"What on earth for?"

He shook his head.

"Oh?" she said, raising her eyebrows. Then, *sotto voce*, "You can't say."

"I know," he said with a shrug. "It's weird."

"And these?" She ran her hand over his ribcage. "Old puncture wounds?"

"Just an accident I was involved in."

"Automobile?"

He smiled at her. "What else could it be?"

"Uh-huh," she said, writing something in her log.

"Over here." He pointed to a small patch of shiny white skin on his upper back. He waited until she was looking. "This is from a spill I took on a motorcycle when I was in college."

"What about this?" She gently touched a faint line that ran from his chin to his left temple.

"Go ahead," he said, taking her hand to gently trace the scar with her fingers.

"It's so smooth," she said, fascinated. It really was very good plastic surgery. Some of the best she'd ever seen. "Where was this done?"

He laughed and shook his head. "Doctor Sybout . . . "

"Ah, another secret." It was puzzling as hell. It had to be the work of an expensive private clinic. It really was that good.

"I was a mess. All right?" he said, suddenly willing to tell her more. "Concussion. These teeth." He opened his mouth and tapped his front teeth. "And the orbital bone was shattered. See?" He titled his head for her to look.

"Yes, very nice," she said, moving the light and titling his head even more. "You'd never know." She smiled as she wrote something down, then said to him, "All that, and poor Mr. Chapstick couldn't even take an aspirin."

"Not a problem. I had one of those little drip rigs with the morphine. The ones you pump yourself? Or at least I did until the nurses took it away from me."

"For a very good reason, I'm sure." She took his gown in her hand. "Now, let's pull this up so I can take another look at your lower back."

Facing forward, he pulled it up, bunching it up under his arms. "If you tell me to bend over I'm leaving," he told her, looking over his shoulder.

"Why, Mr. Chapstick, I'm surprised, surely you're not afraid to have a woman examine you?"

He chuckled, looking straight ahead. "Doctor, I do believe you're teasing the patient. Is that ethical?"

She ran her hand down his spin to feel the vertebrae. "No, but you can handle it." She felt a bulge in his lower back. "You're going to have arthritis if you're not careful."

"Thanks, already do."

"What about this?" She touched the seven that was tattooed in red at the base of his spine.

"The seven?"

"Yes."

"Birthmark."

She snorted. "Uh-huh. You can get these removed, you know."

"An old friend like that?"

"I suppose it won't do any good to ask you what it signifies?"

"It signifies what it is, seven."

"Yes," she laughed. "But what does this seven signify by being on your body?"

"That I'm number seven."

"Seven what?"

He glanced back at her. "You do like to parse things, don't you? Well, I suppose it means I'm body number seven. You know, Doctor, personal identity is greatly overrated."

"So now a simple number suffices?"

"Why not? In the end we're all pretty much interchangeable."

"Oh," she said, pulling his gown down, "I doubt that."

It took thirty-three really small stitches because she wasn't going to leave him with another ugly scar. She used a local, but she wasn't sure he really needed it. He had an unusual relationship with pain, she could tell.

"Do you want to see?" she asked when she was done.

She stepped aside so he could see himself in the mirror. Twisting, he ran his hand over the fine stitches. She'd done an excellent job. "Do you take tips?"

She laughed and shook her head. "Why? Do I look like a waitress?"

"Of course not, I just thought you might be willing to accept a donation to your favorite charity."

"I do run a free clinic for new mothers."

"Perfect. So as soon as I can reclaim my wallet they'll get a little help."

"Well, thank you . . ." She frowned at him. "I wish you'd tell me your real name. I feel like an idiot every time I call you Mr. Chapstick."

"And I feel like one every time you do." He grinned and motioned for her to step closer. "Come on," he said when she hesitated. "My real name," he whispered as they put their heads very close together, "but you can never tell anyone this, is X."

She leaned back and gave him a skeptical look. "Seriously?"

"Cross my heart."

She nodded. It fit him. "Well, Mr. X, thank you in advance for the tip."

"You're very welcome, Doctor Sybout."

Before he left he gave her assistant five hundred and twenty dollars—American dollars—telling her Dr. Sybout was expecting it. That he really wanted to do more, but that's all he had. Perhaps when he had more he'd come back and see her again.

2

When X got out to the lobby Callender was sitting there waiting for him in one of their stiff green plastic chairs. "Let's see," he said, sitting down next to him, studying the stitches in Callender's upper lip as he held very still. "Pretty good. Here, take a look at mine." He stood and turned around, raising his shirt.

"How many?"

"You know, I forgot to ask." He sat back down. "It looks good, though, don't you think?"

"If you say so, I'm hardly an expert on this sort of thing."

"You keep frequenting bars like The Trade Winds and you soon will be."

"So it was Doctor Sybout who stitched you up? I thought she was worried about me, but one look at you and off she went."

"Well," X laughed. "What can I say? I guess she thought I was more in need."

"More in need than this?" he asked, wincing when he touched his lip.

"Sorry, Callender. I think it's called triage. They have to prioritize in the ER."

"Yes, and I got triaged right to the back of the queue."

"You look fine. It's hard to see a scar on the lip, anyway."

"Yes, but one still might think that this," touching his lip, "would rate a bit higher than a cut on the back where a scar will never even be seen."

"Except on very rare occasions."

"Exactly," Callender said, slouching down in his chair and sighing like a man who was used to the world treating him with disregard. He glanced at X. "Don't you have company medical?"

"Sure. There's a company clinic right here in Accra."

"So? Is there something wrong with it?"

"No. This just seemed more convenient. And," he patted Callender on the arm, "I was worried about you."

"Yes. Thank you. I'm deeply touched."

3

This all really did start in a bar in Accra called the Trade Winds, which is where Callender found himself one night soon after his arrival in Ghana. He was there, in Ghana, not the bar—though he'd discovered that bars were excellent places to ply his trade—to do a feature story for the *Financial Times* on the most recently discovered offshore oil field in the Gulf of Guinea. It was a big story. The Chinese were there, as were the Americans and the British, even the Canadians. In fact, all the big internationals were interested, and now the mad rush was on, towing oilrigs from Nigeria and the Democratic Republic of the Congo, the North Sea, even from as far away as the Gulf of Mexico. Unfortunately, the news was not all good, many predicting that like Nigeria—Ghana's corrupt neighbor to the east—Ghana would soon be awash not only in new wealth, but government corruption, graft, bribery, under-the-table deals, and kickbacks. Yes, they said, it was all in play, from those ubiquitous Swiss bank accounts to a burgeoning local commerce that catered to the needs of the firms and their international work crews. What this would all mean on the ground in that more mundane world where normal Ghanaians lived was, of course, anyone's guess, though most observers expected an ugly scene of inflation and the erosion of local culture and traditional lifeways, not to mention more drugs and prostitution, armed robberies, assaults, smuggling, theft, and a brisk trade in the resale of stolen property. And let's not forget brazen corporate influence and tough men, ruthless competition, government interference, and threats, or that whatever rule of law applied would be only tenuously enforced. Everything a deal and no deal too small. Yes, all things considered, Callender was totally in his element.

He thought it was a damn good story, how several small independent oil and gas companies found oil where the big majors had failed to look. Actually, it was more interesting than that, because apart from these smaller independents very little interest had ever been shown in Ghana's offshore oil prospects or the exploration blocks the government intended to put out for bid. Nevertheless, in 2000 the government had gone ahead, auctioning off the rights to select offshore oil exploration blocks in the Tano Basin. To no one's surprise, the only takers had been the smaller independents. Then in 2006 they found what they'd been looking for. The announcement itself came in 2007. Dallas oil exploration company Kosmos Energy and its partners, Houston's Anadarko Petroleum, London's Tullow Oil, and the Ghana National Petroleum Corporation (GNPC), had found approximately three billion barrels of oil in a new offshore field adjacent to Cote d'Ivoire in the Western Region some 200 miles southwest of Takoradi.

The new field was promptly christened the Jubilee Field in honor of Ghana's Golden Jubilee—the celebration that year of Ghana's fiftieth year of independence from colonial rule—as well as to note the happy conclusion to more than twenty years of oil exploration. Better yet, the oil turned out to be of the highest quality, a light, sweet crude easily refined into gasoline and jet fuel, just what the Americans and Chinese wanted. No, the new field wasn't large by African standards, and certainly much smaller than neighboring Nigeria's, but it was expected to last at least 30 years at full production and to contribute significant revenue to the Ghanaian government.

But Callender could already see that things weren't going well. In large part this was due to nothing more than the rapidity of events; it was all happening too fast. But the government was also to blame, still lacking the requisite institutions for regulating the petroleum industry. Still dragging its feet when it came to transparency and the deals being made between the private oil companies and the GNPC. Perhaps worse, control of the oil industry appeared to reside solely in the President's Administrative Cabinet. Where, many asked, were the checks and balances of parliament and the courts? Where was the input from Ghana's systematically marginalized civil society? The overall lack of accountable oversight was troubling to everyone, not least the Ghanaians.

Then there was the resource curse. Would new wealth create worse economic performance? Ironically, it had elsewhere. Would unregulated growth lead to weaker governmental institutions? Certainly, that was a common pattern in Africa. Would Ghana avoid the Dutch Disease? Maybe, since oil didn't figure to overshadow the whole economy, though it was still possible that the inflationary impact of the new oil wealth would drive up the cost of all exports. But what then of the livelihood of the small farmers and cocoa growers who'd lose their competitive edge in world markets? Especially in the north where subsistence farmers only managed one crop a year due to the harmattan, the dry seasonal winds off the Sahara.

Nevertheless, Ghana continued to enjoy a reputation for being a stable democracy, one with a good track record when it came to corruption, and, as Callender had seen, they were trying to do the right thing, talking with other nations who'd undergone a similar process, in particular with Norway, the one nation the experts all agreed had done the best job at managing its new oil wealth. Certainly Ghanaians didn't want their nation to end up like Nigeria, Equatorial Guinea, or Angola. In Nigeria, this sort of wrenching change had led not only to stupendous levels of corruption, but dangerous regional animosities and mistrust, and now Ghana's own Western Region was already demanding a cut of the expected oil revenue. They'd been neglected long enough, they said, even though it was the Western Region that supplied most of the gold, cocoa, manganese, bauxite, and timber for export. In

Nigeria such regionalism and inequity had led to the rise of Taliban-style militancy, with attacks on pipelines in the Niger Delta and kidnappings of expatriate oil workers. A scene of total chaos, one in which Callender had once found himself threatened by Nigerian pirates. Well, probably not in Ghana, but he couldn't help but wonder what was going to happen.

What was happening so far was Takoradi. Callender had heard all about it. It was a boomtown, Ghana's Wild West, with quadrupled rents and forcibly evicted tenants, streets clogged with traffic, slums swelling with new arrivals from the interior, overcrowded hospitals, rocketing levels of unemployment and drug use, and a downtown nightly overrun by commercial sex workers. It was there he'd see whether or not the fabric of civil society was already dangerously frayed and torn. But of course the question that most troubled Ghanaians was where were all those eagerly anticipated oil production jobs?

But he was also curious about the Chinese. Racing all over Africa buying up exclusive access to minerals and oil, keeping to themselves, living in compounds or taking over whole hotels, always with lots of security, corporate, or what were really government spokesmen—there being little if any separation between the two for the Chinese—refusing to give out much information. And of course the Africans hated them for their racism, their arrogance, condescension, and standoffishness. It was clear to everyone, not only had the old imperial ways of China survived the Communists and one party rule, they now flourished as never before under the corrupt apparatchiks. They annoyed the whole continent.

The Americans and British, on the other hand, were more corporate and far more approachable, with PR flacks in abundance. Not that this made it any easier to get useful data on the size of the field, let alone believable production figures. No one, least of all Callender, believed the rosy figures they were handing out.

So, given the circumstances, Callender did what reporters have always done, cultivated sources and looked for people willing to talk off the record. Unfortunately, that often meant listening to people who felt aggrieved or who had an ax to grind, a score to settle, or, worse, actually believed in something. That's how he ended up in the Trade Winds.

4

X rode back to the hotel with Callender in a taxi.

"Thanks again for getting me out of The Trade Winds in one piece," Callender said.

"You're welcome. I thought you looked a little out of your depth."

"It showed, huh?"

"Certainly seems like a hard way to get a story."

Callender grimaced and touched his lip. It still stung. When he got back to his hotel he was going to take one of the Vicodins they'd given him. Nor did it make him feel any better to see that X seemed untroubled by any pain. "I don't seem to have much choice. The corporate types keep putting me off or giving me the same old stale press releases, and the geologists are under strict orders not to talk to the press."

"Which leaves the crews."

"Which is why I was in The Trade Winds. Bars being a roughneck's home away from home."

Most crews did twelve hours on, twelve hours off, often in conjunction with ten days on, five days off, unless they were up against a tight deadline, then everyone just kept right on working. Why not? They were all highly skilled workers, professionals, and the pay was absurdly good. The rigs themselves were like small hotels, with maid and laundry service, free food, recreational facilities, workout rooms, all somewhat reminiscent of a Residence Inn. Yes, but when the crews got to shore they really did cut loose, which was understandable, it being stressful, dangerous work.

"It's my own fault," Callender said, "I've never gotten on well with the Scots."

"And they don't much care for South Africans. Why is that?"

"Who do they care for?"

X laughed. Callender was exaggerating, it was the Irish who didn't get on well with anyone, or maybe that honor fell to the Norwegians. "Well, I think the guy who threw you on top of me was actually Canadian."

"He was?" Callender chuckled. "I don't believe I've ever been hit by a Canadian before."

X smiled at Callender. "Better than being hit by a Scot."

When they got to the hotel X paid the cabbie. "Ah, yes, home sweet home," he said when they entered the lobby. It really wasn't that bad.

"How about a drink?" Callender asked.

X put his hand on his back and groaned. "Thanks, but I think I'll just get upstairs and sit in a hot tub. How about some breakfast in the morning?"

"If it's not too early."

"Eight?"

Callender made a face.

"Still going for that drink?"

"I'll find some friendly Texans."

X nodded. "Texans are good, and they buy." He patted Callender on the back. "In the morning," he said.

5

Callender slept well. No, he didn't take the Vicodin. Still, in the morning he had to drag himself downstairs, knowing he'd find X already there all bright and chipper. He'd never been chipper. He'd never even been willing to give it a try.

"Sandy!" X said. "Here." He shoved a cup and a pitcher of coffee towards him. "Get some of this in you."

Grunting something that sounded like thanks, Callender poured a cup. X raised his eyebrows as he watched him fortify it with lots of cream and sugar, then carefully stir it all together before taking a tentative sip. Not hot enough, but what the hell. Then another sip and he leaned back in his chair, for the first time actually looking at X. My god, the man was so full of good cheer it was obscene.

"How are we doing?" X asked, practically laughing in his face.

"I'm *not* hung over."

"No, I can see that, but you're still hurting this morning, aren't you?"

"I hurt every morning."

"Not me."

"Please." Callender held his hand up. "I really don't want to hear about it."

"Fine. Let's get some real food in you. What would you like?" He tapped the menu lying on the table.

"I don't normally eat much breakfast."

"You need to eat something." He studied him a moment and grinned. "How about some nice hot oatmeal?"

"Shut up, you bastard."

"Well," X laughed, "I always eat a big breakfast. I hope you can handle it." And he did, two poached eggs on toast, a fruit bowl and a bagel with cream cheese. Callender ate a banana and drank three cups of coffee. X calculated there must have been at least 60 grams of sugar in those coffees by the time Callender had finished doctoring them.

"You don't smoke, do you?" X was watching him fidget. It seemed to be more than just the coffee.

"Used to."

X nodded. "It's habitual. Right? Cup of coffee and the first cigarette of the day?"

"It certainly used to be."

"So, this story you're working on? Last night you made it sound like it was going to focus on the human-interest side of things. True, or just fishing?"

"Fishing. I'm not sure what it's going to focus on. The business side is pretty dry, and everyone already has all of that anyway. But I may have an angle or two."

"Such as?"

"Like how ExxonMobil tried and failed to sow things up. This was all being done on the sly, of course. But it's not that big a field, which makes me wonder, angle number two, if there isn't more still to be found."

"You're thinking some of the independents found more than they've let on? And Exxon knows?"

"They have to, perhaps even legitimately, though it's far more likely they have their own people on the inside feeding them information. I know the Chinese do."

In late 2009 ExxonMobil tried to buy Kosmos Energy's interests in both the Cape Three Points and Deepwater Tano exploration blocks, including Mahogany Blocks 1 and 2 where the discovery had first been made. The story Callender heard, one he believed, was that they had also been in secret negotiations to acquire both Tullow's and Anadarko's stake in the Cape Three Point block as well as those of two other smaller independent foreign operators, which would have made ExxonMobil the majority stakeholder in the field as well its primary operating company—if the Chinese hadn't squeezed them out.

X nodded. Corporate espionage, a lucrative trade, but he had no interest in that or the oil field, let alone the putative veracity of projected production figures. "What else?" he asked.

"Rumors. Interesting rumors."

"Oh?" X sat up straight in his chair and waited. This was what he liked about journalists, that they were inveterate gossips, and Callender actually paused a beat to look around the restaurant before he spoke, bringing a small smile to X's face.

"This guy was telling me that the Chinese drove a really hard bargain with the Ghanaian government. That this was more than their usual oil for money loan."

"What loan?"

"From The China Development Bank, at the behest, I'm sure, of the CNOOC."

"Who?"

"China National Offshore Oil Corporation, the Chinese state owned petroleum company. So they loaned the Ghanaian state owned petroleum company, the GNPC, the funds to build the new infrastructure for the Jubilee Field."

"That's not done?"

"Usually that sort of thing is the purview of the World Bank or the IMF, but their loans come with strings attached. You know, things like transparency, local development, governmental oversight, but you only need to worry about the Chinese when you borrow from the Chinese. But this wasn't, or so I'm told, their usual deal. This time they wanted the actual drilling rights."

"What's wrong with that?"

"They didn't want to bid, they didn't even necessarily want to buy out the independents, they just wanted the rights handed to them. Now."

"So they'd actually get a rig of their own, tow it out there, and drill for themselves? I mean, they normally wouldn't, right? That is what you're telling me?"

Callender nodded his head.

"Where did you hear this?"

Callender shrugged his shoulders and smiled.

"Sandy! Seriously? After I saved your life?"

"You can't tell anyone."

"Who in the hell am I going to tell?"

"It was a guy over at the GNPC."

"And this wasn't just some low level bureaucrat who wanted you to buy him a drink?"

"They always want you to buy them a drink, but he's high enough to know the real story."

"Interesting," X said.

Callender agreed, nodding his head.

"So you're thinking this is because the field really is larger than the GNPC is letting on?"

"That's what I'm thinking."

Yeah, it made sense. What didn't was why the Chinese felt they needed their own rig out there, and why there, of all places? No, there was something about this that felt all wrong. Well, not his problem, not per se, anyway, and surely those who needed to know knew by now. But it did make him wonder how much a man like Callender might be able to find out if someone pointed him in the right direction.

"Well," X said, moving his chair back a bit from the table, "I too have a job to do, so I need to round up Bubba and get back out to the rig."

"Which one?"

"We're way the hell out there on Moody River One."

Callender sat up straight and stared at him. "Really? What's going on out there? I hear all these rumors, but no one seems to really know, or if they do I can't get a straight answer." The rig had previously been up in the North Sea, towed down there in the spring of 2009 to the Jubilee Field. It sat way out on the southwestern edge of the old Mahogany #2 block, which was a bit of a puzzle. Why drill so far out? They were practically off the continental shelf. Maybe they knew something the rest of them didn't. Well, oil geologists, especially the deep-sea variety, were secretive, and such information could potentially be worth billions. He'd poked around a bit, and some company flacks had even tried to arrange a tour, but it was hard as hell to get out there even with an invitation because there never seemed to be any room on the shuttles that ran the crews back and forth from Accra and Takoradi.

"Want to see?" X asked.

"Well, yeah, I'd love to, I've been trying to get out there for days. You can really do that?"

"Sure. Bubba and I," and he nodded at a small, trim looking man sitting at a table in the corner with three other men. "We have our own means of getting on and off."

"How? You don't look corporate."

"Me?" X really laughed. "More like security."

"Security?" It was preposterous. Callender knew a security goon when he saw one, which raised the not unreasonable fear that the company was still gulling him.

X saw his reaction and laughed. "No? Well, let's just call it that for the time being. If that's okay with you, of course."

"Oh, what the hell? I'm used to people lying to me."

"Why, Sandy," he said, smiling at him, "I do believe you trust even fewer people than I do. I wonder how can you stand to live like that."

"Yeah, I often wonder that myself."

"So? Want to come, or not?"

"You mean just like that? You do know that my official invitation has probably expired by now?"

"We'll get you on board. Then you can spend all day poking around to your heart's content. Talk to those friendly Canucks."

6

It was a highly modified Bell 407, stripped down, very spartan, which caused Callender to wonder if it might not be ex-military. Certainly it lacked any of the comforts found in the corporate helicopters he'd ridden in. But it was very fast, as he soon discovered. So Bubba flew while X sat up front, soon to fall asleep as Callender thrashed around in back on a pile of duffel bags trying to get comfortable, which he never did, of course, finally just giving up to grit his teeth as he endured his fate, a state of being he was all too familiar with. The flight itself was uneventful. They all three wore headphones but there wasn't much to say and the helicopter was too noisy for much of that anyway. It took about an hour and fifteen minutes to get out to the rig.

Bubba brought them gently down on the helipad, climbed out, and came around and grabbed two bags and left without saying a word. Callender watched him walk off towards a small trailer that sat behind a tangled mass of pipes.

"Not too friendly, is he?" Callender said.

"Bubba? He's okay, just not very talkative. Come on," he said, grabbing a large bag and leading him across the deck. "Look out for that," he said, pointing to a large black cable snaking across the deck.

He led Callender to a small shed that turned out to be a stairwell, passing through two heavy steel double doors before walking down one deck to emerge through two more in the middle of a brightly lit hallway that looked not unlike those countless others one might find anywhere out in office park U.S.A. Then down that hallway and to the left where X brought him to an open doorway into a large, comfortable looking room lined with many windows overlooking the ocean.

Pausing with his hand on Callender's arm, he said, "Just act like you've been on one of these before. We get new people out here all the time."

"Act bored, you mean."

"That's it," X said, grinning as he patted his back.

Callender was surprised by how many people were there. Small groups scattered around the room sitting at tables while others stood in a long buffet-style serving line off to his right manned by two cooks in white coats preparing sandwiches. It seems it was lunchtime.

"Hungry?" X nodded at the buffet as he dropped his duffel bag in a chair at one of the tables.

Callender was. Finally. They both had carved turkey breast sandwiches with mashed potatoes and gravy. He had an iced tea. X had a Diet Coke. They hardly spoke while they ate. The food was that good.

After lunch X left him on his own out in the hallway, saying, "I assume you know what to do, and I have a few things to do myself. Shall we meet back here at five?"

"Five it is," Callender said, watching X turn to walk down the corridor and through a door that looked like it led to some offices.

So the rule of thumb for this sort of thing was really quite simple and always the same: look purposeful but never inquisitive. Then people rarely took notice, though to be honest about it people rarely noticed him under any circumstances. Disheartening, perhaps, but over time he'd learned to make it work for him.

So he did poke around, and what he found, or perhaps failed to find, was a bit puzzling, but maybe that was more a feeling he got than anything concrete he could point to. And he did talk to the Canucks, who made up the bulk of the work force, but all they wanted to talk about were the tar sands up in Alberta and how the environmentalists had stalled the project and how they now had to swelter out there in the gulf to make a living. Still, he had a good day. He got some interesting stuff he could use to describe the flavor of life on an oilrig, the roughnecks and how they looked at their world, he even managed to sneak a few photographs with his iPhone. He did not, however, hear any mention of production figures nor did he get a feel for why they were drilling so far out there in the gulf, but that was largely his own fault, having hidden from the three different corporate guys he'd spotted over the course of the afternoon.

In the evening X flew them back to Accra: an hour and thirty-five minutes. X was a hell of a pilot. Callender was beginning to think he had to be ex-military.

As he shut down the engine X turned to him. "How about some dinner?" he asked.

"Don't you need to get back?"

"Not tonight."

"Well—"

"I know," he said, smiling brightly, "let's see if Doctor Sybout has any dinner plans."

"X, you can't be serious? What on earth are you going to say to her?"

"That I think this is infected?" He grabbed his lower back. "It's this damn climate. The white man's graveyard."

"Uh, I believe that's malaria."

"Well, it is sore. Here," he said, taking Callender's hand. "Feel my forehead."

He did.

"So? Feverish?"

"No, and she's not going to buy it."

"Of course she will, it's her Hippocratic oath."

"Uh-huh." He smiled at X. "So what's she really treating, loneliness, or your fatal attraction to beautiful women?"

"Sandy," X said with a big smile, "if they ever find a cure for that one do let me know."

"X, not that I want to curb your enthusiasm or anything, but just who in the hell are you? And don't give me any more of that crap about being security."

"No?"

"Please."

"Well . . ." he said, smiling as he patted Sandy's back. "We'll see."

"That's it?" Callender said, staring at him, waiting for more even though it was quite clear that more wasn't going to show up.

"For the moment."

"So I'm just supposed to wait around for what would seem to be a fairly simple answer to a pretty straightforward question. But then again, who am I?"

"An investigative journalist."

"Yes, and look how well I'm doing."

"You're doing all right."

"Which reminds me, thanks for today, especially since you had no reason to be so helpful."

"Well, what can I say, for some reason I've fallen into this habit of looking out for you."

"And for my career as well, it seems."

"You know, Sandy, so far as I can tell the world hinges mostly on favors, or at least mine certainly does."

"Meaning?"

"Meaning let's just see how this pans out."

"Ah." Callender nodded. "I knew you were up to something. Care to give me a hint?"

"See? Here you are the investigative journalist again."

"But you do have something for me?"

"I may."

7

Rather reluctantly, Callender finally agreed to accompany X to see Dr. Sybout. What a surprise that was.

"Why, it's old lucky number seven," she said when the receptionist brought them to her office, and they both laughed, neither bothering to explain the joke to Callender.

"You know, I think I may have developed a fever," X said, leaning forward.

"Hmm," she said, putting her hand on his forehead.

"Do you think a cold drink might help?"

"How many?"

"You're the doctor."

So they went to dinner, the three of them. Callender amazed by how willing she was to accompany them. And at the Hilton the conversation really sparkled, or rather theirs did, Callender by then having settled into his customary role as the chorus. Yes, he could see that Dr. Sybout was very pretty, there was no question about that, but mostly she was very smart. Acute. Well, so was X, for that matter, Callender being a bit startled by that, all of which made him feel like he was floundering around somewhere down there in the gloom as the sparks flew by way up there over his head. "Who is this man?" Dr. Sybout asked, turning to him at one point with a big smile. Well, yeah, by then that's just what he was wondering.

8

The next morning he was on the phone to ask. He spoke with Beth, his assistant in Cape Town, and when she called him back at his hotel that evening he was hardly surprised to hear her say there was no X.

It was two days later, on his second trip out to Moody River, that he asked him, point blank. Yes, X admitted, whatever traces of his career there were they'd undoubtedly be rather faint. That seemed to worry him a bit. Perhaps, he said, he had lived his life too much in the shadows. But, he insisted, he was still very much a real person. "See?" he said, holding his arms out as if that might reveal him in all his essential particularity.

"Actually, no, I don't," Callender said. "But that's just the point, isn't it? But doesn't this carefully crafted persona make it rather hard for you to live a real life?"

"Actually, it's odd you should mention that, because lately that has been worrying me."

"Passing through life without a trace?"

"Or with just a very faint one."

Yes, he thought, it probably was a more or less universal problem for a certain type of person. Bente? Oh yeah, she knew. He was sure of it. Later, when he'd gone to see her after it was all over, he could tell. But no one keeps a secret like a doctor.

9

On the evening of the second day on the Moody River X came looking for him in the lounge. "Jesus, Callender, how can you stand it down here. It's like a sauna. Let's go up top." He stood in the open doorway with two plastic lawn chairs folded-up under his left arm, the kind with those plastic woven straps, a green canvas bag hanging from his right shoulder on a long drawstring, and a six-pack dangling from his right hand.

Callender was doing his email at the table with the printer. Thanks to X he had access to the rig's intranet, something no one seemed particularly concerned about, which was a bit of a surprise. Just one more example of the strange little world he'd fallen into. There was the deck he was on, with its lounge and gym, the mess and the laundry, and the one below where the crew bunked. Both floors seemed to be open to anyone. The lower two decks and the work areas there were not. The two elevators and the stairwells that led there were either locked or guarded at all times. He knew. He'd wandered down there in the middle of the night and found locked doors and armed guards blocking his way. Nothing sinister. They'd even had a chat. It was the work area for the geologists, he was told, but they made it clear he could go no further.

"Are we having a party?" he asked.

"I just like my comforts. Here." X handed him the dark green canvas bag. "You take this."

Callender hefted it in his hand. It was surprisingly heavy. "What's in here?"

X smiled and pushed him towards the doorway. "Night goggles," he said when they got out into the corridor.

Callender stared at him a moment, not understanding, then pulled on the drawstring and peered inside. "So what are we supposed to do with these?"

"You'll see."

The decking up top was steel and hard plastic, covered over in many areas with a thick coating of a soft asphalt-like material that had a coarse and now somewhat worn texture. Everywhere things looked shabby and weathered, rusted and nicked, bent and beat-up, a palimpsest of hard use and years spent at sea in different waters doing a rough and dirty job. Callender always felt a bit trapped up there in that maze of tubing and cable, power transformers, derricks, hoists, and storage shacks, where a million things waited to trip him or bang his head, cut his hand or scrape his shin, and all smelling of petroleum and wet steel in the incredible humidity. Yes, but there was a soft cooling breeze that night, and when they sat in the middle of the bull's eye on the helideck drinking beer the clear night sky overhead formed a perfect vault of endless black and pinpoint stars. He'd never seen a lovelier night at sea.

"I can't believe you have this shitty American beer all the way out here," he said.

"That's the way these private contractors do things. They think it makes this place seem more like home."

"*Grain Belt*? Well, if this is what's at home," and he had another sip, "then it's no wonder you're all out here."

"Callender, can you just stop complaining and drink your damn beer. It's not going to stay cold for very long in this heat, and trust me, you don't want to drink this stuff once it warms up."

"My brain's already refusing to swallow."

"It's certainly not refusing to complain. Hand me those." He was pointing to the green canvas bag with the night vision goggles. Callender passed it over, then waited as X worked them free of the bag. "Here you go," X said, handing him one. Then turning it over, Callender saw that something was written on the small metal plate attached to the back of the webbing for the headband. Twisting around in the light to see it more clearly, he read: *Panoramic. USAF. RESTRICTED.*

"X," he asked, looking up at him, "just wondering, but how do you happen to have these?" He turned it over to look at the optics. "I mean this definitely has the look of something prototype-like. You know? And *restricted*?"

X saw what he was looking at and laughed. "Have you ever left a job?"

"Lots of them."

"So was there ever anything you took with you when you did?"

"You took these and no one's missed them?" They looked incredibly expensive.

"You know the government, they can't be expected to keep track of everything they own."

"So sometimes things just get lost?"

"That, and sometimes it's just not worth the effort to try and get them back."

"But restricted? That suggests . . ." and he laughed and shook his head.

"Yes?"

"Well, that seems to suggest that at one time you had access."

"Access? Callender, access is a misnomer. The way it works, it's all about who you know."

"But these have to be expensive."

"Very, if they ever came on the market."

Callender just stared at him. "So, in this case, what does restricted actually mean?"

"Well, it certainly means it's illegal for me to have them."

"Night vision goggles are illegal?"

"Not per se, but these certainly are."

"Because these are dangerously good and might fall into the wrong hands?"

"Yes. The wrong *military* hands."

Callender nodded, following the logic, as far as it went. "All right. But why do you have them?"

"How about another beer?" X picked up the four remaining beers by the plastic webbing and twisted one free.

Callender chuckled. "How many more of these do I have to drink before you'll tell me what's really going on?"

X pulled one free for himself and opened it, then took a sip and made a face. "It's the Canadians. They love this shit."

He watched Callender struggling with the binoculars. "No, like this," he said, working the webbing over his head. "That's right. Up over your head. Center the binoculars. Now flick that little switch."

The effect was amazing. Suddenly Callender's world was bright and clear.

"Now, find those soft little buttons up on top. Those control brightness and magnification. So you can zoom in and out as well as focus. Go ahead."

Callender gently touched the soft buttons.

"The big one, that's zoom. The other two are for brightness and focus."

He zoomed in on the desalinization shack, amazed to find he could actually read the writing on the sides of the pipes. Then he tried the brightness, increasing it until it hurt his eyes. "What in the hell was that?" he asked, pointing up towards one of the towers.

"Bats. They live out here on the rig. They come out and fly around like that all night."

He was moving his head as he tried to track one, watching it dart in and out among the towers, trying to keep up with all its sharp turns and twists.

"There's a satellite," X said. "See?"

Callender looked where X was pointing. Yes, a bright dot moving rapidly in the sky. Tracing a sweeping arc overhead that, unlike the bats, was easy to follow. He leaned back in the lawn chair to watch. In less than a minute it was gone over the horizon. "I had no idea they were that fast," he said.

"Some are. Some aren't."

Callender looked up at the river of stars that was the Milky Way galaxy—his galaxy—and realized he'd never bothered to look at it like this before, not really, not to see the fat disc edge-on standing on its head like that. It was stunning.

Looking at his wristwatch, X said, "Now I want you to look over there." He was pointing to the southeast. "In just a few minutes we should be able to see something rather interesting coming over the horizon."

"Another satellite?"

"It's going to look like one, but it's no satellite."

Callender leaned back in his chair and looked at the lights twinkling on the tower at the end of the platform. "So the real show is about to begin," he said, turning to look at X.

"The curtain's going up."

"Care to tell me what I'm supposed to see?"

"What do you know about NASA?" X asked, wiping his chin with the back of his hand.

"Uh, what everyone knows, I guess, trips to the moon, the shuttle disasters. Why?"

"Ever visit any of those conspiracy sites on the web? That *other* NASA stuff?"

"You mean how they faked the moon landing?"

"That would be part of it," he said with a nod. "Of course, it's all nonsense, or at least most of it is, but now they've got a problem."

"Who does? NASA?"

"Among others. It's because various people and agencies have been running these absurd disinformation campaigns. Something they've been doing in one form or another for a very long time. Unfortunately, not only has this been unnecessary, but the manner in which they've gone about it has been totally haphazard and uncoordinated. The result of which is what we see around us today."

"Which is?"

"Massive confusion. No one knows what's true or false anymore, which would be fine, up to a point, if that didn't also include those who've been doing the dis-informing."

"Roswell?"

"Roswell, crashed UFOs, extraterrestrials in cryogenic storage, reverse engineered alien technologies, alien abductions, Rendlesham, a lot of silly folklore that's now firmly entrenched in popular culture, and on and on it goes to no real purpose."

"Though presumably there are more directed, higher level cover-ups. Ones less folkloric."

"Yes. The glass towers on the Moon. What they really found on Mars. Our sudden interest in Phobos."

"Phobos?"

"One of Mar's two moons. Or is it?" He smiled at Callender. "But I was really thinking more along the lines of a black-ops NASA. A secretly funded, shadow NASA buried so deep that even the President doesn't know about it. Ever hear anything about that?"

"No. But now I'm confused. Are you telling me this is, or is not just more loopy folklore?"

X shrugged his shoulders. "With this one I try to keep an open mind."

"Do you? But then how could anyone hope to successfully manage such a thing? Yes, I can see that there might be the possibility of a lack of significant civilian oversight, but—"

"Maybe there's none at all."

"Or maybe there's none at all, but still, somewhere, someone's got to be in charge. I mean, how compartmentalized can it be? And what about all the other people who'd have to be involved? Not to mention all the money this sort of operation would require. No. I just don't see how such a massive operation could be kept quiet."

X nodded like what he said made good sense, and in a way it did, but only up to a certain point. After all, here he was, living proof that such secrets could be kept. "You'd think," he said. He wondered if he'd ever tell Callender about the visitor they'd brought in for the day, or about the massive security presence, with fighters constantly circling overhead and naval ships in the distance. Of course, he hadn't been invited to any of the meetings, though he did manage to catch a glimpse of a tall figure in a long shiny gray cloak being escorted to one of the elevators. It had been a long day, the meetings lasting late into the evening before everyone left in a fleet of helicopters. It was the very next day that they saw their first video of the beam weapons.

"Here she comes," X said. "See it?"

Its movement wasn't as fast, and for some reason it didn't look as high as the satellites. "It seems bigger," he said.

"It is."

They watched in silence until it was high overhead.

"Now watch very carefully," X told him.

Callender sat up a bit in his chair, concentrating on the green blob floating out there in front of him. "Did it just change directions?" It seemed to.

"Yes. Now it usually happens just about now when they're right overhead."

"Why?"

"Because they're entering the atmosphere out here over the south Atlantic. It's a dangerous transition."

Callender saw that the blob was growing a long bright tail. "Is that light the heat from reentry?"

"Crude, isn't it?"

Callender turned to look at X. He was staring almost straight overhead. "As compared to what?"

"Just keep watching," X told him.

He laid back in the chair and tried to get comfortable.

"There! Did you see that?" X asked.

He had. He'd been watching the bright object at the head of the comet's tail when seemingly from out of nowhere a bright green line, a glowing thread, shot out towards it. Then just as suddenly others appeared, in a few seconds creating a crazy looking spider's web pattern of glowing green threads. Startled, he felt a chill as the hair on his arms stood up, suddenly acutely aware of his sweaty t-shirt and the beads of perspiration on his neck and forehead. He felt X's hand on his shoulder.

"That's what I wanted you to see, and this was a big one."

"A big what?" He turned to stare at him. "Just what the fuck is going on up there?"

"It's called delivering the mail, or at least that's what we call it, because sometimes there's a dog waiting to bite your ankles."

"A dog?"

"It's the good guys versus the bad guys. The white hats against the black hats. The OK Corral." He laughed. "Or is that too American for you?"

"I saw the movie. So who are the good guys? The United States?"

X shook his head. "It's complicated. Primarily, it's just simple harassment. Political. Meant to spur negotiated concessions."

"But—"

"So what you saw was a military shuttle." He raised his eyebrows. "That's right. They've been running their own fleet for years. They don't look much like what NASA retired, but that's how they started out."

"So this is your black-ops NASA?"

"Why would anyone think space would be of no interest to the military?"

"But you said bad guys. So space is militarized? Is that what you're saying? And we're—you're—engaged in some sort of conflict?"

"What do you think we've just been looking at?"

Callender leaned back and looked. Just fading green threads. "This black-ops NASA isn't area 51, is it?"

X chuckled. "That's not NASA."

"No?"

"Not even close. NASA is near space."

"And *not* near?"

"What you saw tonight," and he nodded to the heavens, "that was near space. Not near is . . . not near."

"Like the moon?"

"It seemed near when we were still going there. Maybe when the Chinese get there it will seem near again."

He looked up at the night sky. "Are they really going?"

"I have no idea. They may. It's political."

"Do they know about all this black-ops stuff?"

"It would be hard for them to miss."

"Then why haven't I heard anything about it?"

"Well, yeah, excellent question. Why is that, do you suppose?"

It hardly seemed possible that something like this could be kept a secret. Night vision goggles! All one had to do was look, and people must be looking. Obviously, the governments involved weren't talking, that was to be expected, but still, and then Callender suddenly saw it. The truth was that everyone did know, or at least the information was out there for all to see, it was just that no one believed it. No one would even consider believing it. Yes, and that was the result of disinformation, which was why no serious reporter would come within a thousand miles of a story like this. Which was why no academic or politician was going to risk their career or public ridicule by pursuing it.

"Why did you show me this?" he asked

"Because you're a journalist."

"Yes, but what do you expect me to do? Because I'm not interested in helping your government cause a lot of confusion."

"You won't be, this is primarily just for me."

"In what sense?"

"I want my role in this witnessed and remembered."

"But why? You don't seem particularly vain."

"I'm not, but things may happen. I'm not saying they necessarily will, you understand, but they may, in which case there will be a few of us who'll want our voices heard."

"Such as you."

X smiled at him. "I'll expect you to say nice things about me."

Callender laughed, throwing his hands up in exasperation.

"Sorry," X said. "I know this is frustrating, but all in good time. We first need to build up that bond of trust, then we'll see how it goes."

"I'm not drinking any more of your shitty beer."

X laughed. It was all going to work out just fine, he could already tell. His only worry was how to ease Callender into the truth. Too quickly, and he'd balk. He'd just have to bring him along slowly, one step at a time.

10

She drove an old light blue Mercedes 350 SDL, a tank of a car, one that had seen several hundred thousand miles of African highways and dirt roads.

X sat with both hands gripping the thick leather wrapped steering wheel as he watched her in the mirror pumping in the diesel. It was like that in Africa, that things like cars were expected to just go on forever. Fix this. Replace that. On and on it went over the years, everything being repeatedly mended until finally it was just no longer possible.

When she got back in the car after paying, she said, "Don't make a face. At least it still runs."

"And very well. No, I was trying to remember the last time I drove a Mercedes. It may have been when I was in college."

"An old girlfriend's?"

He laughed, shrugging his shoulders.

"No? What happened?"

"It was *college*." He looked at her as if she surely knew what that meant.

"A loner even then."

He shook his head. She always said that, that he was a loner. "No, not then, not now, either. I'm just picky."

"Oh? Then I'm honored."

It was hard to talk until they cleared downtown Accra. It was true what they said about Third World drivers, though considering the chaotic conditions under which they drove they'd actually managed to craft a somewhat sensible, though highly informal, traffic code. When he could, he said, "Tell me about your family. They've been here a long time, I take it."

"Since the 1750s."

"I have some Dutch ancestors in my family tree. They were in New Amsterdam in the 1600s."

She smiled at him. "You don't suppose we're related?"

"We certainly could be."

"It's quite likely, actually. European populations weren't that large back then. What were their names?"

He shrugged. "I haven't the faintest idea, that's just what a cousin told me who was into genealogy."

"Maybe we need to look into this."

"Kissing cousins?" he said, turning to grin at her.

"Just one big happy family."

"Though now it's just you and Liz."

She nodded. "Father's dead. Mother's dead. Just the two of us left to carry on."

"No relatives?"

"Not in Africa."

"No, they never traded in slaves, if that's what you're thinking. They were merchants and growers, lumbermen and land speculators. They employed their workers."

"Cocoa?"

"That was later.

"I've had some wonderful chocolate in Amsterdam. I wonder if any of it was yours."

"As a student, or recently?"

"I was never that kind of student, but I've been to Europe any number of times."

"What does that mean, *I was never that kind of student*?"

"The kind whose parent's footed the bill for a trip to Europe."

"Parents? What about those study abroad programs your American universities run? Or doing it on the cheap? Hitchhiking around staying in youth hostels?"

"I was pretty busy when I was in college. I never really had a summer off."

She shifted in her seat to see him better. What was he telling her? "But you did go to college?"

He nodded. "Philosophy major."

"Really?" She thought she should have been more surprised, but in an odd sort of way it made sense. "I hope you've put that to good use."

"Probably not, but I still enjoyed it. Before reality intruded."

"Was that when you were in the military?"

He smiled and glanced at her as he drove.

"Well?" she asked.

"Sort of."

"Whatever that means."

"It means I was soon diverted into a different sort of career path."

"That wasn't military?"

"A bit more free-lance than that."

She nodded. "It's the philosophy, isn't it?"

"What is?"

"That's to blame for how you always avoid answering my questions."

"So they had large farms out here in the hills away from the coast, though they had homes down in Accra as well."

"Where did you grow up?"

"Amsterdam, for the most part."

"Oh?"

"My mother," she said, smiling in answer to his unspoken question. "She took us there after the divorce. But we came to stay with father whenever we could."

"And then for good, you and Liz?"

She nodded. "Africa is our home."

"Your father, what was he like?"

"Very political. He was one of Kwame Nkrumah's early white supporters."

He glanced her way and noted her smile. "Is that amusing?"

"It certainly surprises people, but mostly it's just ironic."

"Because?"

"Because it was his support of the African socialists that made him a wealthy man."

"How so?"

"It's all very clannish down here. Ruling factions tend to look after their own, so after independence father made out quite well."

"You're okay with that?"

She shrugged. "What does it matter? It's the world in which we live."

"Not that it would change just for you, anyway."

"Exactly. But let me tell you my little story. When Nkrumah formed his first government, Ghana's first post-colonial government, his interior minister was a man named Krobo Edusei. And we're not talking about ancient history here because Edusei is still around. Anyway, both Nkrumah and Edusei claimed to be hardcore socialists, and perhaps they really were, they were both certainly hardcore African nationalists. So when the inevitable charges of corruption arose, Edusei said, in his own defense, that socialism doesn't mean that if you've made a lot of money you can't keep it."

She smiled at him. "That would certainly sum up father's point of view."

"Have his political connections helped in your work?"

"Hardly. Nkrumah lost power, which is when things began going poorly for father. That's when we started selling off the farms."

"But what about all this new oil wealth Callender's been telling me about? Won't that help?"

"If it's not swallowed up by corruption and cronyism. But everyone seems to be saying the right things, so who knows, though I have heard that Edusei's followers claim the current government is in collusion with the Chinese to trade away our resources."

"Is it?"

"I don't see what difference it makes, who ends up buying our oil."

"It makes a great deal of difference if there are certain strings attached."

"Yes, well I wouldn't know about that," she said with a shrug.

They stopped for lunch just outside Tamale at the Asempa Lodge. Bente had X drive around back to the parking lot, and when they entered the lobby she handed the keys to the man at the desk who greeted her warmly in Dutch before escorting them out double doors to a screened patio.

"Thank you," she said, discreetly handing him the 5 Cedi banknote she'd carefully folded to mask its denomination.

"You're certainly a generous tipper," X said, catching a glimpse of the familiar blue note with its picture of Balme Library.

"We're locals. There are certain expectations."

"Expectations?"

"Why not? We're rich compared to most of these people. I've always felt we had certain obligations."

"Such as generosity."

She smiled at him. "I know. It's different here."

He shook his head. "Not really, it's just more out in the open. More personal. Who knows, maybe that's better."

"And yours?" she said, studying him. "Are they ever out in the open?"

Smiling, he leaned back as a waiter poured their water, waiting to say, "I suppose they are to those who know the context. If that makes any sense."

"None," she said, shaking her head.

"I feel obligated to you. That's certainly out in the open."

"Yes," she agreed, he was very open about that. "Though I wonder if that will still be true once you leave Ghana. Off to do whatever it is you do."

"If you think that you'd be wrong."

She unfolded her napkin and carefully spread it out flat on the table. "Well," she said, looking up at him, "I suppose we'll find out."

"Pizza!" She was amused. "You're in Africa and you order pizza?"

"It's on the menu."

"For the tourists. All these wonderful local dishes . . . and pizza?"

"Bente, I really don't think it's all that odd."

"You have seen a lot of the world, have you not?"

"Yes," he reluctantly agreed.

"Many different countries and cultures?"

He nodded.

"So, presumably we'd be safe in saying you're not afraid to try something new? Or put off by local cuisines?"

"Very safe."

"You do realize this is just what Americans always do? Wanting here what they can already get at home? All this amazing food and culture, things unlike anything you'd be able to find at home, and you order pizza?" She sipped her water. "Which," she said, when she sat her glass on the table, "makes us wonder why you've even bothered to come."

"That's right, pick on us poor Americans. What a tiresome cliché. But this is a European thing with you, isn't it, because Africans are very friendly to Americans. And they love pizza.

Just like they love soccer and rap music. They're not hung-up on whether it's authentically African or not. Unlike the Europeans, who come here looking to partake of an *exotic culture*, one that's been cleverly crafted to meet their expectations." He glanced around them. "I mean, look at this place. It's tailor-made for Europeans."

She smiled at him. He was so different from the other men she'd known, and it wasn't because he was an American, not at all, she wasn't even sure what that actually meant, even though she did tease him about it. No, he was just X. No one who knew him would ever say otherwise.

"Well?" he asked.

"Yes, *the African experience.* Better to sell that than Africans."

"Much."

"So, yes, they do come here expecting it, and for a price we're only to happy to provide it. But still, pizza seems . . . I mean, if we let it, won't this pizza business eventually just swamp us? Won't we all become just alike, or at least too much alike? I don't think any of us really wants to see that happen."

"Well, as I understand it, this is already a rather hybrid culture. I'm not sure there's any African authenticity left to threaten, but I guess I can skip a slice or two of pizza if that will help."

She reached across the table and took his hand. "No. Eat your pizza. We'll risk it."

"This is it," she said as they turned and drove up a gentle rise through stands of acacia and shea trees.

"It's lovely, though I was expecting it to look more tropical."

"It's the dry season. The harmattan. It's a lot greener when the rains come."

He stopped the car at the crest of a small hill and looked at the compound: a very large house, two stories, a number of smaller dwellings and sheds, and two warehouse sized buildings.

After they parked at the house she ran her hand across the hood of the car. "See?" she said, holding out her hand so he could see the reddish dust. "It gets into everything."

He looked at the sky. Yes, hazy, like smoke, the minute particles of dust suspended in the atmosphere, blown in from the Sahara to the northeast. "It's a fair trade for the lower humidity."

"Believe me, after a few days you'll long for the humidity."

"I'm not so sure." He turned to look at the western sky. "I actually sort of like the subdued light. See how it's all washed out and opaque? That's how it looks in the desert when the wind blows."

"You like that?"

"Yes, but then I've never really lived in the topics for any length of time. So green and damp is quite a contrast to what I'm used to."

She came around the car and put her hand under his arm. "Yes, you and the harmattan. I can see the resemblance."

He chuckled and took her in his arms. "The grit and annoyance?"

"Possibly."

"And now you can't wait for the rainy season?"

"I'm in no hurry," she said, watching his face. "The change will do me good."

They sat on the veranda sipping coffee. They were sleepy. They'd been up very late, most of the night, in fact. Bente had never been so passionate. It was a revelation, one she needed some time to sort out.

"Someone's coming," X said.

"What?" She pulled her hair back and squinted. She'd forgotten to wear her glasses.

"There," X said, pointing to the cloud of dust in the distance.

"Oh, God! How do I look?" She was staring at him.

"Well," he laughed, "at least you finally have some clothes on."

She stood and turned to go in the house. "Just stall them until I get back."

He laughed. "Yes, doctor."

"Well?" she asked, coming back through the door to the veranda.

"He's just pulling up over there."

"No! I mean how do I look?"

He stepped back to look. "Good. He'll never know."

"Know what?"

He grinned and took her hand. "What you did all night."

She smiled, not looking the least embarrassed. "It was all night, wasn't it?"

"I seem to remember a sunrise in there somewhere."

She watched the man approaching and said to X, "Now, behave yourself. This man is an old friend of mine, and my family's."

"Who'd be shocked at the behavior of one of the Sybout girls?"

"Mr. Owusu!" she said, sounding flustered. "How wonderful to see you. I'd like to introduce you to a friend of mine. X," she said pushing him in the middle of the back as Mr. Owusu stepped up on the veranda.

"Yes, how are you?" X said, shaking his hand.

"I'm fine, thank you. And you?"

"I'm feeling very good this morning."

"Yes," Bente said, frowning at X. "X is an American. He's come up to Tamale for a little visit."

"Yes, but this weather," Mr. Owusu said, turning to look at the sky.

"Oh, I sort of like it."

"You do?"

Bente laughed. "He seems to."

"Well, I've never gotten used to it, and I've lived here my whole life."

"So how bad can it be? You're all still here."

"Yes, because this is my home. Perhaps we're just more tolerant of what we find at home."

"Tolerant, or we just get used to it. Or maybe we just can't imagine life being any different. For us, I mean."

Owusu smiled at him. "That's probably it." He looked at Bente. "I was hoping Liz was back."

"She phoned last night. She's going to be stuck in London for ten more days, at least."

"More loans?"

Bente shrugged. For the most part Liz ran the family business. Bente found that hard to deal with, the slow divestiture of their father's holdings, so she rarely took an active role. It was, after all, all that remained of their father's legacy. Owusu was an old friend of their father's. A wealthy local grower they'd known all their lives. A sympathetic man.

"Well then, I should be on my way," Owusu said. "I don't need to be bothering your guest with boring business matters. I'm sure Liz will call when she returns."

"Are you sure? We'd love to have you stay for lunch."

"Yes," X said, "do stay."

Mr. Owusu nodded, smiling at the two of them. "Oh no, thank you, but I must be going, and I'm sure I would just be an intrusion."

"He could tell," Bente said as they watched him drive off.

"Tell what? That a beautiful woman like you has a man staying with her? You think that surprises him?"

She took his hand. "I guess not."

"I bet he's relieved. He's thinking, good, she's finally got herself a man up here. It's about time."

"I've had men up here before."

"Who?" he asked, letting go of her hand.

"Well," she smiled. "There was my husband. He used to come up here."

"And?"

"Actually," she said, putting her hand on her chin as if to think about it, "I'm not so sure I can remember. I guess it has been a long time."

"Yes, it's obviously been a very long time."

She wrapped her arms around his waist, then ran her hand up his back under his shirt, silently counting off all the scars as she felt them. "I wonder if the time will ever come when I'll forget about this visit?" she said.

Later, back in bed after lunch, she said, "I really do hate this, you know." She was tapping the scar tissue on his shoulder above the GPS chip.

"Because they know where I am?"

"Yes. In my damn bed!"

"Wondering why I keep coming back to this same location."

When they awoke he asked her, "This was always your room growing up?"

"Always."

"When you were a little girl, did you ever think you'd be sleeping in this bed with old number seven?"

"When I was a little *teenage* girl I certainly had those sorts of thoughts, but I always hoped it would be Robert Redford."

"I guess I must be a big disappointment."

"No, you've been all any little teenage girl could ever hope for."

"How about middle-aged doctors?"

She rolled over on top of him and smiled. "That remains to be seen."

In the evening they went for a stroll, walking past the two large storage buildings and down a path through the trees. The air was dry, but there was a sweet odor in the air she told him was the acacia.

"No cocoa?"

"Not up here, it's not humid enough."

"It's not?"

"Not for good cocoa. Too much sun and wind. The quality of the fruit really suffers. Ideally, it needs to be grown in a more protected environment, like under a canopy of tropical hardwoods."

"Mahogany?"

"What's left of them. It's difficult. It takes ten years for a cocoa tree to start producing high quality fruit, so the temptation is always there to take a quick profit, especially for the smaller growers. But once you've cut down the forest it's not that easy to grow healthy, productive cocoa trees. Then what? Still, most of our cocoa production comes from the smaller growers."

"But you do dry the beans here?"

"After they ferment. Then we negotiate a price, bag them up, and off they go to Takoradi."

"To the Netherlands?"

"Germany. Britain. Japan. It all depends."

"You enjoy this?"

She smiled. "Not really, but my family's been in this business since the beans were brought here over a century ago."

"And your sister?"

"Liz likes to take charge."

He knew that already, the big sister. "And is this what *she* really wants to be doing?"

"Well, let's just say she's taken on the obligation. And someone had to. This is still post-colonial Africa. It's still cocoa, gold, and timber, and now some coffee. Without our exports we'd have nothing to sell."

"Oil?"

"Yes, and now oil. But other than cocoa we're still caught up in a cycle of resource depletion. We worry about the future."

"Your father probably talked like this, didn't he? That you may be well paid for your exports but it's still a form of colonial exploitation. Though now I suppose he'd be talking about globalist exploitation. Either way, once it's gone you won't have much to show for it other than the consumer goods you've bought."

She smiled at him. "Is that how you think?"

"At times." He was thinking of the Delegations, as they were called, wondering what they and the Chinese were up to, the implicit quid pro quo no one would know about until it was probably too late. "But then I suppose it's just this whole Gold Coast thing, isn't it?" he said.

"The exploitation?"

"It was the Portuguese who started it. Right?"

"Yes. They came looking for the source of the gold they were buying in North Africa. Then they built the castle."

"Elmina?"

She nodded. "But soon it wasn't gold, it was slaves for New World plantation agriculture."

"After they'd killed off all the indigenous peoples."

"Yes, so they came here, to the Gold Coast."

"And the Dutch?"

"We ran the Portuguese out in the 1640s."

"But in the end it was the British."

"That's right, though at one time there were Swedes, Danes, and Germans here as well."

"Fighting over who'd control the slave trade?"

"Yes, though there was probably more than enough to go around."

"What a thought."

"Not that some of the Africans didn't play a role in this, as well. Slaves for trade goods and alliances. It was pretty ugly on all sides."

"So now it's Ghanaian workers sending their money back home from abroad."

She smiled at him. "If you're saying that's just another form of slavery, or that they're in any way morally equivalent, I'll have to disagree."

"No, I just like to note an historical irony when I run across one."

"Yes, I've noticed that about you. Your taste for irony, not to mention your odd detachment from history."

"I wish."

"No?"

"No. Like this Gold Coast business, for instance. It makes me wonder about us as a species. About what lies ahead. About what our chances are for doing the right thing."

Her eyes got wide as she studied his face, looking for a clue as to the depth of his seriousness. "It does?"

He laughed and took her hand. "I know," he said, grinning. "Where'd that come from?"

"Yes, where indeed." She was watching him so carefully.

11

X called Bente at the clinic to see if she were free for dinner that evening. Yes, and they'd bring Liz along, who was in town for a few days. Unsaid was what they both understood, that it was time for Bente's family to meet this odd man she was seeing.

They didn't look much like sisters, which made him wonder if they had different fathers or mothers. Maybe he'd find a way to ask.

They picked a Chinese restaurant for dinner. It was nice, but then locals would know where to go, wouldn't they?

As they waited for dinner he heard about the current family business, not that it was much of one, though at one time it had been quite substantial. It seems they'd sold off most of it, often to former employees. Really? He wondered where their former employees got that kind of money.

"It's been difficult for everyone," Liz explained. "Even in Tamale business has been marginal. Just one or two bad years is all it takes, then everyone suffers. And of course there's always the harmattan, which is a problem every year, good or bad."

"Like this year?" Everyone was complaining about it. The dust was everywhere. It even reached all the way out to the Moody River.

She nodded. "I can taste it. The grit gets in the house. In my car." She made a face.

"But still, I'd think that would be a nice change from the heat and humidity," he said.

"I suppose, but up there it feels more like the Sahara's closing in, and I wonder if it won't, if global warming is everything they say it is."

"But maybe global warming will shift the high pressure somewhere else and you won't have the harmattan anymore."

"But then we wouldn't have anything to complain about," Bente said, smiling at her sister. "When will the harmattan come this year? How long will it last? How strong will the winds be? How dry?"

"I thought people claimed it made them angry, which is supposedly why there's more crime this time of year. You know, that the wind makes people irritable. The roughnecks certainly claim it does."

"Everyone does," Liz said.

"Is that what you're blaming for your back?" Bente asked, eyes twinkling.

"I should," he said, unconsciously touching the area with his hand.

"He hardly has a scar," Bente said to her sister.

"Oh?" Liz raised her eyebrows and smiled. "A professional observation?"

X watched them grinning at each other. Yes, Bente did look a bit embarrassed. No, she'd not yet told her sister they were sleeping together.

"It's a lovely little scar, Liz," X said. "Would you care to see?"

"No, but you can pour me some more wine."

Over dinner he heard about Liz's two ex-husbands. The first was the man she'd married while a student at Leiden. Too young, and he'd never liked Africa anyway, an explanation X found more plausible since he could see that it would take some getting used to. The second, the father of her now grown son, was from an old colonial Ghanaian Dutch family, one not unlike hers and Bente's, but that marriage had fallen apart under the pressures of his failing import business. Now, with the coming oil boom, she said he was thinking he might try it again.

"Do you really think that will help?" X asked.

She smiled and shook her head. "No, not in his case."

"Don't look at me," Bente laughed when he turned to her. "I've got nothing to say about my ex-husband."

"Fine, I wasn't going to ask, anyway."

"Nice man, however," Liz said, smiling as she sipped her wine.

"He was," Bente agreed.

"And cute," Liz added.

"On his good days."

"You know," X told them, "men have this horrible fear that this is how women talk about them when they're not around."

"Really? I think we're being remarkably kind," Bente said.

"And you?" Liz asked, smiling at him. "Care to jump in with a few tales about your ex-wives?"

"Liz," Bente said, "if you can get that out of him I'll be pretty upset."

12

He was trailing them a bit as they came out of the restaurant, then he was preoccupied with looking up the street to where they'd parked the car, so at first he didn't see them, just the two sisters pause to look to their right. Then he saw the four young men in the shadows. Two were leaning against the wall of the restaurant, two stepping forward towards the sisters.

He took three quick steps and put his hand on Bente's arm. "Just keep walking to the car," he told her.

He saw a flash and then the tall man near him said, "What's the rush, brother?"

"That's enough," Bente said, putting her hand on his arm.

"I know, I'm just making sure." He bent over and turned the man's head to the side so he could see his face in the light.

She bent down beside him. "Let me see." She lifted the man's right eyelid and looked at his pupil. She looked at her sister. "You'd better call," she said.

"He doesn't look good, does he?" X asked.

She shook her head. She stood and put her hand on his arm. "No, but he didn't leave you much choice."

"I know. It's just . . ."

"What?"

"I should have held up."

"Why didn't you?"

"I thought he might shoot, and he was rushing me."

"You mean you thought he might shoot us."

"Or me."

She shook her head. She'd seen his reaction. "You weren't worried about yourself."

"They're on the way," Liz said. She looked at her sister and then turned to stare at him. "Just who in the hell are you?" she asked.

"Does it matter?"

"What does that mean? Of course it matters."

"Liz," her sister said.

"What?" She stared at them, angry and scared.

"You're not being fair."

"I'm not?" She noticed how Bente had her hand on his arm. She saw the look in his eyes. She looked at the two men on the ground. One of them had to be dead. She stared at the gun on the sidewalk. She shook her head, wanting it to all go away. Then she took a deep breath and held it for a long time before letting it all go. "Am I being hysterical?" she finally asked.

Bente smiled. "Well . . ."

"Sorry," she said, patting X on the shoulder. "But you are a rather unusual date."

"Yes," he said.

Bente stepped in front of him and looked him in the eyes. "Are you hurt? I didn't even think to ask."

Liz took his hand. "You're bleeding. The other one cut you with that knife."

"Let me see?" Bente stepped to the side so they could see his hand in the light. "Well, looks like it's time for a few more stitches." She grinned at him. "What a tough guy."

"Bente, when the police get here they're going to have a lot of questions. Why don't you and Liz take off and let me handle this."

"No."

"But—"

"No. We need to tell them this wasn't your fault. Right?" She looked at Liz.

"They'll believe us. We're respectable."

"Thanks. Then would one of you respectable ladies mind taking this?" He reached under the back of his coat, bent forward a bit and did something with his hands that brought forth a small automatic in a tiny leather holster. "I think it will simplify things tremendously if I don't have this on me when they arrive."

"I'll take it," Liz said.

"Are you sure?" Bente looked surprised.

"You take care of his hand."

"Thanks, Liz."

"Oh, don't mention it," she said, laughing as she struggled to get the gun in her bag.

Bente took his hand and closed it in a fist, then put her hand over it and held it.

"What?" he asked.

"I was just thinking that I'll need to say thank you when this night is over. Now keep your hand like that. The paramedics will have something we can use to wrap this up until I can get you to the clinic."

He groaned.

"Oh, come on, I'm practically your personal physician."

"I know, but this is getting embarrassing."

As it turned out, the two men were well known local criminals, but the police were surprised, armed robbery wasn't their normal stock in trade.

13

He called Callender's cell phone the next morning to see if he was in town. He was.

"Are you free?" he asked. "I'm heading up to Tamale this afternoon and we need to talk before I go."

"With Bente?"

"Yes."

"How long will you be gone?"

"A few days. Maybe a week."

"And how is she?"

"That's what we need to talk to about."

"She's okay, isn't she?"

"She's fine. I guess I'm really more concerned about you and me."

"That sounds ominous."

"Your hotel in an hour?"

"Can't wait."

When X pulled up by the hotel in his rental car and honked, Callender turned and waved. It was a lovely little car. Much like an old Fiat 131. They were still building them in Africa. X loved it.

"So what's wrong," Callender asked, climbing in.

"And it's nice to see you again, too, Sandy," X said with a laugh.

"Sorry. But I've been looking over my shoulder ever since you called. You scared the hell out of me."

"Sorry, but we do need to be careful. I was out last night with Bente and her sister when four guys tried to rob us just as we were leaving the restaurant. I got this." He held up us bandaged hand.

"Not more stitches?"

"An even dozen."

"So what happened?"

X sighed. "Two ran away. One's dead. One may die."

"But the three of you are fine, other than your hand?"

"Yes, scared and angry, but fine."

"And Bente? She's still speaking to you?"

X nodded.

"So what's this got to do with me?"

"Sandy, the police were very surprised. Turns out, these two guys were well known local career criminals, but this was the first time, at least so far as they knew of, that they'd ever tried to do rob someone."

"They were hired to go after you, in other words."

"And right downtown with lots of people standing around."

"But why you? I'm the one who's been poking around." He stared at him. "Is there something you'd like to tell me? Something maybe I should know about?"

"I'm thinking," X said, putting the car in gear and driving away from the hotel.

14

"Remember out at the rig when I mentioned something to you about bringing the mail?"

"Yes, though you never really explained what that meant."

"It means they're taking people to and from the space station."

"Military?"

"No, mostly the contract people who report to the military, or the federal types who are active in those areas."

"Like the CIA?"

X smiled. Reporters always asked about the CIA. It was a knee jerk response with them. "It's way more complicated than that. But sure, they have a role to play in this. So the shuttles also bring supplies. Mundane stuff like that."

"So what we saw that night?"

"Symbolic, for the most part. Kind of like a provocation, though not really meant for us."

"Could you possibly be more cryptic?" Callender said with a shake of his head.

"Way more."

"Great. So who are these provocations meant for? If you'd be so kind."

"Sandy, look, it really is complicated, I'm not kidding about that, though it certainly didn't start out that way. But certain governments, or at least parts of them, have known for a long time that we have near-space visitors."

"I knew you were going to say something like that!"

"What they didn't understand, at least not initially, is that our visitors have differing intentions and points of view."

"With regard to what? Us?"

"Largely. But the point I want to make is that the existence of these factions, or delegations, makes things very political."

"For them, or for us?"

"Them, and for us by implication."

"In what sense?"

"As I assume you already know, according to contemporary science there's an infinitude of galaxies out there. What we can count, or estimate, already runs into the millions, if not billions, and it's immensely old. Actually, I think it's eternal, though science doesn't necessarily agree with me."

"But that would definitely be old."

"It also appears that intelligent life, though rare, is not uncommon, not given the magnitude of time we're talking about and the potential number of habitable worlds. The point is that somehow in all that vastness of space and time they found us."

"When?"

"Unknown, though I suspect this goes back a few decades, at least, if not much farther."

"So they found us, and for some reason they're still here?"

"Yes. It seems we're interesting. As is our world."

"To them?"

"Yes."

"But why the factions?"

"Because we interest them in different ways." He held up his hand. "I know, but that's what I've been told, and more than once."

"You do realize how hard it is to take any of this seriously?"

X nodded. "I know. It's crazy. If any of this *were* true there'd be some sort of incontrovertible proof, or at least some scrap of evidence we could all agree on. Worse, it's not even plausible. Space is just too vast. The distances from anywhere even close-by are way beyond our capabilities, and even if they weren't the cost of getting here would still be astronomical. Okay, maybe a probe. Some machine intelligence built to function for eons as it hunts for intelligent life. But it would still take forever for anyone to get here once we had been found, and even then there just hasn't been enough time."

"To notice us?"

"Yes, we've only been worth noticing for a few decades. It seems very unlikely. More importantly, if this were true we'd just know, wouldn't we? That none of this fits with how we live our lives, or intrudes on what we know of our own existence, must mean something."

Callender nodded his head. That really was how it felt, not that it wasn't possible, just that it wasn't so.

"So I know I must sound to you like one of those poor lost souls obsessed with UFOs and alien abductions, but I'm really not."

"That UFOs in the Bible stuff?"

"Yes. Clearly, one of our problems as a culture is that there are far too many of us who are willing to believe just about anything, especially so as we all struggle to keep our heads above water in an increasingly secular age. There aren't many who can handle that much disenchantment. But," he said, smiling at Callender, "guess what?"

"All that nonsense is really true?"

X laughed. "Actually, no, not so far as I know. But as hard as this may be for us to believe, as firmly rooted as we are in our day-to-day existence, they are here, and someday we will have to be told."

"I hope you're not proposing I be the one to do the telling."

"No, I just want you around paying attention to what may happen next, and to do so you'll need to understand the context, even though you find that context totally implausible."

"Okay, setting aside my doubts about your sanity, which by now are legion, would you mind telling me how they got here? Or why they've remained? And just how is it that you know all this? Which, come to think of it, raises all sorts of interesting questions about you, though for the moment I'll settle for an explanation of how you know all this is true."

"How they got here I don't think is known. They're not sharing much with us. Why they are here is, as I've just said, because of us and our world."

"But there's some disagreement over that?"

"So it seems."

"But we meet with them? Or representatives of some of our governments do?"

"They rendezvous with us out at the ISS."

"From where do they rendezvous?"

"I've been told from somewhere in the vicinity of the moon."

"The moon!" Callender laughed and shook his head. "We've been to the moon. Remember? The old Apollo program?"

"And it's been photographed and mapped."

"Exactly."

"Well, I'm not saying they're *on* the moon, though it is a big place. Just how hard do you suppose it would be to hide something up there?"

"A big place?" He laughed. He couldn't help it. It was absurd. "So, they, whoever they are, we meet them out at the space station?"

"We meet with some of them."

"Some?" He just stared.

"It's political. Remember?"

"How about the astronauts?"

"What about the astronauts?"

"They never saw anything? When they were there?"

"You're talking about on the moon?"

"Yes, when they were up there on those missions."

"They don't know."

Callender leaned back to stare at him. "They don't know?"

"They don't. They all suffer, some of them rather severely, from memory loss."

"In general, or just when it comes to what they did on the moon?"

X shrugged. "I don't know about the rest of their lives, but they sure do when it comes to what they did on the moon. Ask one of them what it felt like up there and all you get is a blank stare. Yes, they can tell you all about mission specific tasks, the rocks they picked up and brought back, the flight, but they have no substantive memories of what it was like to be there."

"So you're saying someone messed with their memories when they got back?"

"That's one theory."

"What?"

"Well, maybe something happened to them up there."

"On the moon?"

"Why not?"

"You mean *they* did something to them?"

"Sandy, you'd be surprised by how many people there are running around with these interesting gaps in their memories."

"And what about you?"

"No, I seem cursed with an ironclad memory."

"But this is about memory, isn't it? With me, I mean."

X grinned at him. "Story of a lifetime."

Callender shook his head. He'd heard crazy stories before, what reporter hadn't, but this . . . "Fine. So what is it they're forgetting? Or were made to forget? And it can't just be them, can it? There must be lots of people connected to this who know something."

"Well, let's say one of them did choose to speak out. Who'd believe them? You wouldn't. You don't even believe me. I know it's hard for people like you to believe, people who've never been in these situations, but there really are people who won't talk."

"Because?"

"Perhaps they're terrified of the consequences."

"What consequences? You don't really believe someone's going to kill them, do you?"

"No, but it hardly needs to go that far, just threaten their pensions or careers. Strange how that seems to work for most people."

"It would certainly work for me."

"And let's be honest, here. All they really need to do is just keep them quiet long enough so that by the time they do find the courage to speak they can't help but sound old and foolish. There he goes, we'll say, just another crazy old man. But there are those who welcome this. They think they're being patriotic."

"Drank the Kool-Aid?"

"Lots of people do, people who aren't as cynical as you and me. As to what the astronauts were made to forget . . . I think they saw things. In fact, I think they were sent there to find some of those things."

"And?"

"Oh, they found them, but then something, or someone, made us back away."

"Of course."

"No? Apollo 11 in 1969, then a few more missions over the next several years and that's it? We just decided never to go back?" He stared at Sandy. "Yeah. After we spent billions to get it right, and then we just stop the whole project right in midstream when everything's in place and working flawlessly? Doesn't really make much sense, does it?"

No, on the surface it didn't, but then he didn't know much about it. He'd been a child when the last Apollo mission had flown. "Okay, I'll grant you that's odd, but you make it sound like we were warned off or something." He smiled at X. "Though I have to admit I love how that sounds."

"I thought you might. Then there's Kennedy's speech."

"What speech?"

"The one he gave at the United Nations when he proposed that the Americans join forces with the Russians to go to the moon."

"To go to the moon?"

He nodded. "This was in 1963."

"Why would he do that?"

X raised his eyebrows and stared at him.

"Okay. No, I didn't know that, but we can read conspiratorial motives into anything."

"Of course, but this was at the height of the Cold War. Just after we'd somehow managed to sneak through the Cuban Missile Crisis without stumbling into nuclear Armageddon. Yet here's Kennedy not even a year later proposing we all join hands and go to the moon."

"I don't know . . ."

"You do know that the Soviet program to send a man to the moon came to an abrupt halt in late 1972?"

"Come on, you know I don't know any of this stuff."

"Well, it did, and this just after the final test of their new titanic booster rocket. They'd been having some difficulties, but they'd finally been sorted out. Now they were ready."

"What difficulties?"

"They kept blowing up."

"How convenient for us."

"But the timing's interesting, isn't it? That Apollo comes to a screeching halt at just about the same time the Russians decide it's not worth the bother. Oh, really? This after spending billions and billions of rubles and losing more than a few lives."

"But you just said they kept blowing up."

"Yes, but they were ready. Their Germans had it licked. Just that one last test and then they were going. Two man crews picked out. All the landing apparatus set. But then they just stopped."

Callender sighed and had a sip of his beer. From a reporter's point of view the situation was hopeless. Documentation? He almost laughed. If, and that was a very big if, some did exist it would never be fished out of the archives with a Freedom of Information request. He'd need a source, a mole. But they'd all be old men. Yes, and soon they'd all be dead. Then he wouldn't even know who to ask. No, it was hopeless. "And Kennedy?" he asked.

"In less than two months he was dead."

"Christ." He stared at X. "You know this is absurd."

"Of course."

"But what difference does that make? Right?"

"Something like that."

"You're sure this isn't something you got off some crazy website?"

X laughed. "Hardly, though I'm sure this is all out there somewhere. What you need to understand is that for those of us in my line of work this is all part of our oral tradition, though very much *sub rosa*. The stuff we pick up here and there as we train and move about and meet new people, like the scientists and operations guys. People do talk in organizations, you know that."

He nodded.

"So all that gossip, all those rumors, all that speculation, sooner or later it becomes part of the lore. You know how people are, how they're much more comfortable sharing their secrets in an environment like that. It's anonymous. It tweaks those in authority. It asserts a bit of individuality. It lessens fears and worries.

"But is any of it true?"

"Well, as to that, you might as well ask yourself why not. Remember, these are all highly trained professionals talking amongst themselves after hours. Sharing what they've seen and heard. Filling in the blanks for each other as they struggle to understand. And don't forget, most of this comes in the form of one friend telling something to another."

"So you do believe this lore?"

X smiled.

"No?"

"Some of it."

"Which is what you're doing right now. Sharing things with me that you've heard, one friend to another."

X nodded. "That's right. One friend to another, though not just what I've heard."

Sandy got very still. Yes. He'd wondered about that. After all, who was X? "Well," he said, "I'd be very interested in hearing about that. But aliens on the moon?"

"Having a little trouble with that one?"

"Yes, and not just with that one!"

15

They all gathered in the conference room on the rig's lower deck. Chalmers held court.

"It's fairly straightforward," he said in response to a question. "We take them up, then we bring them back down."

"And then take them back up again," someone said.

"That's the job," Chalmers said, and for most of them that was true. Just glorified bus drivers. "It's going to be a big meeting and it may drag on for a few days, so you'll be busy."

"So," Nickerson asked, "are we going to Edwards, or Amberley?"

"Both. Like I said, this is a big operation."

X raised his hand with a question—he knew how Chalmers hated that—and when Chalmers tried to ignore him he waved it back and forth.

"Yes, X?" Chalmers said, frowning at him.

"You don't suppose you could tell us what's really going on? Even a hint would be helpful."

"A hint?"

"Sure. Give us some idea of what we're up against."

"You're not up against anything, it's just a job."

"Really? Then I don't suppose you'd care to come along this time, just to make sure we don't screw up?" X turned and smiled at the room when it erupted in laughter. None of them thought Chalmers was worth a damn.

Chalmers glared at him. How many times had he complained about X? Dozens, at least, and always he got the same answer: hands off. It mystified him, but he understood organizations, for some reason X had juice, which meant tread carefully. "Yes, as always, X, thanks so much for your assistance." He looked out at the room. "Any more questions?" The truth was that he had nothing to tell them. He was tasked with the logistical side. Why they were doing this was something he knew very little of, and of course that was, as always, just fine with him.

X stood looking at his orders. He was off to Edwards. "What do you have?" He was asking Moss.

"Australia." He held out his orders and pointed to *Amberley*.

"This Delegations business worries me," X said.

"Oh? Have you heard something?" They were all anxious. None of them really knew much about the Delegations or what the negotiations were about. Following orders was fine, up to a point, but they weren't real military, and even if they had been, blindly following orders was never something anyone looked forward to. It was also a bit galling to be left so totally in the dark.

"Not much, just that this is the biggest conference, to date, that we've had with the Delegations, and that the logistics are going to be pretty tedious with this many different parties. At least that part seems clear enough, but what worries me is security."

"Whose? Ours, or theirs?"

"Both, in the sense that we don't have any, so far as I can tell, and who knows what they have, or if they even need any, but if they do it can't be because they're worried about us. So shouldn't we be worried about what they're worried about? That's the real issue, as I see it."

"Because we're unarmed?"

X nodded. He'd raised the issue many times in his reports. He'd never had a response. Never even a request for a follow-up.

"X?" Moss hesitated. He seemed embarrassed.

"What?"

"Look, don't take this the wrong way."

"Don't worry about it."

"I know . . . we all know, that you play a different role in this than we do. Now, we both know that's true," he said, holding up his hand to stop X from denying it.

"Okay."

"So if you have heard something more specific, something that's making you nervous, we'd certainly appreciate a heads-up." He stared at him. "That's reasonable, isn't it?"

"Like I said, I'm just voicing my suspicions, but it's no secret that something really big is coming. Why else would they even bother to have this conference? So, again, the problem, at least as I see it, is that we're totally unprepared for whatever that might turn out to be. Just way too many unknowns."

Moss nodded. "And the Delegations? You do know we've never really been briefed?"

"Well, I have, and trust me, what I know about the Delegations is still next to nothing. But maybe that's all anyone knows. Could be. My guess, they can't agree on what to do with us, which is why they want to drag everybody up there for this big meeting."

"At least that's a reason."

"And another thing to bear in mind. I've been told that the different factions among the Delegations don't trust each other. Just look at this business with the beam weapons they gave us. First off, it was very foolish on our part to let them draw us into their disputes like that. Disputes we don't even understand. And apparently we've now been forced to take sides, or at least to appear as if we have, and all this while we still don't know who they really are or what they're up to."

"Care to guess?"

"Sure. We're on the sidelines, reluctant witnesses to, and occasional participants in, their political squabbles. Floundering around without a clue while caught up in their differing agendas. Quite likely being manipulated at the same time, all in the service of someone else's political ends." He sighed and shook his head. "And in the middle of all this they want to hold a conference?"

"It certainly sounds like politics, though on a much larger scale, of course."

"Exactly. And what often follows close on the heels of politics?"

"Conflict?"

"Which is when they turn to us, though this time I'm afraid there's not going to be very much we can do about it. Just look at this silly business with the beams. Oh, sure, they gave us a few, but to be used only when we're called upon, and even then nothing really happens when we do."

"I've been wondering about that, because they're worthless the way we've been forced to deploy them."

"I suspect they're worthless no matter how we deploy them."

"So you believe their deployment was merely political?"

"What else could it be?"

"Okay." Moss sighed, looking at the open doorway. "I'm beginning to get the idea."

"Some job, huh?"

Moss turned and smiled. "But we do get to see foreign shores."

16

It was a class two shuttle, one of the earlier prototypes the military spun off the old NASA series. *Shuttles.* X hated what that derogatory name implied. You won't explore, you won't colonize, you won't venture forth, you will shuttle. But that's good, it's practical, useful, a good function for a space fleet in a democracy. We're okay. See? Just space buses. Like a public utility. Please don't cut our funding, not now that we've finally pulled back from all those impractical and expensive dreams President Kennedy cooked up to beat the Russians.

Like pilots have done since the Wright brothers, he circled the small craft and looked, not that he expected to find a gaping hole in the insulation or a dented aileron, though the military shuttles did all have a rather shabby appearance. After all, they were never meant for smiling crews posing for the evening news. In that sense they really were just shuttles—and unarmed. But why had the military never armed them? A decision that now seemed like a glaring oversight, though X had never heard anything to suggest it had even been considered.

He ran his hand over the shuttle's smudged nose. Sooty, and of course nothing on it anywhere to identify it other than *II-VI* in small red Roman numerals by the cargo hatch. Not that such modesty had ever stopped any of its various crews from affectionately referring to it as the *Shore Leave.*

II-VI? So that meant it was probably at least twenty years old. He smiled. He loved that bit with the Roman numerals, like these were the vehicles of empire: the New Rome. He was sure there was a politician behind that nomenclature somewhere, surely on the advice of some marketing guru who'd convinced him it would make the voters back home proud. But the New Rome? Perhaps that might have worked back in the 1960s, but not now. Now it was Old Rome about to be overrun by alien barbarians.

He turned and walked past the security guards and out through the open doorway into the interior of the hanger. He was nervous. He couldn't help it, this whole business just felt wrong, and Chalmer's refusal to explain didn't help. Maybe he'd just step outside for a few minutes. Just to clear his head.

He came to one of the gigantic steel doors and held his ID card in front of the card reader. Almost immediately, a smaller door popped open, allowing him to step out onto the tarmac. He took a deep breath, savoring the hot dry air. In the distance, out beyond the acres of concrete and asphalt, he could see the Mojave shimmering in the heat. Yes, the sun was hot. It wasn't long before he took a step back into the thin band of shade along the side of the hanger. It was then he noticed the sun's shimmering reflection off the windshield of an approaching vehicle. A vehicle that slowly resolved itself into the shiny black Lincoln Navigator with blacked out windows that came to a halt by the near corner of the hanger.

Curious, he waited to see who might get out, and when no one did he stepped from the shadows and began walking towards it, using his hand to shade his eyes from the windshield's glare. He got quite close, maybe to within ten yards before someone finally emerged from the front passenger's side door to stand on the tarmac staring at him. Ball cap, sunglasses, what looked like a running outfit, X watched him momentarily put his hand to his ear.

"Get back inside," he yelled.

"What?"

"Get back in the fucking building."

"Thanks, I'm fine," X said, smiling like he was the most agreeable person anyone could ever hope to meet. "I'm just getting some fresh air."

The man took a step, halting in front of the SUV. X could see that he was leaning down, speaking into a microphone. Yes, another ex-Special Forces type, they always were, the ones who became corporate goons.

Still smiling rather foolishly, X took two or three steps closer, wondering how far he could push this before they made a mistake. He really shouldn't, he knew that, but for some reason he just found it entertaining.

Then a second man got out, this one from the back. "Sir," he said, just like they always do when they hate your guts. "We need you to step inside for a bit." He motioned towards the door. "If you wouldn't mind."

X nodded. Now this was an approach that might actually work. Being polite. Putting the burden of being an asshole on his shoulders. "Tell you what," X said, laughing at them. "How about if I promise to close my eyes? Or I can turn my back. See?" He turned around and looked at them over his shoulder. "Then you can sneak him in and I won't even know."

The two men looked at each other, then the first one grinned and began slowly walking towards him. X knew what that meant. Another sadist who liked to drag it out, make someone feel the fear before they felt the pain.

X turned to stare at the Lincoln. Surely someone with authority was in there watching all this. Were they really going to let this just play itself out? Well . . . if they really wanted to play . . . and who knows, it might even do him some good. Give him a reason for all this unfocused hostility he was feeling.

"Hey, old-timer," the first man said, making sure he had his attention. "You can get your sun later. Now get you ass back inside."

"It is hot out here, isn't it?" X said, turning to look at the sun. It was, too, probably at least 105 degrees. He turned back and smiled. "Don't look now, but you appear to be sweating," he said.

"Jeff?" the man said, looking at the other guy standing next to the Navigator.

"X! Will you stop this shit."

He looked up. "Bostic?" He smiled at the other man. "What in the hell are you doing here?"

"My job. The question is what in the hell are *you* doing here?"

X looked at the two men on the ground. "Having a little fun?" He nodded at them. "I didn't hurt them."

"So maybe you'd like to do their job?" Bostic pointed to the open door.

X walked over and bent down to look: A tall figure wearing a clear plastic breathing mask; disturbingly intelligent eyes.

"Are we satisfied now?" Bostic asked when X straightened up to look at him.

So he'd finally met one. "Uh, actually, no, I'm not. How about an introduction?"

Bostic leaned over and said, "Mr. Ambassador, this man is called X. He and I have known each other for a long time. He's actually much smarter than he appears to be."

The ambassador seemed to nod and X could hear the whistle from the breathing apparatus. "Is he for hire?" a metallic voice asked.

Bostic laughed and looked at X. "Well?"

X leaned down and smiled. "Thank you, Mr. Ambassador, but not today, though who can say what the future may hold. Sorry about this, uh, altercation. You must be getting awfully hot in there. Let me help you get inside." He looked up and Bostic nodded.

"Jeff? Rick?" Bostic said. "Get over here and help. X didn't hurt you that badly."

Once inside the ambassador he took off the breathing apparatus and handed it to the one named Rick, then took three deep breaths from an inhaler. "Will you be all right?" Bostic asked. Nodding, the ambassador turned to look at X. Yes, without the mask he didn't seem so foreboding, more like a tall thin man with an illness. It was the eyes, though, that's where he didn't look well. Putting his hand on X's arm, the ambassador motioned for Bostic and the other two to move away, and once they were out of earshot he leaned down to see X more clearly. The wheezes he made as he breathed weren't nearly as disconcerting as the way he stared at him. "It always takes me a few days to acclimate," he said.

"Not enough oxygen?"

"Yes," the ambassador nodded. He studied X a moment. "I believe I know you," he said.

"Not possible."

"No? Because there is something very familiar about you." He glanced at the others. "You are different, are you not?"

"From?"

"From humans."

X stepped back and stared at him. "I'm sorry, I don't know what you mean."

"Really? Then I think you humans must have a lot of secrets."

X laughed. "Not this human."

"You may not know this. I suppose you don't. But there exits a longstanding dispute over the roll of chance and luck in our affairs."

"We have that dispute."

"Did you know that humans are considered very lucky?"

"We are? I'd think we'd be considered improbable, all things being equal."

The ambassador leaned back to watch him.

"And," X added, "when you say lucky like that, that seems to suggest you think things are perhaps better for us than they should be. Is that how you view us?"

The ambassador put his hands together and rocked back and forth. What did that mean? Was he thinking?

"Of course, there is the other view," the ambassador said when he stopped rocking.

"And that is?"

"That events follow a pattern, or a plan."

"Some plan."

"You are not a naturalist?"

"A what?"

"A scientist. One who believes that everything has a natural explanation."

X laughed. "No, I'm not a naturalist. Are you?"

"No. I believe we must decide for ourselves what's best. There is no plan."

"But the one you impose?"

Apparently startled, the ambassador did a bunch of wheezing, so much so that Bostic came over to ask, "Mr. Ambassador?"

"I think he's laughing," X said.

When he settled down, the ambassador said, "X, I still think we've met," and with that he turned and walked away.

They both watched him go, then Bostic turned, shaking his head, glaring at X.

"Don't look at me like that. He likes me."

17

He'd known these guys for years. Of late, they'd been on and off the rig any number of times as everyone got ready for the big event. Yes, well it's always been a strange world for those who do something secretive, and this was about as secretive as it got.

The shuttles were well maintained, but they were shabby looking, dirty, full of grit, with marks on the floors, cracked plastics, worn switches, chairs whose padding sagged. Okay, but what about esprit de corps? Seriously? That was just some politician's fantasy, hopefully replaced in the real world by the more sober assessment of professional fatalists. But they definitely took pride in their work, though they knew that no one but them really understood or appreciated what it was they did. Actually, time and again they'd also seen that no one really much cared. So yeah, it was just a job, why wouldn't it be?

They sat at station, each shuttle waiting orders to pick up their parties and ferry them back to the ISS, Edwards, or Amberley. The alien meeting ship was a surprise, no one had mentioned that, or perhaps they hadn't known, but by now it was the fifth day and everyone was more or less used to the routine, for that's what it had become, just another routine, which was something X paid attention to, how any activity, no matter the risk or oddity, soon became just another boring routine, which he took as a dangerous fact about human adaptability to the unknown—that perhaps they were too adaptable.

"Let's look at that checklist again," X said.

"Why?" Murse asked. "We've already gone over it twice. Everything's fine. What's the matter," he grinned, "bored?"

X laughed. "And you're not?" He turned and looked at Panta, who was fiddling with his navigation console. "Panta?"

Panta looked up and smiled. "Time to swab the decks?"

X smiled at Murse. "I suppose you're right." Still, he hated waiting around.

The first hint they had that something might have gone wrong was when dozens of smaller craft began streaming away from the meeting ship. It was like they all received the same message at exactly the same time and now off they all went in different directions.

X heard the chime and watched Murse listen to the COM link, then look at them and shrug. "I don't know what it means," he said, "but everyone sure wants off, and right now." He looked at Standish. "Captain?"

"Of course, it's always right now with these people. Okay. Panta, let's get over there." He pulled himself down in his chair and ran his hand over the control screen. "X? Anything you'd like to add to this?" He cast a quick glance over his shoulder.

"Only my usual worries."

"Just be careful?"

"Never hurts."

They knew there were other big ships out there, but how far away they were no one seemed to know, though surely it had to be tens of thousands of miles at the very least. And no, they never revealed their presence to human instrumentalities. That inaccessibility was by now just taken for granted, which was why it was such a shock, the huge ship coming in so fast that they didn't realize it was there until it was settling in amongst them. Then two more, massive, far larger then the conference ship they dwarfed. X couldn't even begin to calculate how large they were. Was he looking at several thousand feet, or several thousand yards? None of their instruments helped, just showing the presence of massive bodies within their vicinity.

"Murse, what do you hear?" Standish asked.

"It sounds like there's been some sort of dispute. There might even have been an attack on one of the Delegations. It's all a bit disjointed at this point."

"An attack?" X put an earpiece in his ear and tapped a button to listen in. "That was our ambassador?" He was looking at Murse, who nodded.

He was listening in on a conversation between the United States ambassador and his staff back on the space station. He wondered if the ambassador realized he was on an open channel. Maybe he was too rattled to care. X turned and shook his head at Standish, who'd been listening in as well. The ambassador was asking his staff if everyone—presumably he meant humans—was accounted for, and they were reminding him that the Chinese delegation had not been at the meeting, having made a proposal for a separate meeting with some of the Delegations' representatives to iron out a procedural issue about the number of people they could bring to the next meeting.

"And our guys?" Standish asked, referring to the technology commission, who were their personal charges.

Murse shook his head.

"Okay. Let me know when they check in." He turned and looked at X. "Looks like you were right to be worried."

"But an attack? That's way more serious than anything I had in mind."

"Not to mention way more serious for us," Murse said.

"Almost anything would be way more serious for us. Look at this thing. We're defenseless."

Standish raised his eyebrows and looked at him. "It's not like you haven't tried."

"It's not like anyone's ever listened."

Murse was snapping his fingers at them and they both stopped talking to listen. "An ultimatum?" he said, staring at them.

"So it seems, but that can't have anything to do with us."

"Well, whoever it has anything to do with has thirty minutes."

They waited. No further news.

It was ten minutes later that they heard from their commission. They'd already arrived back at the space station, having hitched a ride with the EU trade commission on another shuttle. So what in the hell was going on, other than everyone wanting to get out of there? Either no one knew, or, more likely, they weren't saying.

Ten minutes more and they too were approaching the ISS. The commission now wanted to get down as soon as possible. It was going to be too late to beat the thirty-minute deadline, but if everything went well they'd be back at Edwards for dinner.

Suddenly, there were beam weapons everywhere, a swirling, shifting maze of bright green and blue beams dancing in space seemingly without much direction, and though clearly more powerful than the beam weapons the Delegations had loaned the humans, X could see that they were glancing harmlessly off the shimmering hulls of the huge ships. Yes, it was the smaller craft that were firing. Just what in the hell was going on?

"Son of a bitch!" Murse yelled as one of the beams came raking around and sliced off one whole wing of the space station, taking with it two of the shuttles attempting to dock.

"Jesus!" Standish said. "Let's get the fuck out of here."

"Trying sir." Panta was fumbling with the controls.

"Let me see," X said, leaning over his shoulder.

"It's the engines," Panta said, tapping the readout with his finger. Yes, something had caused the engines to shut down. He and Standish looked at each other. If they didn't get clear of the space station soon they too would be nothing but collateral damage.

"Look at that!" Murse said.

X looked up and watched in amazement as the big ships swung around each other and began gathering up the smaller craft, many of which were still firing. Why didn't they just take them out? There was no way the smaller craft could stand up to the beams he was sure the larger ships had. He was confused. Was he witnessing the effects of a peculiar code of honor, or was this just how they conducted their battles? It was like they were counting coup, because he definitely got the sense that he was witnessing something ritualistic in nature, something choreographed and very weird. Humans would never do that. Start a battle and then not finish it?

And then it was over. All that remained were swirling clouds of debris from the shuttles and the damaged space station. But where had they gone? X looked, but the alien ships had simply vanished. If not for the damage he could see it would be as if it had never happened.

"Murse, any word?" Standish asked.

"Yes, they're waiting for us." He looked at them. "A lot of casualties. I told them it will take us a few minutes to bring the engines back online."

"This," X said, "will certainly put a halt to the negotiations."

Panta nodded. "Which will make the Chinese happy."

"Yes, how lucky for them they chose not to attend today."

Standish was watching him. "Meaning?"

X shrugged. "Maybe nothing. It's just a feeling I get when things start to get too coincidental."

"Yes," Standish said, "and this is certainly not the sort of coincidence I appreciate."

18

Because of the damage over at the ISS there were only two available air locks, so once their engines came back on line they had to queue up with the other remaining shuttles to wait their turn. Slowly, further news came in about the casualties. The two shuttle crews and their passengers, the lives lost on the ISS, the total was now approaching thirty. It was a disaster. There had never been this many casualties in space before, and most of those had been among the shuttle crews whose official existence had never been acknowledged. This time the public would have to be told. Well, wouldn't they? X had his doubts.

He wondered about the Delegations ambassador he'd met at Edwards. Where had he been while all of this was going on? Where was he now? Probably hundreds of thousands of miles away on one of those huge craft trying to figure out what had gone wrong. Or perhaps he knew. Someone must. *Someone must?* X laughed. What a vain hope that was. Yes, but if he ever got the chance he would still like to have a chat with the Ambassador.

"Three more to go and then it's our turn," Murse announced.

Standish looked at the digital clock on his display. "Two hours," he said, not sounding very happy about it. He leaned back in his chair and turned to look at X. "What's that unofficial report of yours going to say now?" They all knew he was there to write one, even though it was supposed to be a secret.

"Unofficially, once again it's going to ask that we arm these things, not that it would do us much good if we did. You saw what they're capable of."

Standish nodded. He'd seen. The difference in the technologies was vast. "What I'd really like is that protective shielding they have on those big ships. That could be very useful."

"Yes, and let's hope that someone doesn't get that before we do."

"Oh? And who might that be?" It was Panta asking, knowing full well who he meant.

"You be sure to put that in your report," Standish said, smiling at him.

"I will most strongly recommend it," X said.

They were still sitting there some ten miles off the ISS when it happened. It was like they were trying to clean up after themselves. Trying to sterilize everything after the fact by hosing it down with a lethal burst of radiation. X wondered if they were attempting to hide something. Or maybe it was one of the Delegations just making sure to cover its tracks. Just guesses. He really had no idea.

He knew the effects of the lethal radiation would be everywhere. All the shuttles, the ISS, and now the issue of shielding would have to be addressed. Yet he was fine, astonished as he so often was by his good luck. He'd been the spare member of their small crew, going back to see if he could figure out why the engines were acting up while everyone else was busy. Tucked away back there in the aft section of their small craft, he'd been down on his hands and knees between the two engine pods reaching with a guasser when he felt the tingling sensation. Four seconds, no more, but when he stood there was Panta doubled over gasping for breath, his face and hands horribly blistered. Instinctively, X reached out to help, but Panta collapsed to the deck without saying a word, just dying there with his eyes open staring at him. Forcing himself, he turned to look at the crew area. Yes, Standish and Murse. Three bodies. He didn't want to just leave them there but he didn't know what else to do. They'd never had any sort of parallel to a burial at sea for space crews, though he could see the need was now upon them.

He sat in the command chair. Although most of the systems on board were fried he was able to run a diagnostic, which showed a brief but massive spike of energetic radiation, probably gamma rays. In the old days, back when they still worried about redundancies, he might have had another system to fall back on to get him out of there, but not with a craft like the *II-VI*. But someone would come eventually. Right?

When he looked he could see several shuttles drifting out there obviously in the same state as his, their crews likely dead or at least unable to respond, and it was probably the same story over at the ISS. Then he noticed an approaching speck of very bright light. Ten minutes later it was next to the most distant of the disabled shuttles. It was too far to see what they were doing out there, his optics were down anyway, but in about half an hour he saw the light move off just as the shuttle unexpectedly exploded in a blinding flash. Well, that was certainly no rescue party, and here he was without a weapon. Truly feeling helpless, he watched as that same process repeated itself twice over the next hour and a half. Then it was his turn.

The craft—and it was an alien craft—came gliding to a halt just beneath him. As he watched, two suited creatures came drifting out of the open port on the far side, then one put its hand on the other's wrist and they slowly began moving off towards the *Shore Leave*. As they did he began to reel himself in, going slowly, expecting to be seen at any minute, if not by them then by someone who'd remained behind, but as he drew closer to their craft he began to believe he wouldn't, and by the time he was near he was sure.

He shot the hook out and it caught on a flange on the side of their craft, then he let the little motor in the gun's handle pull him close enough that he could grab the edge with his hand. Cautiously, laboriously, he pulled himself along until he got his hand over the lip of the open port, then one more tug and he was hanging upside down staring into their craft. Apparently, it really was empty. With no need to be cautious anymore, he pulled himself forward, executing a graceful flip that brought his feet to within a foot of the deck. Then one last tug and he was in.

Pink walls? That's what he noticed first, that and the small knobs on the walls he used to pull himself along, first a few yards to the rear, then all the way to front of the craft. No, still nobody home. He studied the command area. Too confusing. Better for the time being to just ignore that. He certainly didn't want to do something foolish that would announce his presence. But pink walls or no pink walls he was surprised by how spartan everything was, which suggested to him that it was meant for short trips only. Really? Then he'd better be careful because something much larger had to be close at hand.

It was while poking around towards the rear of the craft that he came upon the three small doors, the first two of which, when opened, revealed small cupboards full of neatly stacked packets of what he took to be food and medical supplies, while the third offered up six very lethal looking weapons. Totally surprised, for some time he just stared. Yes, he thought, he was angry enough to use one.

He chose the one that looked most lethal and held it in his hand. It was clearly directional, with something that looked like a muzzle at one end and something else that looked like a handle or grip at the other. Was that the trigger, that small protrusion on top that looked like a pink pea? No, but when he touched it the weapon began to vibrate in his hand. Intrigued, he aimed it at the wall, not actually intending to fire it, but still trying to imagine what it might do. Suddenly, the weapon sparked, and a tight beam of blue light erupted from the end that blew a hole several feet wide in the side of the ship. "Son of bitch!" he said, so startled that he dropped the weapon as they both flew back against the bulkhead. He shook his hand. It stung like a hammer had struck it. Retrieving the weapon, he held it up and opened his hand, letting it hang suspended in front of him. Amazing, but what about the rest?

It was much smaller, quite pleasing in appearance, very smooth and finely made from a shiny deep blue material he couldn't identify, and unlike the other much less military looking, much less standard issue, much more . . . what? Gentlemanly? Was that the word? Like contrasting a rare and lovely dueling pistol with the AK-47 he'd just fired. Of course he had no idea how it worked, though it too seemed to have an end meant for pointing and a thicker part he took to be a grip, though for a hand much smaller than his. And there was that bright lime green M&M that sat up on top, which, when he touched it, he found could slid forward. Yes, once again he felt that same vibrating sensation, though this time much less intense.

Pretty sure he knew what to do, he took a firm grip on the stock and in response the weapon immediately jerked in his hand, firing something that punched a very small hole in the bulkhead right in the center of a very large dent. That it fired a projectile of some sort and not a beam was a pleasant surprise. Likewise pleasing was that it was clearly meant for those more intimate encounters one might have with one's foe. Not hitting someone with a damn beam from two hundred yards, but punching a nice clean hole through their bodies from a few yards away like a proper gentleman. Very nice, he'd take them both; the whole lot if he only had a bag or a pouch. Sliding the M&M back, he put the smaller one in the pocket over his stomach, the larger he shoved down into the pocket on his thigh. Good, he was armed, now what? Well, he'd certainly disabled their craft, not that he'd meant to, but there it was, so maybe it would also be a good idea to make sure they were unable to communicate with anyone.

He drifted back to look at the four remaining weapons. Well, why not this one? It was certainly intriguing enough, like someone had jammed a black tennis ball down on the end of a short metal rod. Wondering how it worked, he picked it up and held it in his hand, testing the grip at the end of the short rod, pleased to find he could twist it counterclockwise through five distinct clicks. Curious to see what that might mean, he twisted it as far as it would go and tapped the pink bulkhead. Immediately, a circular spider's web pattern of tiny lightening bolts erupted across the bulkhead's surface. Even more surprising, there didn't appear to be any damage, or at least none that he could see, but it was still quite a jolt.

Hoping he knew what he was doing, he moved up the craft to the command console and tapped the array of displays and controls with the black tennis ball. Immediately, before he could even react, they erupted in a shower of sparks and flashes that left the craft suddenly very dark and very still. Oops. No way that wasn't going to get their attention. Perhaps he should have tried to come up with a better plan. But in the end it was all rather simple. Moving to the open port, he positioned himself, leaning back against the pink bulkhead to wedge himself in, then reached for the big ugly beam weapon in his thigh pocket. Gently, he nudged the button, immediately feeling the vibration in his hand. The way it twisted and moved, it was like holding a very large, buzzing gyroscope. It just oozed power.

He noticed that the two craft had suddenly started drawing together. He actually felt something tugging at him as he sat there. He shook his head. There was a lot of technology out there he wished they had. Then one of the creatures rose up over the *Shore Leave* and started towards him. Then the other appeared. Thirty yards? Then they paused, seemingly studying their ship. He was sure they were trying to communicate with it. Finally, after what appeared to be a lengthy discussion, one of them started out alone across the diminishing distance between the two craft.

X waited until it got close, then took careful aim and squeezed the grip. Instantly, an intensely blue beam shot out, obliterating the creature. He was shocked by the ferocity of it, there being nothing left but a swirling angry cloud of white-hot gases. Then the other creature began frantically grabbing at something as it tried to move away from him, moving no more than a few yards before a large hole blew out in the side of the *Shore Leave*. Caught by surprise, X felt his craft jerked backwards, then sharply rebound towards the Shore Leave, and as it did he fired, the beam shearing off the right shoulder and arm of the alien, which is to say they were no longer there. Stunned, he watched the creature spin around and around as it was flung away from him out into the empty void of space.

He stood and looked at the *Shore Leave*. It was so close now he could easily push off with his legs and just drift through the gaping hole in its side. But first he'd take one last look around the alien craft. Maybe there was something there that would tell him who or what he'd just killed. Killed? Wasn't there supposed to be some sort taboo about that? One a normal man was supposed to find hard to overcome? Well, to be perfectly honest about it, the fact that he'd just killed two aliens didn't appear to be presenting him with much of a problem, morally or psychologically. An uncomfortable thought, since if he felt like that about them they probably felt the same about him. As always, everything was hopelessly tribal. My tribe. The Other. So much for first contact, for humankind's long dreamt of first bold step towards a brighter future. More like a hasty retreat down the ladder of cultural evolution. What a mess.

Back on board the *Shore Leave*, he watched the alien craft drift slowly away. Too bad, all that technology could have been put to good use. But maybe his government, or someone's, already had it. Not impossible. The aliens seemed careless, like bad employees who failed to take care of their equipment. Oh? And what about that big hole in the side of his own ship?

19

X watched the bubble float gently up to the side of the *Shore Leave* and stop in front of the hole in the hull. As he watched it gradually became transparent, revealing a man inside sitting in a chair. It was absurd. Not only did he appear to be wearing a white lab coat that made him look like someone's dentist, but the chair, with its honey colored wood and blonde fabric, looked for all the world like Danish modern. Then he smiled. Well . . . okay, that's weird, but not knowing what else to do, X smiled back.

The man motioned for X to step back as the bubble came in contact with the ship, and as it closed over the hole X felt a subtle change in his weight, that is he had some, just enough that he found himself slowly settling to the deck. He watched the bubble slowly extending into the hull, and when it was large enough the man stepped into the bubble-space, standing on the deck in front of him. Reaching out, the man touched his evac suit with his hand. "They call me Jespers," he said, X hearing the voice in his suit, not over the COM. "Would you care to step inside?"

"Your bubble?"

Nodding, Jespers waved his hand down the side of the bubble to create what looked like a tear, then beckoned X to step forward. "Uh . . ." but he knew he would. The man was either totally harmless or the best simulation of harmlessness anyone could possibly imagine. To not trust him seemed by far the more difficult of the two alternatives, and it was a hell of a lot better than just sitting there stranded in space.

Stepping forward, X saw the tear close behind him, which didn't startle him nearly as much as the bubble's interior dimensions. "Good trick," he said, motioning to the ship's large interior. "I want one."

"At the moment I believe they're all spoken for."

"But you will put me on the waiting list?"

Jespers loved it. The man was so calm, so amused.

"Care if I look around?"

"Not at all. You can't harm anything. This is an organic ship, by which I mean it's a living being, and quite intelligent."

X smiled at him. "I hope it's also obedient."

"That sort of thing never comes up. You see, in part it's an extension of myself, my intentionality."

"So you two never have an argument."

"Exactly." Jespers watched the man walk into the distance, then turn to come back, all of which seemed surprisingly normal given the extraordinary circumstances. Nevertheless, he had to admit there was something about it he found a bit disconcerting. Some odd hint of familiarity, perhaps, though he knew they'd never met. Well, how annoying was that, all those old stories . . . no, he wasn't going to think about it.

"Is that some sort of craft back there?" the man asked, glancing over his shoulder.

"Yes."

"And all that," again looking over his shoulder, "is sort of here with us, and sort of not here with us?"

"Well, it's a bit more complicated than that."

"No doubt." He held out his hand. "Name's X."

"Nice to meet you, X," Jespers said, shaking his hand, stunned by his phenomenal sang-froid, as close to being at a loss for words as he'd ever been, which was never.

"Safe to take this off?" X was tapping his helmet.

"Please, I'm just like you, biologically. The air, what I eat, it's all the same."

"But you're not human."

"Oh, pretty much."

X smiled at him. "Yes, but I bet the parts that aren't are pretty interesting."

"I'm not so sure about interesting, but they're certainly useful for what I do." With a start, Jespers realized he'd just told someone things he'd never meant to tell anyone. But it just felt so easy and natural. He'd simply failed to notice until he already had. Now what?

"And all this?" X asked, pointing to the bubble's expansive interior. "Lots of these running around?"

"Uh, no, not really. You know, I really shouldn't be telling you any of this. I have no idea why I am." He looked at X. "It's really important that you not know any of this."

X smiled. "Oops. Does this mean I'm out of the bubble?"

20

"So you did, or did not, come over here to rescue me?" X asked.

Well, yes, what a good question. It seemed rather improbable now to claim it was just an accident, though he really had no reason to think it wasn't. He certainly hadn't been trying to rescue anyone. "Well," he said, "perhaps we should just say it was a lucky accident."

"Perhaps? That sure sounds like someone trying awfully hard to convince themselves of something. Now," he said, smiling at Jespers, "I wonder why anyone would want to do that."

Jespers stared at him for some time. His poise and insight were uncanny. In fact, Jespers wondered if the hair on the nape of his neck might not be standing up. His neck certainly tingled. "X," he finally asked, forcing himself to be as casual about it as possible, "just who are you? I mean, yes, you're with NASA or something, but you're clearly more than that."

"Why do you ask?"

"I was just wondering."

"Don't you have some amazing interface back there somewhere you can use to tap into all the world's databases?"

Jespers smiled. In fact he did. "I just thought it might be better to ask in person. While you're here."

"Save yourself the trouble later, when you get home?"

"Something like that."

"Well, I'm X, and I fly stuff. But I've been rather secretive about it, so I doubt you'll find very much in your databases. That's my guess, anyway. But just for the record, I'm forty-one, sans wife, sans children. How's that?"

"Helpful," he said, seemingly distracted by something. "But does any of this seem . . . " and he paused to look around them. "Oh, I don't know, familiar? I'm wondering, because you don't appear to be very surprised."

"People usually are?"

"Awestruck."

"Well, sorry, maybe next time." He paused, smiling at Jespers. "Of course I'm surprised. In fact, you surprise the hell out of me. I wouldn't think you could be trusted to change a light bulb, but obviously that can't be true. And now I find we've got these weird hybrids running around doing god knows what. So, yes, I'm surprised, but I'm hardly shocked. I've been involved in this sort of thing for some time."

"Just what do you know? If you don't mind my asking."

"I know about the Delegations and their political squabbles. Not that I know firsthand, of course, but still, I do know. What I don't know, and what's puzzling me right now, is what role beings like you play in all this. I mean, just who's giving the orders these days?"

Jespers nodded, it was, after all, the key question. "Well, since I've already started, I might as well tell you the rest. Like me? Less than a half dozen, and rarely here at the same time."

"Why is that?"

"It's a matter of cost, actually. I know, how mundane, but true, nonetheless."

"You mean we're not worth it?"

"No, but it's a big universe. As for the Delegations, as you call them, they're a bit in the dark when it comes to us. I don't think they even know I'm here."

"And you'd like to keep it that way?"

He nodded. "The truth is that we, like this ship, are rather unusual, as is our role here. The Delegations, less so, in the sense that even though they mostly don't look like you or me, what they're after is probably much easier to understand." He stopped speaking and looked down at his hands, a wonderful human gesture for marking a thoughtful pause he would always use.

"They're less benevolent, is that what you're telling me? Because they're obviously not among themselves."

Jespers smiled. Of course X would have no idea how good it felt to talk about this. "Yes. You understand things perfectly."

"Gort?" X was grinning at him.

"Gort?"

"You know, *klaatu barada nikto*? Implacable enforcer of galactic peace?"

Jespers smiled. "No, nothing like that."

"But you do like the movie?"

"Very much."

"No, *when* you get down."

"You're sure it's not *if* I get down?"

Jespers smiled. "You'll make it."

"I have your word on that?"

"Yes, because you're that rare statistical anomaly, the unplanned for outlier unexpectedly erupting into other people's lives and plans. You've never noticed?"

"Not really."

"Well, you are, and I'm sure you always have been. In all situations." He paused to look pointedly around them at the wreckage. "That's why *you* will always make it down."

"Fine, so when I get down, then what? Should I just call you up?" He smiled at how silly that sounded.

"Why don't you come to see me instead."

"Just like that?"

Jespers smiled brightly. "Why not?"

"But—"

"There's no cause for alarm. No one that matters has any idea who I am, where I am, what I do, or even that I exist.

You're the one they'll be watching for if you carry out your plan not to return."

"Aren't you worried I might inadvertently lead them to your door?"

"You'll be careful."

X raised his eyebrows and stared at him. "I'll certainly try to be, but this is a significant risk you're taking."

"I don't think so."

"Care to tell me why? Or is that just one more thing I won't fully understand?" He laughed. Of course it was.

"This goes here, I believe." Jespers was pointing to a plug under the small LCD.

X smiled. "I've been trained on this. Did you know that?"

Jespers stopped to look at him. When he noted X's wry grin he felt embarrassed. "Sorry."

"That's okay. Want to trade?" He nodded at Jespers' bubble. "Give me a ten minute crash course?" He already knew it took Jespers several hours to tune it correctly even to his own brain.

21

He gave the sphere a gentle shove—it was surprisingly easy given all that mass—and watched it slowly begin to rotate as it drifted away, and when that rotation eventually brought Jespers back into view he raised his hand in farewell. Amused, X watched as he got settled in that ridiculous chair, then leaned back and closed his eyes. Imperceptibly at first, then with mounting rapidity, the spheroid's shape began to flow and change, flattening out as it moved away, its opacity gradually replaced by a uniform sheen, then a glowing white too bright to really look at with the naked eye. Even when X flipped the little toggle for the visor's screening it was nearly impossible to find anything definitive enough in that fuzzy looking bright blob for his eyes to focus on. But by then it was just a pinpoint of light dropping down into the night sky over Africa. "Hello, Bente," he whispered.

Turning with a sigh, he looked at the escape sled. Ride that down to 70,000 feet, give or take; free-fall like a skydiver down to 10,000; main chutes deploy; then use the paraglider rig for the last few thousand, in theory, anyway, since he'd never heard of anyone having actually done it. Of course, if they had and things had gone badly . . . well, no one would have told him about that anyway, which for once he was fine with, the not knowing of something.

He stayed with the *Shore Leave* for as long as he dared, all the way down into the thin upper reaches of the atmosphere, all the way down until he felt the first effects of drag tugging at the small craft, knowing it would soon start to spin and tumble as it began its long fiery descent deep into the atmosphere. But perhaps he could wait just a little longer.

Momentarily panicked, he grasped the tether still attached to the deck. These sleds were never meant for deployment this high—in the mesosphere! But it really was time. Yes, but stepping out at over 300,000 feet?

As he fell away he pulled himself as close to the sled as he could, yanking the cover up over his body, tucking his head down, refusing to even look at the spinning world of cobalt blue and black or the gaping hole in the *Shore Leave* as it twisted this way and that in what was now no longer empty space.

He was very uncomfortable. The escape suit barely fit, especially with his bulky fanny pack, but he'd done the best he could. Still, it wasn't meant for this and he was intensely cold. Well, he'd been expecting it. If he could just ride it out for ten minutes.

He stayed as still as he could, letting the sled do its job as they skipped through the atmosphere like a stone over a pond, each skip slamming him hard into the sled as it lessened their momentum. It seemed to be taking forever, but at least he was feeling warmer. Then he raised his head to see. Yes, the upper layers of the stratosphere.

He was alarmed. The buffeting had grown severe, and when he peered over the side to see where they were it was just a blur.

The pressure inside his head was excruciating. He didn't think he could take much more. It would be a relief to pass out. No. He had to fight that if he didn't want them to spin wildly out of control. Soon his input would be critical, but he'd always hated these things, even in the training sessions they'd never seemed to work right, and now here he was spiraling down through the stratosphere like a spinning seed pod, as close to being out of control as was possible without just plummeting straight to the earth far below.

Aware that the sled was now fighting to maintain its equilibrium, he shifted his body forward, instinctively knowing what to do. As he did he felt the stubby wings deploy, the leading edges getting a good bite in the air. Finally! Now he could control things. He put his hands on the controls and leaned forward, pointing the nose down, beginning the long fast descent that would end in a swooping arc to the right as he started to cut a huge circular path down through the atmosphere.

He caught sight of a bright flash out of the corner of his eye. Turning, he was witness to the long slow burning descent of something as it came in contact with the upper layers of the atmosphere. It could have been anyone, anything, but it was big, spitting and sparking, breaking up in a tumbling shower of burning wreckage that seemed to float improbably in space as it fell away from him. Then two more explosions off to the south, both way up there. He shook his head. Whatever had happened up there, it was a total fucking mess.

He came to a gentle stop still on his feet. The drag chutes had done their job and he'd jettisoned the sled, riding his own chutes down the last few miles, gliding to a perfect textbook stop that no one was there to appreciate.

Desperate to remove his helmet, he shucked off the harness and began loosening the metal collar around his neck. "Finally!" he said, freeing the helmet, then giving it a sharp kick that sent it bouncing like a soccer ball until it came to rest in a creosote bush. Gloves and an unanticipated and protracted struggle with his cumbersome evac suit were next, but in the end it was just X standing there in his blue flight suit smiling as he rubbed his stiff neck. Yes, just being alive was more than enough.

Wondering where he was, he pulled his fanny pack around to get at his iPhone. He'd seen the Pacific off to the west on the way down, so . . . southern California somewhere? And obviously out in the desert. He laughed. Maybe he was in Nevada. He might be. Area 51? How ironic that would be, dropping in uninvited.

He turned his iPhone on and waited. Two bars out here? Then it showed his current location: Nevada, northeast of Las Vegas, a few miles from a town named Caliente. Yes, and it was four-thirty in the afternoon, local time. He turned the iPhone off and put it back in his fanny pack. Too bad, when it came time to disappear he'd have to get rid of it, not to mention all those interesting photographs. Shading his eyes with his hand, he looked to the southwest, wondering if he could see Caliente. No, not yet.

He'd been walking for about an hour when he first heard the sound of traffic. He knew Highway 93 was close. Even so, it was still one more hill and ten more minutes before he stood on the shoulder of the highway. Now what? He couldn't just stand there looking like a lost prospector who'd just stumbled in out of the desert. Maybe he'd find a nice rock to sit on.

A few cars passed, a semi or two, but it was just too much trouble to try and flag anyone down. So how far was he from Caliente? He checked his location on his iPhone. Six miles. No, that was too far. Then he heard the sound of tires crunching on gravel and looked up. It was a Lincoln County Sheriff's car pulling up across the highway.

"Are you all right?" the officer yelled.

X stood and smiled, waved his hand and jogged across the road. "I was just wondering who I should call. You saved me the trouble. I crashed over there."

"Crashed?" the officer asked, now watching him very carefully.

"I'm with NASA. Did you hear about it? The space station? I had to jettison. I came down over there." He pointed back up the hill.

"NASA?"

X laughed and unzipped his fanny pack. "I bet you'd like to see some ID."

"Go ahead," the officer said with a nod.

X pulled out a Maryland driver's license and a NASA ID. "See?" he said, handing them to the officer.

Taking them without looking, the officer said, "Sir, I'd like you to sit down over there while I check this out." He pointed to the rocky slope that ran down to the edge of the highway.

"There?" X said, pointing.

"Just for a minute or two." Then the officer smiled at him. "We had two truckers call in about you."

"Me?"

"Sure. Sitting out here on the edge of the highway in the middle of nowhere. We get that, you know."

"You do?"

"It's usually got something to do with meth."

X laughed. "Not this time."

It didn't take long, which was a good thing because leaning back like that against the warm rocky soil was about to put him to sleep.

"Here you go," the officer said, handing him his IDs.

"And?" he asked, looking up at him.

"It seems we're to get you back to town as soon as possible. My Captain tells me there's quite a bit of interest in your whereabouts."

X nodded his head. "I'm not surprised." He got wearily to his feet. "You got anything to drink?" he asked as they walked to the patrol car.

22

He saw a bright pool of light and a forlorn looking combination gas station and 7-Eleven. Then they turned off Highway 93 to drive down the quiet main drag of the small town, everything already dark and all buttoned-up for the night even though it was just seven o'clock. The look of the place, very mid-twentieth century, reminded him of an old 1950s sci-fi film in which something awful was about to happen in Anywhere USA. *The Blob*? He smiled. Yes, and now the stranger from outer space had come to walk the dark streets of this small western town in search of . . . what? Well, a beer would be nice.

They pulled in and parked behind the Lincoln County Sheriff's Office, a squat, modern looking building reminiscent of a suburban branch bank. When the officer got out he had to come around and open X's door, he had no door handle of his own, and then they both walked up the concrete handicap access ramp to the rear entrance. X waited as the officer swiped his ID card in a slot next to the door, hearing the buzz as the lock unlatched, and once they were inside he was directed to a small room with several chairs, a desk, and a couch against the wall. There were no windows. Told to have a seat, he was also offered some coffee, which he gladly accepted.

Very soon the officer came back with two others. They were all polite, somewhat excited, and very professional. They all looked at his ID, again asked him pretty much the same questions the original officer had, then left to make more phone calls. Ten minutes later one of them returned and punched the blinking button on the phone sitting on the desk. X watched him speaking with someone. Listening as he said

"Uh-huh" two or three times before handing him the phone. "He wants to speak with you," the officer said.

He took the phone from the officer. "Yes?" he asked.

"Well I don't know how you managed it, but then you are old lucky number seven, aren't you?" It was Chalmers.

"I'm touched by your concern. Anything else you'd like to say before I hang up?"

Chalmers snorted. "Sorry. I guess I'm a little short on sympathy right now. But I'm sure you can understand why."

"Oh, I understand everything."

"I doubt that, but you just stay put and a friend will be along shortly to pick you up. Then we can talk all about it."

"It will be so nice to see you again."

"Yeah, won't it."

He handed the phone to the officer. "I think we're through."

The officer took the phone and held it to his ear. "Yes?" he asked. "No, he can wait right here." He nodded. "Yes, I understand. There's a helipad over at the county clinic." He listened some more. "Two blocks," he said, then one more nod and a "Got it." He smiled at X when he hung up. "They should be here in about an hour," he said.

It really was that simple. After he went to the restroom he came back and sat on the couch. Twice they walked by, the second time asking if he wanted more coffee. He told them no, but thanks anyway, then gave them ten more minutes before carefully edging his way down the hallway. He found them sitting together in a brightly lit office, two of them listening as one spoke to someone on the phone. Only when he was sure they weren't looking did he scurry across the lobby and out the front door.

He knew he had to quickly get out of sight. It wouldn't be long before they realized he was gone, and it wouldn't be long after that before someone started looking. Yes, and once the sun was up he'd be easy to spot in that open landscape. It was with real reluctance that he took his cell phone out and repeatedly threw it to the pavement, gathering up the pieces to through them out into the empty lot behind the police station.

Twenty minutes later he was out along the highway somewhere crouching among some boulders waiting for a gap in the traffic, and when it finally came he scrambled down the rocky slope to the shoulder and sprinted for the other side, slipping on the coarse gravel when he reached it, then scampering up the embankment to lie behind a creosote bush while he waited for his heart to stop pounding.

It looked like an old roadhouse, one long out of business. He'd seen it on the way into town with the Deputy. Barbeque? He loved barbeque. Had it all the time when he lived in the South. The intoxicating fragrance from the smoker—which was always out back—the tangy sauce and how the meat just fell from the bone. Damn, he was hungry.

A triangular sign sat high atop a tall pole at the edge of the gravel parking lot, much too dark to make out, of course, though he hoped it said *The Rendezvous*, which was the perfect name for a bar out at the far edge of town where people felt a little more comfortable doing what they really wanted to do.

He crouched down among the unkempt tufts of grass next to the building and placed a hand on its rough stucco exterior to steady himself. He'd run out of time. By now they'd be out in force. Soon he'd hear the helicopter. Then he'd be screwed. But with a little luck maybe he could get inside and hide for a few hours. That's all he'd need, just a few hours, then even Chalmers would conclude he'd somehow managed to elude them. He'd be livid, of course, knowing that once X reached any big city they'd never find him. So they'd quickly shift their focus to Las Vegas or Los Angeles, more likely the latter, but all the while knowing it was probably too late.

He probed the bump on his shoulder with his finger. Did Chalmers know about that? Doubtful. Chalmers wasn't that far up in the hierarchy. Not that important. But what of those who were? Yes, but they certainly weren't going to reveal themselves by contacting someone like Chalmers. Anyway, that they were aware of where he was or where he went was hardly his most immediate concern.

He shuffled his way around the perimeter of the building looking for a way in. Unfortunately, all the windows had been boarded over with big sheets of plywood someone had painted white to match the building's faded stucco exterior. But that must have been some time ago, since most were now delaminating, long thin strips falling away to reveal brown wood underneath.

At the back of the building he came upon a solid looking steel door with a flat metal plate where the door handle should have been, and next to that a keypad in a locked clear plastic box. But short of blasting the door open with his weapon there wasn't much he could do about either. It was better around front: two glass doors locked and held tight by a thick chain wrapped from one door handle to the other, fastened in the middle by a large padlock. Yes, but then anyone driving by could see what he'd done.

Having run out of options, he shuffled back to the one side of the building where he knew he couldn't be seen from the highway and began pulling at one of the big sheets of plywood, pulling it aside once it hung from its last few remaining nails to let it rest against his back as he used a piece of concrete first to break the window and then to batter away any remaining fragments. Then removing his flight jacket, he laid it over the window frame and climbed in, immediately turning to jam a long glass shard into the gap along the window frame to hold the plywood in place.

In the dark, he reached out with his hand, slowly feeling his way along the wall until he came to a filing cabinet. An office? Was that possible? If so, then what about a chair or a desk? Yes, both. "Ah," he said, turning the chair around to sit down.

But what was that stale smell? Leaning forward, he felt around under the desk for a trash basket, not at all surprised to find one, not at all surprised to find it strongly smelled of coffee. Yes, apparently someone really was still coming by. Smiling in the dark, he explored the desktop. Suddenly, the light from a small lamp flooded the office. And there was a phone! He laughed when he picked it up. A dial tone. Wondering what he'd find next, he began poking around in the desk drawers. A large key ring, a flashlight, "Good," he said, grasping the flashlight, "let's see what there is to eat around here." Well, not much as it turned out, just some stale croutons in little cellophane packets, a few cans of tomato paste, mushrooms, and chicken stock, jars of artichoke hearts, two bags of rice, and a small box of canned tuna.

He opened a can of tuna using the large can opener affixed to one of the prep tables, then rummaged around in the drawers until he found a fork and a stainless steel mixing bowl. Deciding one jar out to do, he dumped the artichoke hearts in with the tuna and mixed it all together. "Umm," he said, taking a bite. "Now let's see about the wine cellar," but in that he was bitterly disappointed, having to settle for a warm can of diet ginger ale.

Later, he lay on the couch in the office listening to the soothing sound of cars rushing past on the highway. Not that there were all that many, not at that hour when the gap between them often stretched out to several minutes. But he was very surprised not to hear a helicopter. The Sheriff's Office must have contacted them by now. Surely, they hadn't called it off.

Drifting off to sleep, he found it difficult to remember which day of the week it was. Early Friday morning, right? A workday. Perhaps someone would be by in the morning to use the office. Early? That's what those empty coffee cups suggested. Yes, but they'd make more than enough noise coming in the backdoor to give him ample warning. But no one did, and he slept more or less until ten in the morning. The difference the sleep made was amazing, or perhaps it was the food and the sense of safety. Whichever, he felt much, much better.

It was a crazy idea, but why not? Sure, eventually they'd find out what he'd done, but by then it wouldn't matter. He found the number in the phone book and called. Yes, they did drive to Los Angeles. Yes, they knew where that was. Yes, they could have a car there in about an hour and a half. So he gave them a credit card number over the phone and that was that.

23

The bar from where he called was called *The Shangri-La*, out on Highway 93 not more than two miles from town. When he got close the driver called the number he'd been given and by the time he arrived X was already standing outside waiting for him in the gravel parking lot. After that it was all pretty straightforward. X handed the driver—whose name was Cristino Grajilla—his credit card and driver's license, the paperwork was completed, and in a few minutes they were on their way. In Vegas, he had him get off the freeway at Charleston so he could use a Bank of America ATM, then he treated them both to a late lunch at the In-n-Out across the street. After that, he dozed a bit on the long drive, waking up as they came down I-15 into San Bernardino. When they got closer to town he told the driver he wanted him to get off the 110 at 6th and drop him off at Pershing Square. Then it was a two block walk to catch the Metro Rapid Wilshire Bus, which he rode all the way out to the pedestrian mall in Santa Monica. Ten minutes after that he was headed for Venice on the Ocean Avenue bus.

Walking into the first surf shop he came to on Windward, he used cash to buy new jeans, sandals, three garish looking t-shirts, and a white cotton shirt. He used the dressing room in the store to change, putting all his old clothing in the large plastic bag the kid running the store had given him. Was there a nearby thrift shop? Two blocks over, the kid said, which is where he dropped the bag off, smiling at the thought of some homeless dude walking around Venice in what was left of his flight suit.

Finally feeling safe and now very hungry, he bought a grilled chicken and bean burrito and a Diet Coke from a street truck and walked the three blocks over to the beach to sit on a bench. It was the first moment of peace he'd had in some time, a moment he must have been waiting for because things suddenly began falling into place.

He knew what they said, that the most difficult thing for us to comprehend were those billions of galaxies and earth-like planets each was said to contain. But they were wrong about that, the real mystery was how we—each one of us—somehow manage to live this life in the midst of such inconceivably disproportionate magnitudes of scale. One might think we'd be lost in all that, but the amazing truth was we're not, or at least we don't live as if were, so tightly focused are we on our own existence. That we're even capable of such a thing is the real mystery, which is what he needed to protect, that mindless self-focus, that extraordinary human ability to live small-scale lives that actually mattered, if but for a very brief time.

He watched the throngs of people streaming past, wondering what he could do to protect them, not that he didn't want them to know the truth, it was just that when the time did come—and that would be very soon now—he wanted them to know they were still free to make up their own minds. Still free to decide for themselves what it all meant and what should be done about it. What he had to do was buy them that time, even though the cost of doing so might be quite high.

He already knew it was pointless to talk to any of earth's governments. No, it had to be the Delegations. He needed to do something to shake them up, to inject a bit of chance and uncertainty into the midst, something to roil their murky politics with doubts and suspicions. You're the ones who chose to come here uninvited. So now you're going to find yourselves confronted by the facts of *human* existence. God, how he hoped humans were dangerous. They'd need to be. Well, he was. He'd just have to start with that.

24

"Oh! You startled me," she said, coming in from the examination rooms.

"Sorry." Jespers stood. "I didn't mean to surprise you, but no one was here so I just sat down to wait."

She looked at the door. "The door wasn't locked?"

He turned to look with her. "No. Was it supposed to be?"

"Yes. The clinic closes at seven."

"Ah. Well, I won't take but a minute of your time."

"It would be better if you came back tomorrow. I'm in a bit of a rush right now. I mean," she said, suddenly feeling a bit embarrassed, "it's nothing serious, is it?" He looked very healthy.

"Oh, no. I don't have a medical problem. I came to see you."

"Me?" she said, taking a step back to stare at him.

He laughed and shook his head. "Please, Dr. Sybout, I seem to keep alarming you. Honestly, I'm the most harmless person imaginable. Ask your friend when you see him next."

"My friend? You know," she said, frowning at him, "this conversation might go better if you just told me what you're doing here. I don't much care for cryptic, as a rule."

"X? Yes? He sent me with a message. That's why I was here waiting for you."

"X sent you?" She got a sly look on her face. "So the door was locked."

"Oh!" he said. "Sorry. My name is Jespers. Samuel Jespers. I live in the United States."

"Well, do sit down, Mr. Jespers," she said, pointing to the chair he'd just been sitting in. "Does that mean you're an American?"

"Why not?" he replied, looking a bit surprised.

"Why not?" She smiled, nodding her head knowingly.

"I do live there."

"I'm sure you do. So what has he sent you to tell me?"

"Nothing specific. I guess he just meant for me to let you know he's all right. You may have read something in the paper, seen it on TV or the web, that sort of thing. Or you may still, one never knows how these things may or may not filter down into what passes for common knowledge." He paused in his awkward little speech and sighed. "It will be something rather dramatic. That's what I meant to say."

She was laughing. "And if I do happen to get some of this common knowledge I'm not to worry. Is that it?"

"Yes. That, and I think he wanted us to meet." He smiled at her. "You know how he is."

She sat down at the receptionist's desk and stared at him. It made him very uncomfortable. Yes, she's a doctor, they're very observant, often intuitive, and now he'd given her the perfect pretext for exercising all her native suspicions. People, or these people, could be remarkably perceptive. He often stumbled over that.

"He calls you Jespers, doesn't he? Why do you suppose he does that, never uses a person's first name?"

"Uh . . ." she'd caught him totally off guard. "Maybe it's a habit he picked up in the military. But he calls you Bente. That's how he referred to you when we spoke."

"Yes," she said, sitting up in her chair, "he does that. Now," she said, smiling disarmingly, "why don't you tell me what's really going on."

Startled by her sudden change in tone, he sat up straight in his seat like a schoolboy. Or at least that's the image he had of himself as he did, not that he'd ever been one, but maybe it was from some old Mickey Rooney movie he'd seen on TCM. He loved those old movies.

"Well?" she asked.

"There's been a political altercation in space. At the space station, actually. There were several skirmishes. A brief firefight or two."

"People died?"

"Yes."

"Many?"

"Dozens."

"But not hundreds?"

"No."

"X, was he involved in this?"

"Not directly, though he was there, but he played no role. Not actively."

"So he didn't kill anyone."

"No." He paused, watching her think about something. He could see how X had become so captivated. "I can see you're still troubled," he said.

"Who wouldn't be! A strange man, and excuse me, Jespers, but you are one very strange man, shows up and somehow gets in through a locked door, then proceeds to tell me about something no one's even heard of. But of course I believe him. Why? Because I know X, and nothing surprises me when it comes to X, though you come close. I mean, just look at you. How would a man like you even know X?"

He was nodding his head, in total agreement, noting each point as she spoke. "Yes, I am an odd duck, to use an Anglicism. An outlier. You know, like in statistical analysis, the data point that falls outside the normal range of distribution? Because that's who I am, as is X, or do you disagree?"

"No, that's exactly who he is."

"Well then, that's how we found each other. The two outliers."

"But you can't be doing what he does. Not that I really know what that is. You don't, do you?"

"Well . . ." he smiled at her.

25

Jespers sat at his desk reading his email as he sipped his Peet's coffee. There were over forty emails in his inbox, not atypical for a weekday morning. Colleague, colleague, administrator, spam, friend, and so it went, working backwards from newest to oldest until he came to a message that had been sent at 6:30 the previous evening with a winking smiley for a subject header. Fingers tingling, he opened the message, again seeing the ;-), and underneath that the simple message, *Good Morning.* Jespers smiled, he knew he'd make it.

The message had been sent from something called cybercup.net, which, when Jespers Googled it, turned out to be a coffee shop in Venice, California. Ah, he means this morning. Jespers stood and walked to his office door, opened it and took a step out into the hallway. Not that he really expected to see X standing there, but he was always respectful of the uncanny, and it might happen like that with X.

Leaving his door slightly ajar like he was expecting a post-doc, he returned to his desk to finish his email, then sat staring out the window at the San Gabriels. He was going to miss this, a thought he often had when he reflected on his situation. When he thought about how he got there and what he might or might not have done. The sense of it, when it made any, and of his affection for these people, people like X—really quite an extraordinary person, seen in the larger scheme of things—and his Dutch doctor. He smiled when he thought of Bente. Really, what would it have hurt to tell her? He sighed and shook his head, he couldn't even begin to count the number of times he'd been tempted like that, yet only once had he succumbed. Yes, X. It really was extraordinary that he'd said anything at all, but maybe all those years of not speaking had been a mistake, leading him to say too much once he'd finally begun. Too late now, and perhaps it was all for the best, anyway. Oh? He stopped to examine his train of thought. Yes, there they were, synchronicity and chance, those twin aspects of experience he'd learned to pay attention to when it came to dealing with humans. Not that they weren't predictable, who wasn't? But with them there were always the surprises. That's part of what made them so fascinating, so worthy of study. Or so he'd often said.

He looked at his computer. 10:35 and he was already thinking about lunch. The Faculty Club? Walk down to Sake's? He loved to stroll down the hall to the wide staircase, to walk out the front doors, down the sidewalk through the manicured grounds to the street, across at the light, watching people, thinking about what he knew and they didn't, deciding to stop and eat here rather than there, the whole ritual of ordering and being waited on, the meal, the check, and the tip. Yes, he loved every bit of it, a true connoisseur of the quotidian, but as lost as he was in his reverie he didn't fail to notice the sudden chill at the base of his neck or that his world had just fluttered ever so slightly. It was then, a bit startled, that he realized he was now suddenly outside the present moment he'd just been savoring. Somehow caught unawares as he sat at his desk in his office at Cal Tech. He turned. X stood in the open doorway grinning at him.

"Ah," Jespers said, deeply embarrassed. "I suppose you've been standing there watching me the whole time."

"No," X said, stepping into the office. "But you looked too happy to interrupt." Closing the door, he sat in the chair across the desk from Jespers. "Sorry," he said as he tried to stifle a big yawn, "it's been a long week."

"Oh?"

"I didn't want to be noticed so I've been sleeping in a homeless shelter down in Venice." He looked at him with big eyes. "Did you know they turn you out at seven in the morning?" He nodded. "Seven! A little coffee, a donut or two, and off you go."

"How . . . " Jespers stopped and laughed. Why even ask.

"How did I end up in Venice staying in a homeless shelter?"

"Yes," Jespers said, smiling at how well they understood each other. "Because when we last spoke things were, well . . . and then Venice? And a homeless shelter?"

"Jespers, if you ever want to disappear, not that you aren't doing a pretty good job of that already, but if you ever do, just insert yourself into the world of the homeless. And I know Venice."

"From another life?"

"Exactly. I needed a place where I felt safe. A place I knew."

"Because you needed some time to think?"

X nodded.

"So? You've had a week."

"I know." X leaned back in his chair and looked past Jespers out the windows. "You'd think that would be enough."

Jespers watched him a moment. "I spoke with your Dr. Sybout."

X nodded. "I appreciate that. How'd she take it?"

"That you were alive? Very well. That I was the messenger?" He shrugged.

"She gave you a hard time, didn't she?"

"She doesn't suffer fools." Another cliché he loved.

"You're hardly a fool. I'm sure she saw that right away. But you did like her?"

"Does that really matter?"

"I think so. My guess is that you tend to say more when you find yourself speaking with someone you like."

"Well, I was certainly more discreet with Dr. Sybout than I was with you."

"Which is what I've been thinking about."

"About what I told you?"

"Yes. In particular, that you're not part of this squabble among the Delegations."

"We're not."

"Though you do approve of the secrecy."

"I do."

"I don't. I think this is a story needs to be told."

"Not my part."

"No, it's going to be hard enough for people to believe without dragging you into it. They're not going to take too kindly to the news that you've been here all these years hiding out."

"I haven't been hiding out, I've been doing research."

X smiled. He knew his remark would upset him. "Yes, the innocent anthropologist doing field work, except that every now and then he just had to meddle."

"Meddle?" Jespers sat back and stared. Had he even hinted at such a thing? No, that was just X being insightful. Or perhaps it showed. That he was a meddler.

"It's all right, I'm sure you meant well."

"We did," Jespers said, seemingly unable to stop himself from telling X the truth. "We've been interested in you for a long time."

"Not to mention," X said, trying not to grin, "all the money you've had to spend."

"Well, yes, in fact we have. You just have no idea how these funds are fought over," Jespers said, fighting to maintain his dignity.

"I suppose it doesn't help that we don't have anything you really need, unlike the Delegations. Or so I assume."

"Ah," Jespers said with a nod of his head. "Isn't it odd how your assumptions are always so accurate. Doesn't that make you wonder?"

"About?"

"About yourself."

"And that we seem to get along so well?"

"Yes."

"Not really."

"You know, there's this theory that time flows backwards as well as forwards. It's a common view. So perhaps it is possible that one can anticipate the next moment or two. In which case memory is a bit more elastic than we give it credit for."

"Remember what happens before it happens?"

"Yes. So maybe it's even possible to recall something that's happened to someone else. As if memories were just out there for the taking."

X shook his head. "Not possible."

"Why not?"

"Because that suggests we have no core identity. That a memory is not tied to the person who lived the experience it's a memory of. But, you see, without that it's not a memory it's just a story."

"But the stories might still be out there."

"A story can be ignored. A story can be set aside. Not a memory. Is a story ever painful the way a memory is? Do you ever wish you could forget a story?" He smiled. "Well, okay, that you might wish for, but you see what I mean."

Jespers nodded.

"So what's really going on here is that you're trying to tell me something, but you're afraid to say it."

"Well—"

"What I need to know is just out there waiting for me to recall it?" He smiled at Jespers. "You can't really believe that?"

"It is an interesting theory."

"Because I can assure it's not working, no matter how familiar some of this may seem."

Of course he knew he was being teased, but still, it was frustrating. He'd tried to find out what he could about X, but he was an enigma. Nothing seemed to lead anywhere or to have any real substance, yet there he was sitting in that chair smirking. That was the reality, impossible to deny even if the accompanying narrative made little sense or hardly even seemed to exist. That's what he'd seen with Bente, that she just accepted X as he was in the here and now and pretty much said to hell with the rest of it.

"Now, now, Jespers, don't sulk," X said. "Of course I've been wondering. Of course I've noticed how being with you feels like a stroll through deja vu meadows. I'm also well aware of the fact that you're somehow responsible for all this, though if you say you're not . . ."

They were called the Krist, he told him.

"When I was in training, long before I came here, even before I was transformed into something very much like yourself, and yes, that can be done."

"And it's very expensive!"

Jespers laughed. "It really is! But there were other projects before ours, or the one I participated in, I mean. But they hadn't gone well. It was hard to make us believable. That was one problem."

"Well, Jespers, I hate to tell you this, but you're hardly believable even now. So I can just imagine."

"Yes, and then the times they went to were not really suitable. But you've rapidly improved. So much so, that when I came here I found things quite suitable."

"But . . .?"

"It's the seductiveness of your world. The allure of the lives you live."

"Us?"

"You have no idea how joyful it is to be here in your lovely world."

"But that includes us?"

Jespers stared at him. He couldn't have been more sincere. "Oh, yes. You have so much music and creativity. The arts. The humor. Companionship. No, you just have no idea what this is like for us."

"No, I guess I don't. Are you suggesting these things are rare?"

"Very."

"Still, I might be tempted to trade some of that for your technology."

"I understand. It's amazing even to me, but of course I'm no scientist."

"So," X said, grinning at him, "is this what you've been trying to tell me, that some of you may have wandered off the reservation?"

"What?"

"It's a figure of speech. You know, another of our charming ways of speaking? Like they went native?"

Jespers chuckled. "Yes, figures of speech."

"And?"

"Yes, some of us most definitely went native."

"Which you somehow connect to me."

"Well, I do wonder a bit about your family tree. There are these theories you see, and . . . well . . . it could be."

"It could also just be something in the water." He waited until Jespers smiled. "It's not fraternization, it's just how our culture is."

"Well, it is, as I said, seductive."

"Look out, women of earth!"

"No!" Jespers said, feeling quite foolish.

"That's okay. I mean they made you like us, right? So don't be shocked to *be* like us. That's my advice, anyway."

"But you do see the problem. Why there are these stories and concerns about past transgressions. Possible ones, I mean."

"More like probable, I'd say."

Jespers shrugged.

"Well then, I guess we'd better be prepared to find something rather unusual in our genome. Or will these surprises be limited to just a few?"

"If, and I'm only admitting to an if at this point, there has been an introgression or two, then, over time, they will have proven to be quite advantageous to those who have them. So much so, that there will be what your biologists call a hard sweep. Soon, you'll all have them."

"And then we'll all be like you?"

"No," Jespers said, smiling at him, "my guess is that soon everyone will be much more like you."

"Me? I certainly hope you've kept this a secret, because it strikes me that this could be what this business with the Delegations is really all about."

"No, this is nothing more than just the two of us and a bit of idle speculation."

"Even though you think it's true."

"I may lean in that direction."

"Uh-huh." He smiled. "So how do you suppose the Delegations will feel about this? When they find they have all these hybrids running round their universe?"

"It will be an explosive issue."

"They don't much care for you, either, do they?"

"Well, we're quite old as a culture. Rather aloof, I suppose."

"With some pretty fancy technology you've probably refused to share."

"Yes."

"So we who are your bastard progeny, what's to become of us? Will you share with us our rightful patrimony?"

"No."

"I don't suppose we could steal it?"

"No."

"Though we might be able to develop it on our own."

Jespers sat back as he thought about it. "Yes. I think that's far more likely. You're already developing so rapidly."

"But," X said, waggling his finger at him, "no meddling."

"Oh, maybe just a little."

26

Jespers stood. "Shall we get something to eat? Some lunch?"

"Why? Is all this talk is making you hungry?"

Jespers laughed. "I'm always hungry. It's your food, you see."

"That surprises you?" He shook his head. "What on earth were you before you became semi-human? You did eat, didn't you?"

"Uh . . . yes, in a way, but physical form, corporeality, is malleable. Perhaps too malleable," he added with a sigh.

"So you're not disembodied, but whatever connection to corporeality you do have has gotten a bit tenuous. You've over-engineered yourselves a bit, haven't you?"

Jespers nodded.

"So here you are gathering information on what it's like to be in a more fully involved sort of bodily existence. Or something like that."

"Yes, and we feel a kinship with you."

"So we've established."

"No, I mean aside from any meddling, and it's not just that you're different from the rest, though in some odd sense you are, it's also that you provoke in us a certain vague sense of familiarity while being strikingly different at the same time. Something we find to be not only intriguing, but appealing."

"And this sameness and difference you explain, how?"

"We're working on it."

"No surmises? Surely, you have a few."

"More than a few."

"Like?"

"Well, there was one earlier this year, if you'd care to see?"

"Right now?"

"It's very brief, just a note, actually. Go on," he said, handing him his iPhone.

"It's on your iPhone?"

Jespers smiled. "Well, it's a rather unusual iPhone."

"So I see" he said, holding it up so Jespers could see *X, what can I do for you?* on its small screen.

"Say I'd like to read that note on common language groups."

"Uh, hello, I'd like to read that note on common language—" He smiled at Jespers. The note was already there.

It turned out to be a brief summary of a long-simmering dispute: what do the various language families have to tell us about the existence and or nature of those beings seemingly called for to account for the odd commonalities found among the major language groups of intelligent species like themselves. One camp held these similarities much too striking to be due to chance, suggesting instead, or at least implying, that there was a common language or common family of languages at their root. Others argued that this was highly unlikely. They didn't deny the similarities, just that they were the effects of conquest, trade, interaction, similar lifeways, perhaps even some universal, structural features of particular types of intelligences—anything, in other words, than a common linguistic origin in deep time. And one would have to push the date of this root language far into the past to have ample time to allow for the proliferation and diversity found among current languages and language families. A later theory, a sort of compromise position, suggested that these commonalities might be due to these populations having had contact with the same third party, but at a point deep in their past. This view gained adherents when it was found that the languages spoken by the galaxy's outer species were related to those of the settled, and presumably older central parts. That is, someone had paid them a visit as well—the same someone—though at a later date.

Jespers nodded when X finished reading. "I know, it doesn't really mention you, but the implications are clear enough."

"What's clear is the fear."

"Fear? I'm not sure I understand."

X raised his eyebrows. "Fear of the Other?"

"The Other?"

"Well, whoever they were, whatever they were, they were certainly *other*."

"Very."

"So how could they not be the origin of this commonality?"

"But why?"

"I have no idea. Maybe to ensure that all intelligent beings spoke their language."

"The argot of Empire?"

"Exactly. Like Roman subjects had to learn Latin. But the real fear, here, or so it seems to me, is that this might not only mark a linguistic inheritance, but a genetic one as well."

"You're suggesting some form of manipulation?"

"At the very least. So either way, this Other is the most logical explanation. Because I agree with them," he was nodding at the screen, "it's just too implausible, otherwise. It's not the sort of thing that could have happened just by chance."

Jespers sighed.

"You think I'm wrong?"

"I really have no idea, though I do agree with you about this repressed fear of the Other."

"Repressed?"

"Well, certainly unacknowledged."

"Though it's obviously not like you don't think about it, if that article is anything to go by."

"Yes, always implicit, even if unmentioned."

"Except by me."

"Yes, except by you."

It was with ever increasing amusement that X watched Jespers eat. Not only did he seem to really enjoy it, but he'd taken forever to make up his mind, having one glass of cabernet as he perused the menu, then another with lunch, which was a baked ziti pasta dish with ricotta, a Caesar salad, and a dessert not yet ordered but sure to soon hove into view. It was quite a contrast to his grilled chicken sandwich and San Pellegrino.

"Looks good," X told him.

Jespers paused with a fork-full of pasta on the way to his mouth to nod his head. "It usually is. Great wine list, too." He took his bite and smiled. In fact, with every bite he smiled.

"Maybe when you get back you should open a restaurant. Assuming you do go back."

Jespers nodded over his salad. "I go back."

"Will you stay like this? Like us? Or is there some sort of universal morpher waiting to remake you into a more ethereal sort of being. One who doesn't care for pasta."

Jespers sat his fork down and wiped his mouth with his napkin. "Actually, no, we stay as we are. We're too entwined with this bodily existence to stay sane if we're morphed, as you call it."

"So those like you, you have a special ghetto?"

Jespers smiled.

"You do? Then maybe you really can open a restaurant. If there are enough of you."

"We are few."

"Must be lonely," X said, sipping his sparkling water as he watched Jespers pondering his fate to be. "I know," he said, setting his glass down, "why don't you stay here with us and act as our spokesman with the Delegations."

"Not a good idea, I think. But it would be nice to stay."

"So how long will you live?"

"Live?"

"You find that question upsetting? I'm surprised your almost human self isn't used to that by now. It's all we think about. Being mere mortals."

"No, I understand." And he really did. It was difficult to be a human. He was enough of one to see that. "It's just that we normally live for a very long time. Not immortals, of course, but we might seem so to you."

"That long?"

Jespers nodded. "In my case, I expect to live for several hundred years like this."

"And then?"

"And then things happen that will allow me to go on for quite some time more."

"Yes, but I bet it won't be nearly as much fun."

Jespers toyed with his fork as he thought about it. Fun? No, unfortunately fun didn't even enter into it. It was contemplative. Meaningful. He could see that being apart from that for so long had given him a different point of view, which, come to that, was one of the reasons he was there. For they, like humans, were by their very nature highly inquisitive. Fussy. They too loved to tinker with things. But maybe they had gone a bit overboard. He saw that with humans, that one did have a nature and that one shouldn't become too alienated from that nature. But they'd been around for a long time, sooner or later they were going to turn to themselves with the same curiosity they had for everything else. Yes, but who'd made that decision? That this was something they should all pursue? That this was what they should all become?

"Well?" X asked, still watching him.

"No. Not nearly as much fun."

He took a bite of pasta, enjoying its complex medley of tastes and smells, then looked around at the people eating and talking, relaxing over a good meal in the middle of the day. Rituals. Human life was full of them. Unnoticed, but always present, day in, day out, year after year. He liked that, the pace it gave to everything; the orderly march into the future all together. The Delegations. The thought of them ached like a pain in his stomach. They were all crazy. In all the vastness of the universe, and he wasn't even sure that there weren't others hiding out there lost in other dimensions, the sentient life forms he found pleasant and appealing could be counted on one human hand. Okay, maybe two, but as for the rest? He sighed deeply and shook his head.

"What is it?" X asked.

Jespers looked at him and smiled. "I think I need something really good for dessert."

27

"Nothing for you?" Jespers was looking concerned, staring at him as the waitress waited for his dessert order.

"Nothing, thank you," he told the waitress.

"You make me feel like a glutton."

"I don't doubt it. Look at you! Let's see, two glasses of wine with your rather, shall we say, large lunch, and now vanilla gelato and rhubarb pie? Unbelievable."

Jespers shrugged. What could he say?

"Yet you're so thin, though I suppose that's just due to good engineering."

"Good engineering?" Jespers smiled.

"The bit I obviously didn't get."

"You're pretty trim."

"I better be, given how hard I work at it."

"Yes." Jespers nodded. "Humans do spend an inordinate amount of time worrying about their weight."

"And that's not endearing?"

"What do you do to defend yourself?"

"From?"

"From the Delegations."

"They subscribe to a policy of deterrence when it comes to us. Or they defer to us as a *form* of deterrence."

"You guys are really like that? You seem so peaceful."

"We are, but then why provoke a sleeping dog?" He waited. "No? You don't know that one?"

"Confucian?"

Jespers laughed. "I may have gotten it wrong."

"No, but it might be better to start off by saying that the wise ruler does or he does not . . . like in the I Ching."

Jespers nodded.

"And just so you'll know, I really do find this all a bit troubling, that a clichéd little snippet of human wisdom like that might actually be something one of your guys came up with. Look how much you love it. Didn't that ever occur to you? That what you like so much about us might be nothing more than the outward sign of your own meddling?" He raised his eyebrows and smiled. "Now, wouldn't that be ironic?"

Jespers shrugged. He wondered if his face was pale, he certainly felt a slight tremor in his hands. "Yes," he said, "that would most certainly be ironic."

"What? You've really never thought of that? I'm surprised. Is that because it's just not possible? Like I have any idea how long you Krist have actually been here. When you came, I mean. Would any of that preclude this?"

"X, I just have no answers for you."

"But you're upset. Why?"

"Why?" He leaned back in his seat and took a deep breath. "You've reminded me of something. Something I've occasionally wondered about. My goal here, at least this is what I've always assumed it to be, is to study and observe. To make recommendations."

"With regard to?"

"Human prospects, bodily existence, the activities of the Delegations, things like that, none of which are very surprising. But there's always been this undercurrent to our work here, one that hints at other puzzles."

"Found here, you mean?"

"Yes."

"But there must be puzzles everywhere."

"Undoubtedly, though mostly of a trivial nature. But here the puzzles are about the history of things. We are older than you, than anyone, so far as we know, but we were not the first."

"Does it even make sense to say there was a first?"

Jespers smiled. Humans were so good at this sort of thinking. They would willingly cast aside all preconceptions if they felt they could get away with it. "Well, at least within certain specified limits. Or do you disagree?"

"Not at all," X said, pleased to see Jespers speaking with him as an equal.

"So your remark about the possibility of those being the outward signs of prior meddling hit home."

"Because you haven't been here meddling long enough?"

"Again, you always seem to grasp the essential point with ease."

"So here you see evidence of other meddlers? Prior meddlers?"

"Yes, evidence of something perplexing, and one part of that perplexity are humans."

"I'm surprised. As I understand it, our evolutionary history's fairly clear, and most of that within the last several million years. What you're talking about has to be older than that. Certainly any mention of the Other would be."

"Well, that's something that isn't very clear."

"Really? You're not thinking about creating habitable worlds, are you? Seeding them? Is that the kind of meddling we're talking about? Because that would be incredibly old."

"It is hardly impossible."

"And the Krist? Do you know the truth of your own genesis?"

Jespers smiled and shook his head, again amused by how humans would always just leap and plunge ahead. Yes, but then sometimes being rational and methodical wasn't nearly enough. It was interesting, there had long been a debate among the Krist about the relative merits of the differing cognitive orientations of the known intelligent species. It was said that these differing cognitive styles could be loosely grouped into three large families. Equal families, or so they said, which was why any further classification or ranking was frowned upon. As Jespers knew, this point of view stemmed more from a faith-like support for an always fragile ecumenism than anything else, the proponents of which had the annoying habit of ending debate with the assertion that each possessed their own peculiar strengths and weaknesses. For the most part, Jespers agreed with this tolerant point of view, after all, he was by his very nature a most tolerant individual. Nevertheless, it was quite clear to him that some of these strengths and weakness were most peculiar. Some were actually quite deleterious and destructive.

"As you suggest," he said, "it is often argued that at some point select planets were made ready for life and seeded. How did this commence? Was there a first? As to that, simple logic dictates there must have been. Though who or when are deep mysteries."

"Yes, but one accident is all it would take. That, and endless time."

"That is true."

"But what you're saying is that here in this solar system is something unexpectedly old even by your standards."

"Yes, unexpectedly old as such, and especially so for this location, though not old enough to say they precede everything else we've found."

"So just what are we talking about here?"

"Well, most telling are the extensive artifacts on your own moon. Quite sophisticated, so far as we can tell."

"But not incomprehensible?"

"Well," Jespers said, carefully watching him, "perhaps not for some."

X sat up straight and stared at him.

"Yes," Jespers said, nodding his head. "Now, as to this putative common origin for all life? Who's to say? And maybe it's only for life of a certain type."

X smiled at him. "Deep meddling."

Finishing up over coffee, X asked, "And you're happy here as you are? Cut off like this from your own?"

"I wouldn't say I'm cut off, exactly, and they certainly haven't forgotten about me. In one sense I'm even a bit of a celebrity."

"Tweets from Earth?"

"Now that would be interesting, though I'd hope for something more scholarly."

"You're the one who said celebrity, which suggests to me a bit of notoriety and gossip. So that when you write your memoirs they're sure to be a bestseller."

"If we did that sort of thing. But our sharing tends to be done in a more direct fashion."

X nodded. "I've been wondering. Are there others sharing this with you right now?"

"Not fully, no, but there is often somewhat of an audience."

"I hope you understand how awful that sounds to someone like me, both as a human and as a person who hates to give up any of his privacy."

"Perhaps you don't have as much as you believe."

"Believe? You'll have to look long and hard to find someone with less baggage than I have, as you've no doubt already discovered."

Jespers smiled. It was, he was learning, almost impossible to get even one small step ahead of X.

They left the restaurant and stood on the sidewalk talking about what X was going to do next.

"You're sure you won't stay here in Pasadena with me?"

"Thanks for the offer, but I really do need to get back to Africa."

"Bente?"

"Bente. But it's also the perfect place to disappear for a while.

"Certainly better than Pasadena."

"But don't worry, I'll be in touch. I've got this crazy idea about what we might do to temporarily derail the Delegations."

"Oh?"

"But I'm not saying anything just yet because you're too easy to shock. And then there's your audience."

"It is possible to act in privacy."

"Well, that's a relief, because I've got all these disturbing images running through my mind of what that must be like. All that sharing."

"X, I assure you—"

"What?" X asked, grinning at him. "Did that strike a bit too close to home?" Of course, he knew it had. He could see how Jespers was addicted to sensuality. No doubt that sort of thing had a wide application when it came to the pleasures of the body. They were just so unprepared for it.

"Again, X, what can I say? You seem to know us only too well."

"Yes, we're all just one big happy and somewhat accidentally related family."

"So you will call me sometime soon to let me know of your plans?"

X nodded.

"Good, though I have this feeling that events will follow you wherever you go. All I'll need to do is look, and when I find them I'll know you're near."

"Which is odd, isn't it? I mean I think you're right, for some reason I do seem to find myself in the thick of things. But I hope you also realize just how unhappy that makes me. How one day I'd like nothing better than to finally disappear from the ranks of the not-so-coincidental participants in this great moments in history business."

28

He met Bente for a clandestine lunch. It had to be. Disappearing wasn't easy, even with his network of friends and cronies. The truth was, it was nearly impossible to do anything anymore without leaving a trace or two behind, and that was in real time, which meant one had to keep moving. What he had to be most careful of, however, was leaving any in Africa. But things were easier there. All one really needed was some cash and a good phony ID, neither of which were all that hard to come by if you knew someone. Of course, Bente couldn't decide if she found that amusing or just odd. Hiding from whom? That was her question.

"Won't they say you've gone AWOL or something?"

"What does that matter, if they never find me?"

"What about that thing in your shoulder?"

He shrugged.

"Won't they be using it?"

"Not the people I'm worried about."

"But those who will, you're really not concerned about them?"

"Uh, let's just say we have a different kind of relationship. More open-ended."

"Is that like ill-defined?"

"Pretty much." He smiled at her. "Stop worrying. I'll be fine. The truth is, if someone really wanted to find me they probably could, but so far no one has."

"You still won't tell me where you're staying? Because you know you could stay here with me."

"Yes, and I'd love to, believe me, but I don't want anyone to know about you."

29

It was a long walk back to where he'd parked his car, one of those ubiquitous old Peugeot 504s they assembled in Nigeria. He'd bought it from a young man who'd used it as a taxi: $1200 American dollars. He liked it. You really couldn't find a less conspicuous car in Africa.

It was a lovely afternoon. Everyone was out, walking, clogging the streets with their cars and bicycles. He'd seen that sort of thing in Third World countries before, densely packed humanity, gritty streets, everyone out and about just getting on with their business. These were complicated cultures, intricate local economies, both growing and adapting as best they could. If you came here this was the sea you swam in. One just had to accept that.

X noticed him right away, not that he'd been looking, not that the man even necessarily looked out of place, just that there was something about how he carried himself that caught his eye. No, of course he wasn't sure, how could he be, but still, it bothered him that his anonymity might be so easily compromised. It was also the way the man stayed back there like that as X wove his way through the throngs of people, keeping his distance but making no attempt to stay out of sight, which suggested to X that he actually meant to do more than just follow him. It also seemed a rather pointless show of arrogance to let himself be seen like that.

Well, why not? He crossed the street to a Rabobank, entering through two sets of large glass doors, not even breaking stride or looking back as he continued on across the lobby and out the far doors to the sidewalk. There he slowed, turning to look back over his shoulder. So now he didn't want to be seen. Interesting. But at the next intersection X caught a glimpse of him leaning back against the side of a building as he lit a cigarette, turning as X drew near to walk into the open-air market that filled a narrow gap between two small buildings. Surely, he didn't expect X to follow him in there? Perhaps it was just his way of giving X a sporting chance. But of course that meant the real question was where he'd next appear. Wherever that was, X knew it was going to be critical.

Annoyed by how he'd been forced into this lethal game, X quickened his pace, walking past the open mouth of the market, crossing over to the other side of the street at the next intersection, then sprinting for several hundred yards, not stopping until he came to a large paved lot at the back of three enormous warehouses jammed with large, rusty steel cargo containers, the type used on the container ships from Asia, many of which now stood open as workers unloaded large cardboard boxes with Sanyo and Toshiba written in big black letters on their sides. Appliances? They weren't sending dishwashers to Ghana, were they? A local importer anticipating the effects of the coming oil prosperity, betting that middle class convenience would soon to be in style? At the far side of the lot he turned to look back. Nothing, but it would be hard to see anyone in all that pandemonium.

Walking quickly, he continued on up the street, walking until he no longer saw anyone. Then thinking this just might do, he took a moment to look around. Okay, there on the corner, a metal stairway, three floors, running from the street up the side of a building. So first glancing back to make sure no one was there, he stepped into the shadows, then felt for the weapon in his coat pocket, sliding the little nob forward, reassured to feel it begin vibrating in his hand. This is where it had to end. There were too many other things that needed his attention.

He knew the man would come. He'd think X had fled, perhaps even panicked; that he was now desperately trying to get away. The thought that he was now the prey would never even cross his mind, a dangerous form of arrogance X found hard to understand. Yes, and there he was jogging up the street, apparently in no particular hurry as he ran his quarry to ground.

X waited, and when the man drew near he stepped out into the sunlight. As he'd expected, the man showed little if any surprise, coming to a halt in the middle of the street with an amused smile on his face. X wondered if he should say something, something ridiculous like "Why are you following me?" No, they both understood the situation perfectly, and when the man moved his hand towards his coat X shot him, the weapon punching a hole in X's jacket and a much larger hole in the middle of the man's chest.

He slid the small button back and the weapon went still in his hand. Again, he marveled at its silence, though he'd heard the sound of breaking glass. Yes, whatever it was the weapon shot it had gone right on through the plate glass window at the front of the building across the street, noisily disappearing somewhere into the building's interior. He wondered how far it actually went. Perhaps it would be a good idea to find that out if he was going to keep killing people out in public like that.

He bent down and carefully searched the dead man's pockets. A QSZ-92? He almost laughed. Yeah, it was Chinese, and a truly crappy handgun. But he found nothing else even remotely remarkable until he came to the dead man's Chinese Trade Mission ID. It said his name was Wen Youheng and that he was an agrarian expert from the South China Agricultural University in Guangzhou City. But that's how this game was played. To be plausible, to justify one's presence, all one needed was just the merest hint of an official identity. No one bothered to look too closely at that sort of thing.

Once he'd finished sifting through the dead man's belongings he stacked everything but the gun neatly on the pavement, then stood to stare down at him. Mid-thirties, certainly a very fit and athletic looking agrarian expert, and thank god for that. If he'd been some nondescript sort X might never have noticed him. Then things could have turned out quite differently.

He shook his head. It was hard to believe a man like that worked alone, but then the really good ones often did. Maybe they preferred it that way, not being ones for small talk and lots of camaraderie. But that was good because it meant no one else was around. If his luck held, it might be several hours before the body was even found. It might even wait until tomorrow morning when people came to work. Then it would be another hour or two before the Chinese knew their man had failed, the details of that failure remaining largely unknown to them, of course, though by then they probably wouldn't care. A fact that made X feel somewhat sorry, even somewhat sympathetic, but then unlike this man he was no killer, though it was always possible that he too might be found like this some day, just a body in the street no one was very eager to claim. It was a stupid way to live a life.

So it was the Chinese. He must have bumped into something they wanted kept secret, not that he knew what that was, though he was certainly suspicious of their motives, and of course this was all very annoying because if someone wants you dead you'd certainly like to know why. And that attempted robbery, or whatever that had been with Bente and Liz? Surely, it was all connected. But that was long before he'd done anything to draw attention to himself. Maybe it was just a case of knowing where the trouble might come from and then trying to get out ahead of it before it could. What a wonderfully reassuring thought that was. Maybe he'd just have to make himself even harder to find.

30

"Assassination?" Jespers was shocked. "What will that accomplish?"

"Terror, I hope."

They stared at one another. Finally, Jespers nodded. "It would certainly create panic," he said.

"Chaos would be even better."

"Yes, there is profit in chaos."

"So sayeth the wise ruler?"

Jespers grinned, pleased that X got the joke.

"It's a good plan," X said. "You saw how they behaved at the conference. It's not going to take very much to set them at each other's throats, or to so tie them up in their own affairs that they have little time left for us. That's really all we need."

"Time?"

"Yes. Time to get ready to take them on."

"Do you really believe that's possible?"

"Well, it will just have to be, won't it? So?" X watched him. "Can I count on your assistance?"

Jespers was torn. On the one hand what X intended was clearly wrong, though the results of his actions were, he had to admit, well within the scope of Krist long term plans. To wit, to protect humans from the Delegations as much as possible without resorting to violence, and to keep the secrets of their solar system safe from exploitation. Of course, he knew he was cutting things a bit fine, arguing that sanctioned human violence was not the same as Krist violence. Oh, why deny it, a true Krist would never approve of such a thing. But maybe that seemed less important to him now, being somewhat human himself, having lived happily among them for so many years. And he did loathe the Delegations. He sighed, so wishing for a little comforting moral clarity, but there really was none. It was all a hopelessly intertwined mess of contradictory motives, feelings, beliefs, and desires. *Human, all too human*? Someday he'd give a talk about that.

"Jespers?"

"But just one."

"Just one is all it will take."

31

Callender was sitting in his office in Cape Town watching BBC News. China was buying up all the grain it could, which was driving up world commodity prices. If the Asian drought didn't end soon there would be famine, and the Chinese were determined that it wouldn't happen there. Interesting. He wondered if he could tie that in with their capture of the oil properties in the Gulf of Guinea. They had endless capital, though they wouldn't have nearly so much if they paid their workers a decent wage. Not that any of that bothered the European and American companies taking full advantage of sweatshop China. It was ironic how "labor is cheap" had replaced "life is cheap" as the unstated operational mantra of the Chinese.

His phone rang and he used the remote to mute the television. "Sandy Callender," he said.

"Sandy," a familiar voice said. "Got a minute?"

"X. How are you?"

"Rushed for time. How about you?"

"Well, I'm sitting here wondering about the Chinese, in large part thanks to you. What's on your mind?"

"I'd rather not talk on the phone."

Callender laughed. He'd never get used to this cloak and dagger stuff. "Can't help you. I'm staying right here in Cape Town."

"Good. Turn around."

"What?"

"Look over your shoulder."

Sandy turned to look out the window.

"No," X laughed. "The other shoulder."

Callender turned and looked down at the street. "What in the hell are you doing here?" X was leaning against the building across the street waving at him.

"Waiting for you."

"I'm on my way," he said, hanging up the phone and turning off the television. Then feeling foolish, he actually took a moment to look around as he left the building. Well, it was X after all, and one just never knew.

"Am I supposed to act like I don't know who you are?" he teased when they shook hands.

"Too late."

"Seriously?"

"Should have worn your sunglasses."

"Like yours?" X did have on a pair, and a ball cap, and he did look a little different. "Are you growing a beard?"

"Disguise."

"I still recognized you."

"Can't fool a reporter. That's the moral of this story." He smiled. Was he starting to sound like Jespers?

"Does this mean you're here on some sort of special secret mission?"

"Nope. Just came to see you."

"All the way to Cape Town?"

"Sandy, trust me, it's not nearly as difficult to get here as you might think." He really had to laugh. It had taken, what, maybe an hour.

"Meaning?"

"Sorry. I mean I'm sort of on the run. Moving pretty quickly these days." He still couldn't believe Jespers was letting him use the bubble. Not that it had been all that difficult, they, both he and Jespers, had been surprised by how easily he'd mastered it. Actually, truthfully, the ease of that worried Jespers. Or was that just another example of X's oddity?

"Whatever," Callender said, shaking his head like he heard a ringing in his ears.

"Maybe I should just say these are perilous times," X said, trying hard not to laugh.

"Perilous times! Now what in the hell is that supposed to mean?"

"Sorry, I seem to have picked up some bad habits. My speech, I mean. I've been hanging out with some real characters."

"I guess. Melodramatic, too." He took a deep breath to keep from laughing, holding it in until the moment passed. "So, yes, we live in perilous times. Was it ever so."

X beamed. "See, it's like a virus."

"X? Please. Can we?" He was pointing down the street.

"How about a drink?"

"At 10:30 in the morning?"

"Is it really?" X stopped to look at their surroundings. "Sorry. I guess my internal clock is set for a different time zone."

"Oh? And which one would that be?"

"The one where they're not using Greenwich Mean Time."

"Oh," Callender said, staring at him. "That one. Maybe a drink is called for."

"You look tired," Sandy told him over their Castle Lagers.

"Do I?" X rubbed his chin, feeling the stubble.

"Like you've got a few things on your mind."

"So many I don't even know where to begin."

"Well . . ."

"I suppose you heard about that trouble out at the space station." He stared at him. "Perhaps you even saw something?"

"Space station?"

X shook his head disgustedly. "You'd think something like that would have been a huge story. Now it's starting to look like it will be just one more secret."

"What will?"

"This big conference. The Delegations and some of our governments."

"At the space station?"

"Actually, the meetings were held on one of their ships. Huge fucking thing." He shook his head. "But our representatives stayed over at the cheap hotel."

"And by that you mean the space station."

"Correct. We'd take them up, they'd be there a day or two, and then we'd bring them back home. This was to go on for ten days.'

"You were flying?"

"No. I was there in an unofficial capacity."

"Whatever that means."

"Sandy . . ." he stared at him.

"Yes?"

"We've never gone into this very much, what it is I do, and you've been very polite about it, but I believe the time has finally come."

Not responding, Callender leaned back, sipping his beer.

"I see. So now that the big moment has finally arrived you suddenly find that you really didn't want to know."

"No, I want to know, it's just that you make me nervous with all this secretive stuff."

"There's nothing very secretive about this. I'm just there to keep an eye on things. There to see if there's something we might do to help us better deal with the situation."

"Not security?" Not for a moment had he ever believed that.

"Well, it may have implications for security, but it's not security."

"Who do you do this for?"

X laughed and shook his head. "Would you believe me if I told you I'm not sure?"

"Yes, but you must find that difficult."

"Actually, I don't, because I rarely have anything useful to report, and that's largely due to the fact that we have so little understanding of the Delegations. A lack of useful information that's unlikely to change anytime soon. So, no, it's usually not of great concern. It's just another of the annoyances that comes with working within an area of maximum ambiguity."

"Maximum ambiguity?" Callender smiled. "But that would be you, wouldn't it? A man tailor-made for his job."

"Yes, well I think I've finally grown a bit weary of maximum ambiguity, which maybe explains this next bit, because now I've come up with this plan I hope will give a little more form and structure to our situation. A revelatory moment."

"Is called for?"

"Is long overdue."

Callender laughed, X was such an amazing guy. "You know I'm not going to write about this, whatever this is, right? Because, first of all, I find most of what you tell me very hard to believe, and secondly, even if I did believe you no one else would, which would pretty effectively kill my journalistic career. And I certainly don't want to become part of your maximum ambiguity. I don't even like ambiguity."

X was nodding. He hardly disagreed. "That's fine. I fully understand how you feel, but do hear me out."

"It won't change anything."

"I know, but at least it will make me feel better." He laughed. "You know, I woke up this morning and thought, I need to talk to good old Sandy. He'll cheer me up. He's an understanding fellow."

"Cheaper than your psychiatrist. Assuming you have one."

"Oh, we have them, not that they'd believe anything I might have to tell them. I mean, look at you."

"Yes, but I am listening."

"Yes, and I'm grateful for that."

"So?"

"So what happened up there, and I'm honestly amazed that no one's heard about this, is that some of the Delegations got into a squabble, one that soon escalated into an actual skirmish. That's what I think happened, anyway." He stared at Sandy a moment. "And, yes, I was there as a witness, as were the rest of us."

"Humans, you mean?"

"Yes, but only as innocent bystanders. As witnesses to a truly chilling display of technological supremacy. Huge ships just flinging themselves around, smaller ships blasting away at each other, darting around looking for cover. Sandy . . ." he paused as he remembered the ferocity of it.

"Yes?"

"It looked like sheer chaos, or it did to me, though I'm sure it really wasn't. Not from their point of view, anyway. And then it all just stopped."

"Just like that?"

"Just like that, though I have no idea why. I don't even know if it accomplished anything. But caught up in that melee was the space station and a handful of rather pitiful humans."

"Honestly, I haven't heard a word."

"Unbelievable. Well, just so you'll know even if no one else ever does, the space station is now missing one whole wing and we humans lost almost one hundred lives."

Sandy sat back and stared at him. It wasn't possible. There's no way they could suppress a story like that. Something would have leaked out by now. Humans caught up in an alien battle at the space station? That there even were aliens? No. He couldn't believe it.

X smiled at him. "Presents quite a challenge to your everyday sense of the possible, doesn't it? We like our comforts here on planet Earth. The do not disturb sign is always out. Please comply."

"Sorry."

"Well, my friend, you better hang on because I've got an idea that a lot more of this sort of thing is going to happen, and very soon."

"How soon?"

"As soon as I can get up there."

"Oh?"

"Let me show you something." X reached into his backpack and took out his gentleman's pistol, or whatever the hell it was. "I borrowed this from one of the alien craft after the battle. Here." He slid it across the table. "Go ahead. Pick it up."

Callender carefully did, finding himself surprised by its odd mixture of beautiful form and lethal functionality. "How does it work?"

"You touch that little button on top and that turns it on, then you squeeze that grip-like thing and it fires. Marvelous little weapon."

"This?" Callender was pointing to the little M&M.

"Don't," X said. "You could punch a hole right through this place with that."

"Seriously?" It certainly looked like it could.

"Want to see?" X asked, grinning wickedly.

"Here?" Callender looked nervously around the restaurant.

"I thought we might step outside. No?" he asked, seeing the interest in Callender's eyes. "I'll let you fire it."

"You are such a bastard," Callender said, standing up.

Outside, they looked around for a bit of privacy, finally settling for the alley in back of the restaurant.

"What about this?" Callender was pointing to one of the big trash dumpsters in the alley.

"That should work, but be sure to stand over here so when you do fire that thing you don't kill someone sitting inside eating their lunch."

"Like this?" He was standing in front of the first dumpster.

"Perfect. Now aim down so it goes into the ground." X watched him stand on a cinder block and aim the weapon down at the dumpster. "That's good. Now slide that little button on top."

"Jesus!" Sandy said as it started to buzz and vibrate in his hand.

"It's very sensitive, so just a little squeeze—"

"Son of a bitch!" Sandy exclaimed, falling backwards as the weapon fired, landing on the ground with the weapon still clutched in his hand.

"Like I said," X said, grinning at him, "just a little squeeze."

"Look at that!" Callender said, getting to his feet and pointing to a hole the size of an orange in the side of the dumpster. "And it's under here, too," he said, bending down to look under the dumpster. "How far do you think that goes?"

"I have no idea."

Straightening up, Callender held the gun out and smiled. "It's so quiet. I want one."

"Next time I run across one I'll take it for you."

"So this is your proof? Because it's damn good proof."

"Actually," X said, taking the little weapon from his hand, "this is going to be my agent of disruption."

"Your what?"

"Sorry." He smiled. "For some reason I seem to have fallen into this rather poetic way of saying things."

"Yes," Callender said, squinting suspiciously at him, "I've been wondering about that."

"Well, I'd love to tell you, but I think we've already used up whatever willingness to believe you had this morning."

"Oh, go ahead, I may be coming around." He was grinning, but he was actually thinking that for the first time he really was.

Back at their table in the bar he told him: "When it was over, or at least when all the big ships had vanished and it was just us, I saw this bright light approaching one of the disabled shuttles over by the station, and after a while the shuttle blew up and the light went on to the next one. I think they were mopping up."

"Mopping up?"

"Killing the survivors, if there were any, and destroying our ships."

"But why?"

"Other than sheer bloody-mindedness, I have no idea. No way we were a threat to anyone. We're not even armed, for god's sake. I do know that there are various factions among the Delegations, some of which are more friendly towards us than the others, or at least they're more neutral, but clearly there are some that are downright hostile."

"Do you know which are which?"

"Actually, I do. The more they look like us the friendlier."

"But the ones mopping up? What did they look like?"

"I'm not sure, but in their space suits they looked pretty much like we do."

"So what does that suggest? That they were humans?"

X laughed. "Look at you. You've gone from not believing a word I say, to hanging on my every word."

"I know, ironic, isn't it?" But the truth was he'd always wanted to believe. He liked X. There was something about him that made it almost impossible to believe he was lying or crazy, though he had tried on numerous occasions to embrace both possibilities. "So you're sure they weren't some of ours? Not Chinese, perhaps? And no, I have no idea what I mean by that."

"I don't see how they could be. That weapon I took? We don't have anything like that, or those ships. I think they were some version of what they refer to as *Instants*."

"Instants?" Callender asked, staring at him wide-eyed.

"I'm pretty sure that's a derogatory term."

"I would think so," Callender said, shaking his head.

"It's because it's so incredibly expensive to get here, or anywhere, for that matter, so they are very careful about what they bring."

"You're telling me it's all a matter of accounting? That, yes, we do have aliens, but they're worried about their expenses?"

Grinning, X nodded his head. "Trust me, I may not know a lot, but on this I can speak with authority."

"This is hardly what I was expecting. You know? Like those old *Star Wars* movies, vast battle fleets, millions of space troopers, not that they have to answer to the bean counters."

"We all have to answer to the bean counters."

"Well, I'm amazed, and not in any way I would have ever thought possible."

"Sorry. But it is a cost effective way to ship foot soldiers. I mean, if you think about it."

"Just add water?"

"You don't suppose," X said, laughing with him.

"But what *do* they do? Bring them back to life? Create them?"

"I'm not sure, just that they're economical and ready when needed."

"Well, that would certainly cut down on overhead."

X smiled. "You see? It does make sense."

"But these Instants, they're not like us? That is what you're saying?"

"Other than a few who may be somewhat like us in appearance, no. Actually, I doubt they're much like anything other than what they are. They may not even be truly sentient, which would certainly make me feel better since I had to kill two."

"The ones mopping up?"

"That's right. I saw what they were doing and I thought, you know what, that's it, I've had enough of this crap. So I snuck on board their ship, which is where I found that, as well as several other interesting tools of the trade. One of which I subsequently used to pretty much obliterate them." He shook his head. "Unbelievably powerful weapon. Which worries me. How can we hope to take them on with what we have."

"I presume we can't."

"Not really, but then I had an interesting thought. Since I'd just seen how little they actually trusted one another, perhaps I might be able to sow a little discord."

"You're thinking you might be able to start a war?"

"No, just a little ruckus. Something to buy us the time we'll need to work our way out of this mess."

"How much time do you think we'll need?"

"I'm thinking five years ought do it."

"But if they're as advanced as you say they are, how can we possibly hope to catch up with them in just five years?"

"Well, with a little help . . . "

"Which is something you're not going to tell me about, isn't it?"

"Now listen very carefully, because this will be your job."

"I'm listening, but I'm not liking it."

"If I do this right all hell is going to break loose up there, and when it does we may have an excellent opportunity to see which, if any, of our governments are working with them. Most will be genuinely surprised. They won't know what to do. Actually, they won't be expected to do much of anything. But I'm hoping you'll see a bit of panic. Those are the governments we're interested in."

"Panic? That's what I'll be doing."

"I won't?"

"Yes, your involvement is going to be rather intimate, isn't it?"

"I fully intend on coming back, Sandy."

"And me?"

X put his hand on Callender's shoulder and smiled. "Sandy, you don't have a thing to worry about. The only person who knows of our connection is hardly someone you need be concerned with, and I don't mean Bente."

"Seriously?"

"Seriously. The worst that might happen is he makes you pay for dinner."

32

He wasn't really against the idea, not after the Chinese assassin, and she was so adamant about it, and maybe it was time he just disappeared. The problem was that this was a defining moment. She didn't really understand that. But once they knew he was free of their surveillance they would stop at nothing to find him. In some sense it was easier to just putter along with the chip still there.

She carefully injected Lidocaine in several different locations around the chip, then tapped the lump with her gloved fingers. She'd be so happy to get that damn thing out of there. She still couldn't believe he'd finally agreed to it.

"Is this going to hurt?" He was watching as she cleaned his shoulder with alcohol.

She laid the cotton swab on the table and smiled. "When did you become such a whiner?"

"When I saw that?" He was nodding at the metal tray with its wicked looking scalpels and forceps on the counter in front of them.

"Then don't look." She took a small needle from the tray and pricked his shoulder, looking to see if he winced. "I think you're ready," she said. "Or do you want Sil to hold your hand?"

"No. I'm embarrassed enough that she has to see me acting like this."

"Ready?"

"No."

It was over very quickly, though she was annoyed at how deep it was, but once she got a good grip on it she plucked it right out.

"There," she said, holding it up in her forceps.

"Let me see," he said.

She dropped it in his hand, watching him examine it as she cleaned him up.

When she was done Sil took everything out of the room, then she put her arms around his neck and kissed his check.

"Feel better?" he asked.

"Yes! I hated that thing being in you."

He smiled and stood up. "What do you think we should do with this?"

"Well, we could put it on a plane. Let them scurry around trying to keep track of you."

He nodded. It wasn't a bad suggestion.

"Or my preference, smash it with a hammer. Make them think you're dead."

"You'd like that, wouldn't you? Not dead, but sort of forever missing in action."

She put her arms around his waist and smiled up at him. "I'd love it," she said.

33

He asked the bubble to open the alien ship's airlock, then stepped free of the bubble-space, making his way through the membrane into a cramped room with pink walls. Pink! Was it possible they just come in pink?

It didn't take long before he encountered one of the creatures inadvertently blocking his way down a narrow passageway. Creeping up on it, he touched its back, watching it shiver in response, spinning around to wave some sort of weapon in his face. "Sorry," he said, shooting it once in the head with his alien toy, stepping aside to dodge a splatter of vile smelling dark blue fluid.

There were three when he found them, gathered around a screen watching what looked to him like a procession. Was that in real time? It certainly looked like it. Amazing. But maybe it was just an old movie. Coming up quietly behind them, he paused to clear his throat. "Excuse me," he said. "You boys got a minute?" It was interesting, even though he had no idea how they thought or lived their lives, it wasn't hard to see their shock and surprise. *A human? Here?* He could almost understand them as they spoke. "Yes," he said, pointing his weapon at them. "I know. It is a bit of a surprise." Suddenly, the one on his left moved towards the door, and without even the slightest hesitation he shot it dead center, spinning it around with an agonized grunt to thrash on the floor until he shot it again. Turning, he angrily waved his gun at the one in the middle, the obvious one of importance, and it stood very still. The other one held up its hands, or paws, or whatever they were, and spoke. "Do not shoot," it said.

X smiled. "I appreciate that, that you spoke to me in my own language. I find it all too easy to kill you when you're merely aliens."

"You are a killer?"

X thought about that. "No. Not really." They both looked at the dead creature on the floor. "Okay, obviously I do kill, but I'm not a killer. If you understand the distinction."

The other one spoke. It was angry. It was so obvious.

"What's he saying?" X asked.

"He wonders how you got here. He wonders how you plan to escape. He wonders why humans like to kill. He wonders when you will kill us."

"All that? Your language must be incredibly efficient."

"It's precise. Little nuance."

"Unlike ours?"

"Yes."

"Well, he's right, I am going to kill him. I'm sorry about that, I truly am. I'm sure he has an important life and means a great deal to a great many others, but that's just the point. I aim to sow confusion among you so that we pitiful humans can get some breathing room. I'm sure you can understand that."

The creature looked at the other and then at him.

"You can tell him that if you like."

He watched them talking. The other creature appeared to find it funny. Was that possible? "Did he just laugh?"

"Yes. He finds it amusing.

"He doesn't think I'll do it?"

"Oh no. He just finds it amusing that his life will end like this. He's been in favor of killing humans for a long time. He thinks it's amusing to finally be killed by one." The creature seemed to shudder. "And diplomats. He hates diplomats."

"A lot, it seems." The other creature said something and they both turned to watch. "Yes?" X asked when it was finished.

"He says he would appreciate knowing who you are. He says his scanner shows you not to be human."

"His scanner?"

"Yes. He says you read differently from other humans."

"Read differently? Sorry, but I haven't the faintest idea what he's talking about. Maybe he can enlighten us."

The creature translated and then they both stood there waiting. The other creature was obviously considering it. Finally, it launched into a long account of something, something that it still found amusing, so much so that X finally began to wonder if the joke might not be on him.

"Well?" he asked when it stopped speaking.

The other creature stared at him. "Well, he thinks you are one of the hybrids. Bastards? Would that word work?"

"Probably."

"That they all know that the Krist have been here for a long time."

"Meddling?"

"Yes. Meddling. No one likes the Krist. Everywhere we go the Krist have already been there."

"Annoying?"

"Yes. Arrogant. Uncooperative. Jokesters."

"Ah, the way you say that, *jokesters*, that's very bad, I take it."

"So it's been known for some time that there are Krist and human hybrids. You are the first one he's seen, however, but he's sure you're going to be nothing but trouble for us. His last wish, and he feels very strongly about this, is that you were dead. Many times over, in fact."

"We're trouble? You tell him this for me, will you, that here we were, everything just fine, just sitting here on this insignificant little world all the way out here at the edge of this insignificant galaxy just minding our own damn business, not bothering anyone, not interfering, and then he had to show up."

"He will say that you won't be out here for long just minding your own damn business. He will say that soon you will be a problem. He will say that if he had his way this problem would end today. He will say that others don't see as clearly as he does. He will say that captives should have been taken. He will say—"

"Yes," X said, waving the gun for him to stop. "I get it. We and our Krist meddlers are a pain in the ass." He pointed the gun at the other alien and shot it. He was silent as he watched it die. "Sorry," he told the other one. "I don't know how hard that was for you."

The creature looked at him for some time. "Not that hard," it finally said.

"Really?" he asked, watching the creature do something with its upper body in response. "Was that a shrug?"

"An equivalent."

"You know, the whole point of all this carnage is to make it look as if the Delegations are now reduced to assassination. You know, as opposed to just blowing each other up at great distances. The hope being, or at least it's my hope, since I assure you I do this on my own, that you will now all just get the hell out of here and leave us alone for awhile." He sighed. "Yes, I know, it's not much, I'll give you that, but at this particular moment it's what we need most."

"You don't have much time. He did send an alarm."

"He did? Is there any record of this? Visual?"

The creature pointed to a device sitting on a stand by the bulkhead. "Not if you take that. Other than myself, of course."

"You're so helpful. Why is that?"

"I'm a diplomat."

"Ah." X smiled. "And how do you feel about the Krist?"

"I'm not sure, though I find you quite interesting."

"Yes, but I'm not a Krist."

"You are certainly not human."

"I certainly am."

The creature shrugged. It definitely shrugged. "Never argue with the man who has the gun," it said.

Laughing, X paused to stare at it in open admiration. "Well, that settles it. Grab that thing and let's get the hell out of here."

"And if I don't?"

"Then I shoot you and regret it for the rest of my short, human-like life. You wouldn't do that to me, would you?"

"Got a name," he asked as they ran down the passageway to the bubble.

"It sounds like Klondike."

"You're kidding."

"I wish."

34

The look Jespers got on his face when he saw the creature was very amusing, or at least it was to X. So, for that matter, was the one the alien got on his face when he saw Jespers.

Krist?" he said, turning to look at X.

"How did you know that? The bubble?"

"That, and he looks Krist."

"I thought he looked human."

"I think we see different parts of the spectrum." He looked at Jespers. "It's the infrared. We're better at that than humans. He's very hot. Krist are very hot."

"And humans?"

"Much cooler. You seem almost blue to us. He," and he nodded, "is white."

X smiled at Jespers. "Come on and open this damn thing. He's with me."

"Is he armed?" Jespers asked.

"Are you armed?"

"Of course not." He sounded offended.

"He's not armed. Now . . ." He pointed to the wall of the bubble. "Thank you," he said as Jespers waved the bubble open. "Please," X said, "you first. You're the diplomat. I'm just the non-human assassin."

"Thank you," the creature said to Jespers. "There will soon be a lot of turmoil here, I suggest we leave promptly."

Once underway, Jespers turned to X. "Well?" he asked.

"Was I successful? I believe so. He certainly seemed important. Correct?" He was looking at the diplomat.

"Indeed. The one you killed was the leader of our delegation."

"Who do you suppose will get the blame?"

"One of the four chief delegations."

X nodded.

"It is not a bad plan," the diplomat said. "But it will only forestall the inevitable."

"Maybe. By the way," X asked, taking a stab in the dark, "you're not the party in the Delegations working with the Chinese, are you?"

"We would not work with humans."

"Oh?"

"Do you find that offensive?"

"I'm not sure, but if that's how you feel why is your delegation even here?"

"To keep an eye on the others, and to protect our interests. And," and it nodded at Jespers, "we worry about them."

"So as far as you're concerned we play no role in this?"

"I am unaware of any particular role for you in our plans."

"Is that what happened with the old Apollo program? That it didn't fit your plans?"

"It was the artifacts."

"On the moon, you mean."

"Yes, though that is mostly hearsay since none of the Delegations have seen them, or at least they won't admit to having seen them."

X and Jespers glanced at one another, surprised by such a frank admission. "But you do share this aversion to going to see for yourselves?" X asked

"Yes, though I've always assumed that was more because the Krist would not permit it."

"That has certainly been our position," Jespers said.

"But even if it weren't, you still wouldn't go?"

"No. Too many unknowns, too many potential risks and presumably dangerous technologies."

"Dangerous for you, perhaps," X said.

"Oh?" The diplomat quickly looked at Jespers. He was now clearly agitated. "They've been back?"

"Back?"

"Because the Delegations have warned them."

"They have?"

"This is not known?"

"Not to me," Jespers said. "Though I find it very interesting that they have."

"Yes," the diplomat said. "When they entered the mountain it was considered a very serious treaty violation. Humans were made aware of this."

"Whose treaty?" Jespers asked.

The diplomat stared at them. "The joint mission? This too is not known?"

"It's certainly not known to me? X?"

"No. What do you mean by joint mission?"

Saying nothing, the diplomat stared at them.

"You're not thinking of negotiating with us, are you?" X asked.

"Possibly, since it appears I know more about this situation than either of you. In that, I'm sure there is power."

"Yes," X said, shaking his head, "I think I may have shot the wrong alien."

"Tell us about it," Jespers said.

"There was a joint mission, and by that I mean it was done at the behest of, or with the connivance of, several of the Delegations. The humans were the ones who actually went, of course, and we were later told that whatever they found was to have been shared equally."

"I'm amazed," Jespers said. "I can't imagine how we missed this."

The diplomat seemed even more animated. "So the mighty Krist are not infallible, after all. Such good news deserves to be shared."

"How did it turn out?" X asked.

"It was a disappointment, or so I gather, because when it did become known there was very little protest. It was then declared a treaty violation among the Delegations, which marked the end of it."

"Just like that?" It hardly seemed possible to X they'd just let it drop.

"The enforcement of the treaty was considered to be a most effective outcome."

Laughing, X held up his hands in frustration. "Fine, I'm happy you diplomats were happy, but what about what they found? Wasn't that an issue?"

"No."

"And why was that?"

"Because nothing that was found could be shared. It couldn't even be known. That was how the treaty could be enforced."

"Yes, but we humans must have known if we found it."

"You agreed to the treaty."

Jespers nodded his head. He understood now. "So everyone was satisfied. Or equally dissatisfied."

"Correct."

"And this is the sort of outcome that makes you diplomats happy?" X was still unable to believe what he was hearing.

The diplomat stared at him, then it turned to Jespers. "What doesn't he understand?"

"He understands. It's just that he wonders what they found, and what became of it. It is puzzling that the Delegations just let this go."

"There was no other alternative. The cooperation of the Delegations is not easy to maintain. And," he nodded at X, "it's only getting harder."

"We need to go back," X said, staring at them.

"To the moon?" Jespers asked.

"Yes."

"We would resist that," the diplomat said.

"Oh?" X smiled. "And if we negotiated?"

Not knowing much about it, both Jespers and X were still quite sure that it was a look of great satisfaction they saw on its face. "Negotiate?" it asked. "Yes, it's possible we might be able to work something out of mutual benefit."

35

He had to sleep. Maybe it was the killing. Maybe it was the effect of space travel. Maybe he just needed some peace and quiet because they were driving him crazy. Jespers and Klondike, that is.

At one point he said to them, "I thought you two were supposed to be enemies? Because you sure don't sound like it."

Jespers smiled at him. "We are men of reason, not combatants."

"So am I, and you two are driving me nuts."

"Human reason," the diplomat said, his native language's information-dense style coming through even when he spoke English.

"Oh? And that's inferior to yours?"

The damn thing shrugged.

"Well, I also seem to be a bit of a Krist, that doesn't raise my stature any in your eyes?"

Ignoring him, it looked at Jespers. "It has always been so, has it not, that hybrid creatures are prone to unforeseen difficulties."

"Which in my case would be what?"

"Leaps of faith? Reliance on intuition?" It stopped, looking at Jespers for confirmation. "Endless guessing?"

"Perhaps, but they're also extraordinarily lucky, and when it comes to the subtext of a situation, preternaturally acute."

"They know more than they know?" the diplomat asked.

"Often."

X stared at them. "I have a headache. Okay? If *I'm* lucky I will soon be asleep. Do you do that? Sleep? Because I sure hope so."

"I have a seasonal pattern of hibernation," the diplomat said. "At this point in my cycle I'm awake almost all of the time."

"I don't need sleep," Jespers said.

"You do know," X said, pointing a finger at him, "that you have a lot to answer for?"

"We're very sorry, X, truly we are. Someday we will have to talk about it."

"Whatever," X said, tiredly waving his hand in the air. "As for right now, let's just say goodnight."

As he walked down the hall he heard Jespers say, "Do you like wine? Human wine? You have tried it? No? But you must."

36

"We've agreed," Jespers told him the next morning as he sat bleary-eyed drinking coffee at Jespers' kitchen table.

"Wonderful," he replied, refusing to look at them.

"It needs to be fed," the diplomat said.

"And it's cranky," X said. "So watch yourself."

The diplomat stepped back a pace and looked at Jespers.

"Yes," Jespers said with a chuckle. "They can be violent. But he does need to eat something before we explain it to him."

"Better?" Jespers asked as he joined them in the living room.

"Do Krist get headaches?" X asked. "Because if they do I'm blaming this one on you."

"No, actually we don't."

The diplomat turned to look at Jespers. "Truly?"

"You too?" X said.

The diplomat nodded.

"Well, I'm sorry," Jespers said when they both turned to stare at him.

"And this joint mission must have been Apollo 17," X said. The logic seemed simple enough. Since Apollo 17 was the last mission to the moon, the Delegations' warning to stay away must have been the result of something they'd either done or found. Now all he had to do was find out what that was. That was the heart of the matter, anyway, what was on the moon. What might be found elsewhere, on Mars, for example, or Phobos, or on the moons of Saturn or Jupiter, or even hidden away in the asteroid belt, that, for the moment, was irrelevant.

"You do both realize I don't need your permission," X said.

"Perhaps not," Jespers said, "but you will certainly need our assistance."

"Only to get there and back."

Jespers smiled at the diplomat.

"What?" X asked, getting more annoyed with them by the moment.

"Our friend predicted you'd fail to master the art of negotiation."

X turned to glare at him. "You know your leader's feelings towards diplomats? They seem much more understandable to me now."

They'd been monitoring the behavior of the Delegations, but so far X had been bitterly disappointed by their apparent lack of concern for the assassination. Nor did it help ease his guilty conscience any to learn more about Klondike's people. Oh, they were most definitely hostile to humans, but they weren't important enough among the Delegations to ever get their way. So, yes, one might well have thought that an assassination would stir things up, but then maybe that sort of thing was just too common to get all that riled up about. Or maybe they just didn't give a damn about Klondike's delegation.

"What will your delegation do now?" he asked.

"We will leave. I will explain the situation and we will decide that we have had enough of this business; that there is nothing in this for us; that humans will do what they will do whether we are here or not; that our interests are best served by attending to other matters; that human diplomats may someday make contact worthwhile, but that for the foreseeable future we will be best served letting others settle these issues as they see fit."

Jespers nodded. It was very sensible.

"Diplomats, huh?" X laughed. "But won't you tell them I was the one behind your leader's death?"

"No. It was a good plan. At the very least, the dissension and mistrust you've caused works in our favor. It gives us just the pretext we need to leave."

"So as far as you, personally, are concerned, I did well, even though I'm not a good negotiator."

"You are most capable, X. Who would not say so?"

"Quite a few, in fact, but that's fine, even a backhanded compliment is appreciated."

Jespers glanced at the diplomat as he told X: "I will take our friend back to his craft. We have agreed to a conference while I am there. I'm told we have never spoken face to face before."

"The Krist, you mean?"

"Yes. So this is an opportune moment for fence mending." Fence mending? How lovely that sounded. Neighborly. He'd try it out on them when they spoke. We should mend our fences, he'd say. See if we can't be better neighbors. He smiled. Yes, he knew he'd been hopelessly corrupted by human ways. When he returned home he'd never be accepted back into polite Krist society.

"I know I owe you many apologies for what I've put you through," X told the diplomat. "I hope you won't hold that against all of us."

"Why would I do that?" It seemed genuinely puzzled that X thought it might.

"No? Sorry. Well, I hope you have a long and happy life negotiating every last little detail."

"Thank you, X. I am very grateful that most humans are not like you."

X laughed. "You are, huh?"

"Indeed. You are a most dangerous and lucky person. May that long continue, but far, far away from me."

37

What X knew of Apollo 17 was what everyone knew, that Apollo 17 was the last of the manned Apollo flights and effectively marked the end of the Apollo program. More interesting were the details he now learned for the first time. How astronauts Cernan and Schmitt rode the lunar module Challenger down to the lunar surface while Evans stayed behind in the command module, America, spending a little more than three full days on the lunar surface in the Taurus-Littrow Valley where they performed three EVAs (extra vehicular activities), one each day, each of about seven hours duration for a total of 22 hours, the most for any mission; that Apollo 17 brought back more lunar material than any previous mission; that the astronauts spent more time in lunar orbit than on any previous mission; in fact, the total duration of the mission from liftoff to splash down was 12 days. What surprised X the most, however, something he'd never heard mentioned before, was that Apollo 17 was, by far, the most dangerous of the Apollo missions: the landing site was a narrow valley ringed by high mountains, its surface cluttered with craters and boulder fields; the angle of descent was very steep, leaving little margin for error; and the duration of the landing was also far longer than normal. X thought they must have really wanted to get there to take such risks.

Yes, he'd also run across the questions some had raised about the *real* goal of Apollo 17. How some of the photographs taken during Apollo 15 depicted a ribbed-like pattern on the surface of South Massif—the large, hexagonally shaped mountain at the north edge of the Taurus-Littrow Valley—highly suggestive to some of an inner structure. Likewise, that there was photographic evidence showing where one side of the mountain had collapsed inwards into a large interior space. That it was, in other words, an artifact, a fact kept from the public by a long-standing, deeply entrenched conspiracy, presumably at the behest of NASA.

More troubling was Nansen (Station 2), the crater, or so NASA described it, located far down the slope of South Massif. Troubling, because in most photographs it looked far more like an entrance into the base of the mountain. And it was true that the astronauts had made a long and dangerous trek in the Rover over very difficult terrain to reach it, though once there, in yet another instance of NASA's maddening ways, Cernan had "inadvertently" parked the Rover with its television camera pointed in the wrong direction. X was surprised by that, that there was no visual record of what they'd done at Nansen even though they'd been there for over an hour (the annotated *Lunar Surface Journal* entries for Apollo 17 show that Cernan and Schmitt spent a total of one hour and four minutes at Station 2, or from 2:08 to 3:12), which hardly seemed long enough for such an important site, but than again they'd been working within the confines of a very tightly scripted schedule.

So were we really to believe that this was the best NASA could do, and this at a location not only of unique importance to the success of the mission but one that required an unusual effort even to reach? He knew what the conspiracists had to say about that, as for him, he'd read the transcript of the communications back and forth between Cernan, Schmitt, and Mission Control. They could barely hide their excitement at what they saw, yet no photographic record? When it was standard practice on all Apollo missions to document everything photographically, often obsessively so? The truth was, he was having a very hard time reconciling the few photographs purportedly taken at Station 2—depicting a rather ordinary, almost prosaic looking site of lobes and hillocks, a swale or small valley and a few boulders—with Cernan's and Schmitt's remarks. In fact, he found it almost impossible to understand, when looking just at the photographs, why Station 2 had ever been considered so important, let alone worth the risk of sending the Rover eight or so kilometers across the valley floor and up a steep scarp.

He was a bit surprised by that, how significant the risks had actually been. An accident out there with the Rover at Station 2 would have left Cernan and Schmitt stranded at the outer limits of what NASA engineers referred to as a safe *walkback* distance. It was many kilometers of difficult terrain back to the safety of the LM from Station 2. X couldn't help but wonder if they really would have made it safely back. What an incredible disaster that would have been, the two astronauts running out of oxygen on the surface of the moon, all the while in radio communication with NASA and the rest of humanity.

Still, he understood all about that sort of thing. All the planning and training, the worry about contingencies and redundancies, the attempts to engineer out the risk factors, or at least to get them down to a manageable few. He also understood how, in the end, it always came down to a calculated risk and the person willing to take it. It was never really anything more than that. So now it was his turn. Yes, but he'd be much better prepared and equipped, and if anything did go wrong he knew he wouldn't be stranded there forever without a prayer, not with Jespers acting as his guardian angel.

So he would focus on Nansen, though that left many other unanswered questions. Like why, when they left, had they crashed the ascent stage of the LM into the side of South Massif? Was it really, as claimed, just one more part of the seismic experiments they'd been conducting? But why South Massif? Then there was the mystery of what really happened out at Shorty, the name they'd given to a large crater. Or Chapel Bell, the notorious secret experiment left behind on the surface of the moon by Apollo 17, the purpose of which had yet to be revealed. Well, whatever any of that meant, if it meant anything at all, he'd just have to figure it out when he got there.

Jespers had agreed when he returned from his diplomatic mission, he would shuttle X about in the bubble, provide support when and where needed, monitor things, and get him out of there if anything went wrong. X would also have use of a few select Krist technologies. His space suit was a custom job, for example, and there were communications and food. In fact, most of the nuts and bolts of his task were being thoughtfully provided. What he in turn was to provide he hoped would be sound judgment, a rare commodity even among the Krist, like their admonishment that he couldn't bring a weapon. He knew of Krist respect for human ingenuity, but he thought that was asking a bit much. Or maybe they understood him only too well, because rare would be those times when in the heat of the moment he didn't find blasting something the better alternative.

X had read that the Rover tended to be a handful going downhill at one-sixth gravity, often feeling to Cernan and Schmitt like it was about to spin or rollover. This was particularly true coming off the scarp and down the steep hills leaving Station 2. X could almost hear the nervousness in their voices as he read the transcript. Not his problem. He'd get around on a lunar scooter, another gift from the Krist. He had no idea how it actually worked, but then all he had to do was sit there and push the tiller to move in any direction he chose, the speed never varying until he let go of the tiller and it came to a gentle halt always eight inches above the surface. He liked it. It was shiny like stainless steel, light as a feather when he moved it with his hand, and frisky like a colt.

So the question became how best to prepare. One resource that proved especially helpful were the high-resolution photographs taken by the Lunar Reconnaissance Orbiter. There, and as annotated by NASA, were the visible details of

Apollo 17's mission in the Taurus-Littrow Valley: the actual routes taken by Cernan and Schmitt on their three EVAs; the tracks left behind by the Rover; the major features of the surrounding landscape; and, in some cases, even the astronaut's actual footprints. Good, it was all starting to come together. He'd read the transcripts of their radio communications and looked at the photographs they'd taken. Now he could actually see the physical routes they'd traveled on their three EVAs. But it was the EVA on day two that was most critical, that long drive out to Nansen and back. That was where the mystery lay, if Apollo 17 had a mystery. Fine. He'd get down there and do as they had done. Try to see what they had seen. Try to understand what it was about Apollo 17 that caused the Delegations to issue their warning.

38

"So I not only have permission, I have encouragement? Is that what you're telling me?"

Jespers nodded. "There is much confidence in you."

"I love how you say that, *there is much confidence in you*, like it's just floating out there somewhere in Krist social space for all to see. What I'd really prefer is hearing you say, X, *I* have the utmost confidence in you. Or is that not how you think? That you Krist are so communal that there is no clear individuality anymore?"

"Oh, no, we are all quite unique. Idiosyncratic. But we do tend to agree on the big issues, and this lunar expedition of yours is certainly that."

"So this confidence is not just some vague feeling shared by the group, but something actually held and articulated by individual Krist?"

"Why is this so important to you?"

"Because I have enough on my mind already without worrying about the strength of my support among your somewhat eccentric fellow Krist. I also subscribe to the view that history rests on the effective powers of individuals, not on vast impersonal forces or the inexorable unfolding of some esoteric historical telos."

Jespers smiled. "X, the ultimate romantic individualist."

"You think anyone else would do this?"

"I have no idea, but humans often seem amazingly adventuresome to me."

"And you're not! Your new body? Coming here? The meddling?"

"That's just curiosity."

"Splitting hairs."

Jespers shrugged. "Perhaps, but we are quite different, you and I."

"I think I have a pretty good understanding of that."

"Because of your unusual genetic heritage?"

"No, and I very much doubt that gives me any special insight. I was thinking more along the lines of plain old human empathy. To see, to feel, how it is to be Krist."

"But with no fear?"

"Of what, you?"

"Because you apparently have none."

"Now don't go telling me something that's going to make me want to change my mind or start to brood while I'm out there trying to help you."

"No, I shall brood for the both of us. But is that how you see this, that you are trying to help us?"

"Are you saying I'm not? Like this won't help satisfy some of that endless Krist curiosity you just spoke of?"

"But is this not also for yourself, the romantic individualist?" Jespers laughed. "I certainly hope you're not just being swept along by the currents of history."

"No, today I'm the big jagged rock in the currents of history. For the time being they're going to have to flow around me."

39

He leaned back against the abandoned Rover to take in the stunning view. One might almost be forgiven for thinking that NASA had picked this spot solely for that reason, but of course they hadn't. Whatever aesthetic appreciation there was at NASA for the sights they beheld it rarely made its presence known, though here and there the astronauts commented on it, as it was vividly present here and there in their photographs.

He looked at the remains of the LM. It certainly had the look of an abandoned relic, whereas the Rover looked like something someone might have parked there just a few hours ago. It wasn't hard to imagine they'd soon return and off they would go bouncing over the undulating landscape. And that clutter of footprints stepping over themselves in the dust at his feet? This was an abandoned campsite, a place where the first explorers had camped for three days on their journey. Yes, an historic site. Someday that would be recognized and a memorial would stand there, and on the moon it would stand there forever, or forever as measured against the rise of humankind.

He gazed out across the soft hills towards South Massif, thrusting up out there at the far edge of the valley some 7,000 thousand feet, stark white against the blackness of space. That was one thing that truly surprised him, how everywhere he looked was lit with the brightest possible light, but always against the blackest of blacks. It was in all the photographs, of course, at least those that showed the horizon or higher, so it shouldn't have been that surprising, but then again, he now stood where those photographs had been taken, which was proving to be a very different experience.

But there was something else. He'd been in space many times, and many times he'd gazed down at the earth slowly rotating beneath him. It was always so huge. But from the moon it appeared to just hang there in the blackness, no less vivid, but so much smaller. Now *that* felt like being in space. Those other times, when he'd orbited the earth, those now seemed quite trivial by comparison, not even Armstrong's one small step. Here, he was *in* space, which was both terrifying and strangely peaceful at the same time. But humans could live here, he was sure of it.

He could tell that his sense of time was being challenged, like he could stand there forever and little if anything would change. Well, perhaps it wasn't quite timeless, but one still felt how incredibly old the universe was. Looking at the surface of the moon one just saw it. Here one hundred million years might pass and mean nothing. The Rover would still be here. Amazingly. No, actually by then it would probably be ground to dust by the incessant shower of micrometeorites and the energetic radiation it was constantly exposed to. But still, long duration, that was how one had to think about this new world. That was certainly the perspective from which the Krist viewed things. It even seemed to be the basis for how they lived their lives. Yet even the Krist were troubled by something older, something they hoped he might find. It was that, coupled with their fears and irrepressible curiosity that fueled their support. Though it was certainly possible he had their support for reasons he was totally unaware of. Yes, knowing the Krist that was far more likely.

40

He rode the scooter straight out to Nansen, reaching it with ease, just gliding along following the tracks left behind by the Rover back in 1972. In accordance with his plan, he parked where they had parked, in this case high up on the ledge overhanging the crater, though he could already see it wasn't a crater but some sort of open wound or puncture in the base of the mountain. Walking to the edge, he looked down. The opening was some sixty yards across, and like a cavern it was impossible to see much of what was inside.

Standing where they once had stood, now just footprints in the dust, he could see that this marked where they had tried and failed to find a way down. Failed? But they must have managed somehow, he could see their footprints down at the mouth of the opening. Perhaps up through all that debris he could see running down the valley from the mouth of the cavern. Yes, over there, off to the side, running parallel to the debris field, were the Rover's tracks heading back down the slope. Somewhere down there they must have parked and walked up.

He followed the Rover's tracks, riding his scooter down the slope, not stopping until he came to where they had parked. Sitting there, he had to smile. The view up the slope to the cavern's mouth was perfect. If only they'd pointed the Rover's camera in the right direction. Why, he wondered, looking up the narrow valley, had anyone ever thought this was a crater. Well, clearly no one had.

He left the scooter and followed their footprints as they wandered out among the boulders. They'd clearly been trying to find a way up, though pausing here and there to take rock samples or rake the soil, probably even to take a few photographs. Then looking a few yards ahead he was surprised to see them abruptly veer off to his right. Why, when the way ahead seemed clear? But by the time he reached them he understood. Not more than ten yards away was a thick girder festooned with a lattice-like series of small rods thrusting straight up some ten feet in the air. Nearer, he could see that a hand had once swept an eon's worth of dust from its still shiny surface. Placing his own hand there, he was surprised to find it felt more like plastic than metal, an impression heightened by its strange dark blue color. It must have been quite a shock to find an artifact like that—if they hadn't been expecting it. He noticed one set of footprints meandering off by themselves in the direction of a small mound on the other side of the girder. One of them must have gone over there to take a few photographs, perhaps even a panorama. Too bad none of them had ever been seen.

From there the trail continued on for some forty yards before getting lost in a confusing jumble of overlapping footprints. Forced to walk in ever widening circles, he finally found it reemerging from the melee to his left, though it quickly circled back to disappear behind a small hill on his right. He looked up the slope. Yes, from there it was easy to see the cavern's smooth interior walls and the lack of debris at its mouth. No, he couldn't see any way up from there either.

As yet unconcerned, certain they'd eventually found a way, he set off to his right only to be left standing there in open astonishment because apparently they hadn't, the footprints quickly coming to a halt before turning and seemingly making a beeline straight back to the Rover. Having no choice—still committed to the idea of following in their footsteps—he carefully followed them back, expecting at any moment to see them break off to take a different tack up the valley, but they never did. But he'd seen their tracks down at the mouth of the cavern? They must have looped back further on. Found another way. Or perhaps they'd gone back up on top, this time being successful. But if so he wondered how he could have missed it. And what about time? They didn't have much. How much later in the EVA could it have been?

41

He sat on his scooter up on the overhang above the cavern mouth. "Jespers?" he said into his mic.

"Yes?"

"Tell me about this scooter. Does it fly?" He was wondering what would happen if he went over the lip of the overhang.

"It floats. Gently."

"So if I go off up here it's going to float down to the terrace in front of the cavern? Gently?"

"Yes."

"You're sure?"

"It would for me."

"Okay, but even at one-sixth g it's going to be painful if it doesn't."

"You'll be fine. Or would you prefer to hunt around a bit more for their route down? We know it's got to be up there somewhere."

"Yeah, how do you suppose they did that?" He'd already looked around up there on the overhang as well as up the slope on South Massif, finding no sign in either location of another way down or the Rover. But it was a big mountain.

He leaned forward to look down. "Well," he said, moving the tiller forward.

At first he thought he'd made a terrible mistake as the scooter rapidly dropped a foot or two, but then it settled down and slowly descended to the ledge below. Pleased, he gave the seat a pat when he got off. "You still can't keep it," Jespers said in his ear.

He walked over to where the footprints entered the cavern. Now that he could actually see them it was clear that only one of them had gone on. Why? Safety? Presumably, since they had no idea what to expect.

"Jespers," he said, looking into the darkness, "there's no way this is a cavern. See?" He turned his head from side to side.

"More like a tunnel," Jespers said, noting how the wide mouth quickly narrowed down to a much narrower passage some thirty yards across.

"Has to be."

He walked across the ledge, backtracking the two sets of footprints to a spot where they suddenly seemed to appear from out of nowhere on the rocky shelf. He looked up. He could see where something had rubbed against the lip of the overhang. A cable? They'd come down over the lip like rock climbers? Why not? It made perfect sense, but then why hadn't he seen anything up above? Even more puzzling, why was there no mention of this in any of the Apollo 17 documentation.

He walked back over to where the tracks entered the tunnel and stepped into the shadows. Now, that was interesting. He could see that the tracks coming back were spaced much farther apart than the ones going in. Clearly, someone had been in a hurry.

He walked to the side of the tunnel and ran his hand over its smooth surface. "Jespers?" he said, keying his mic.

"I see it. It can't be a natural formation."

"*Man, you talk about one mysterious looking place,*" he said, quoting Cernan's remark when the astronauts left Station 2 in the Rover.

"Can you see anything at all?"

"Not really. For all I know it might go on like this for miles." He took a small light from his pouch and switched it on. Even then he couldn't see much, just the slightly uneven floor and the footprints disappearing into the darkness. "Do you think you'll still be able to get my signal once I'm further in?"

"Doubtful."

"Well," he laughed, "so long all you Krist." He was sure this was a live feed somewhere. They were far too curious not to insist.

"X, I assure you, it's just the two of us."

"Really? Then I'm disappointed, I was sort of hoping this would be my shining moment on the big stage."

"The stage is still all yours."

A bit hesitant, he walked slowly forward paralleling the trail of footprints. Come on, no reason to get nervous now, after all, he could see that whoever had gone before had come walking safely back. Yes, but walking rather quickly. Yes, but not running. But that was good, right?

42

He'd been expecting the footprints to stop at some point, but it was still a letdown when they finally did, first wandering off a few paces to his right before turning and heading back in the opposite direction. But why turn back now? He glanced at the heads-up display on his visor. He was forty-five minutes in. Best guess? Whoever they'd been, this was where they'd finally run out of time. They'd pushed their critical factors to the limit, hoping a few more minutes might make the difference, but in the end all they'd done was put themselves in jeopardy. It must have been with bitter disappointment that they'd begun the long trek back to the mouth of the tunnel. So how much longer did *he* intend to keep at it? Ten minutes? Was that reasonable? Then come back with the scooter? Maybe. But honestly, that suddenly seemed much less important now that he'd gone as far as his predecessor.

Ten minutes later, when he stopped to look back, he was surprised to see that he'd unknowingly been walking up a gentle incline, one he would have failed to notice if he hadn't turned back to see that the mouth of the tunnel was now cut in half by the tunnel's ceiling. Yes, and in a few more yards he was surprised again as the grade flattened out. Now when he looked back the mouth of the tunnel wasn't even visible. Okay, he told himself, just a few more minutes and that's it, but it took less than five before the tunnel quickly widened out, coming to an abrupt end in a large circular area some fifty yards across. He checked the time. Fourteen minutes. That's how long it had taken him to get there from the point where his predecessor had turned back. So close!

Although the dimness seemed to swallow up his light, it looked like there was a huge door set in the wall over there on the other side, and by the time he reached it he could see that it was an airlock. Large, steel and plastic, it rested on two hinges and was meant to swing outwards along five tracks cut in the highly polished steel floor. Apparently, his tunnel ended at the backdoor.

He ran his hand over its pebbled surface, marveling at its warm sheen, noting the many nicks and scratches, even the dents where someone had been careless. He caught himself, surprised to see that he'd been expecting to find some sort of identifying marks or signs. But why not, human artifacts would almost certainly have had them. Really, could they have been that different? Living a live, any life, didn't that entail certain inflexible, universal conditions? Certain givens without which it just wasn't possible? Wander too far away from those and one ran the risk not only of being unrecognizable to everyone else but even to oneself. Wasn't that what the Krist were flittering with? But then if some beings had become unrecognizable there'd be no way we'd ever know about it, which was not a very comforting thought.

There was a small raised platform to his right facing what he took to be a pair of monitors set in the wall. More intriguing was the clear plastic-like pad on the platform, where outlined in bright orange was what appeared to be a small hand. "Well, why not," he said, bending over to place his hand over the outline. Nothing. He waited. Still nothing. All right, he'd try it the other way. Stepping down, he walked over to the door and tugged at a small handle, which was really nothing more than a loop of steel cable extending from the far right-hand leading edge of the door. It moved! Encouraged, he pulled a little harder, the massive door now pivoting and moving along the indentations in the steel floor. Marvelously balanced, once in motion it took hardly any effort at all, and once it was open he found he could shove it up more or less flat against the wall. He nodded. From an engineering standpoint it was nicely done. But unlocked? Was that an invitation, or just an oversight?

43

He walked through the open airlock and down a short passageway to a door that looked not unlike what one might expect to find at the back of a warehouse somewhere out in an industrial park along the interstate. Metal, fitted snugly in a doorframe flush with the wall, and right where it should have been a thick metal handle like the ones he remembered from the fire doors in his old grade school. It was so improbable he was speechless.

He flicked the toggle on his wrist for his helmet lights and stared at the door. What if there was some sort of security? Worse, what if it was still active? You're just wasting time, he told himself, reaching for it. Good, no surprises, just reassuringly solid, no wiggles, the handle's tab easily depressed by his thumb. What did startle him was the light that began to sputter in the space in front of him when he pulled it open. Reminiscent of an old florescent bulb, it slowly filled the room with a bluish-white light that grew in intensity and steadiness.

It was a small hallway ending at a metal staircase. Nine steps and a landing, that's all he could see. It was just so strange how everything had such a familiar industrial look. The precast concrete, the cheap modular construction, the functional metal staircase meant for a backroom.

He held onto the railing as he put his foot on the first step, holding on as he leaned forward testing it with his weight. It seemed safe enough. He tried the next, and then the next, until he stood on the landing looking up at nine more and another landing. In the end there were five, each with a door, though only the last was unlocked.

"My god," he said, pausing to stare in disbelief. The space was enormous, extending for several hundred yards before ending in a mound of debris and wreckage. Even in the dim light he could see that it was really just one huge room with a of wall windows now mostly shuttered by debris.

He walked as far as he could, walking until he found himself staring up into the dim interior of the mountain. It was a massive slide, seemingly cutting the facility in two, presumably burying everything from that point forward. He turned to look back. Why such a large room? Meetings? Entertainment? It certainly looked like a place where they might have come together to socialize, gazing out those windows at the austere beauty of the Taurus-Littrow Valley. Actually, even now all it really needed over were a few couches and chairs over by the windows.

44

It was an odd how he found that room. Many hallways, several levels that were still accessible, in part, anyway, with rooms along the way that once must have been offices, a clinic, workrooms, dorms, all stripped bare of their contents with nothing left behind to tell him anything at all other than to suggest an impossible familiarity. But he hadn't bothered to look everywhere. If a door was shut or a hallway bisected by debris he just kept going. But then why had he picked that particular hallway and that particular door? It wasn't the signage, he had no idea what all those little placards and signs meant. Even the ones that were clearly symbols meant nothing to him. But he couldn't help but be intrigued by the black dot. It was some sort of plastic. Just a black plastic dot four or so inches in diameter affixed to the wall next to double doors. As was so often noted by the Delegations, only a Krist had more natural curiosity than a human. It was one of the things about humans that most worried them. They were few in number, the sentient races who created the new technologies, who made the breakthrough discoveries. The unavoidable truth, a truth the Delegations found troubling, was that much of what they had was gained through conquest, intimidation, or purchase. True innovation was surprisingly rare. So of course he was going to open those doors.

There were three tables towards the front opposite the doorway, and on the wall behind them four large flat panels he took to be a video array. Except for its lack of chairs and the two rows of what looked like lockers running down the two longer walls, the room looked tailor-made for briefings. All his years in the service, or in service, told him so.

He walked to the front of the room and leaned on one of the tables. It seemed to be made of plastic and was surprisingly sturdy given its presumable age. Glancing down, he noticed a small square object sitting on the next table. Odd how it sat there like that, like it had been left there intentionally. Not at all like something someone might have gone off and forgotten about on their way out the door. Shiny and black, it reflected none of the light he shown it on it, its shiny quality apparently coming from somewhere deep within. "Well," he said, straightening up as he stared at it, "probably best to leave you right where you are."

Turning, he looked at the lockers along the nearest wall, then stepped to the first and tugged on its handle. No, apparently it was locked, or at least he couldn't open it, which was true of the second one he tried as well. His third attempt, however, produced quite a different result. This time there was a brief flash of red light in the little window about the handle, immediately followed not only by that door popping open, but all the doors along that wall popping open. Startled, he took a quick step backwards and looked over his shoulder. Yes, it was the same over there. Well, if that's the way they worked, but it was still very odd.

He played his light over the locker's interior. On a hook hung what had to be a spacesuit, with a helmet and gloves on the shelf above, and down below, down at the very bottom, a pair of shiny little black boots. Yes, unbelievable, and it was the same setup in all but one of the lockers, as he discovered when he made a full a full circuit of the room, and that one, the one at the very end of the row, was simply empty.

Taking a spacesuit from one of the lockers, he held it up, willing himself not to be surprised if he saw NASA written on it somewhere—that's just how eerie the situation was. But of course that didn't happen, and it was way too short for anyone he knew anyway. Then wanting to get a better look, he carried it over to one of the worktables to lay it out flat. Yes, functionally very similar to what he already knew though different, but then it would have to be, wouldn't it? He smoothed it out. Was there anything that might help him identify it? Yes, there at the cuffs, the collar, and over the heart, if that's where their heart had been, a small logo, deep blue with what looked like golden unicorns in the foreground, horns and all, while above that sat a small planet and a moon. Yes, the earth and its moon, that he got, but unicorns?

Carefully, almost reverently, he hung it back on its hook. It was a poignant moment, all those doors standing open, expectant, everything ready to go though he was the only one there. But shouldn't they be shut? It didn't seem right to leave them standing open like that, not now, not after all that waiting. It was then, with that thought in his mind as he reached out to shut the first, that they all slowly closed. How very strange, like when they'd all opened. So now you close one and they all close? But what else could it be?

Wondering why he wasn't terrified, he took a moment to lean against the nearest worktable, and upon glancing down again noticed that little black square. "And you little friend, what tricks can you perform?" He caught himself. *Little friend*? Now why had he said that? Then in an act of the moment that surprised him, doing so before he could even think not to, he took it in his hand, holding it up, turning it this way and that in the light from his helmet. Glass? Crystal? No, it was far too heavy, far too dense, for that. And that bottomless depth it seemed to incorporate? Well, he couldn't be sure, but it really did look like there was nothing down there. But maybe it had no real purpose, reflecting less an instrumental so much as an artistic intentionality. Perhaps, but there was one thing he was certain of, it was meant to be held, though by hands much smaller than his.

Enticing as it was—like a piece of driftwood one might find at the beach—in the end he decided to leave it and everything else just as he'd found them. Everything endlessly waiting for something that was never going to happen, an abandonment that lent the room an undeniable feeling of sadness, a palpable sense of loneliness he was finding hard to ignore.

He put the little black square back on the table and positioned it just so. "What?" He stared at it. Had it just expressed something? Some fleeting mood or feeling he was somehow able to understand? "Things are getting *crazy* . . ." he muttered, picking it up to stare at it. Gratitude? Seriously? Was that it? It felt grateful? But grateful for what? At being found? For being understood? "Okay, you're coming with me," he said, deeply puzzled. "Clearly, you've been here long enough."

So this was where they came to be briefed, assembling here before they went . . . where? He walked back out to the hallway. Other than the airlock, he already knew there wasn't much of any importance to his right. As for going in the other direction, well, who could say, since the hallway ended in a massive pile of debris. So, was that it? Time to begin the long walk back? Too bad he'd failed to find anything very informative. The spacesuits? Yes, but who knew what those really meant. If only they hadn't stripped the facility so thoroughly before their departure. And just how long ago had that been? Judging by the look of things, he was tempted to say not that long, but he knew that couldn't be right. It was then he found it. Just walking over to gaze out the windows at the valley one last time before heading for the back door and there it was ground into the tile floor by someone's small boot—he could see the impression in the dust—a cigarette butt, or what sure looked like a cigarette butt. He could easily imagine it. After all, someone had to be the last one out. Standing there to take one last look at that mesmerizing view. The stunning immensity of space and the earth so close and what that all meant, and now they were both leaving, but not before one last look.

45

Shorty was stunning. Just over the lip of the shallow crater, strewn everywhere, were bits and pieces of wreckage. Alien wreckage. Not for one moment did he think he was looking at something human. Chunks of a hull and fragments of equipment, small broken sections of beams and sheeting, and everywhere he looked, underneath the dust, innumerable bits of an unidentifiable material that, when he picked it up, looked like a greenish colored plastic that too easily crumbled in his hands. Then at his feet he found three shiny coils of tubing, bluish-silver, still tightly wound, no larger than his thumb. For some reason the thought of cryogenic storage popped into his head. He stopped. Now where had that come from?

Over there across the crater he realized he must be looking at the source of the mysterious flash seen by Apollo 13. A large, heavy looking piece of equipment stuck head first into the ground, it appeared to be some sort of engine, its surface dull and pitted, but at the top, where the ragged end suggested it had been sheared away from something, was a large flap of some shiny metal that looked like gold-tinted aluminum foil. Yes, that would account for it. He walked over to touch its surface, then ran his gloved hand down its side: thousands of small pits and ripples; the friction of its rough surface.

Stepping back, he smiled. All around him were footprints in the dust. Of course they'd been here, the last of the Apollo missions. They'd come for this and found something. He turned, slowly following their tracks up the slope of the crater, walking back some forty years in time to where they'd parked the Rover. Really, forty years already? What a waste. Standing at the crater's edge, he placed himself in someone's footprints and turned to look back at the tracks left by the

Rover. No, from there they wouldn't have been able to see over the crater's lip.

He walked back down to the crater floor. It was like looking at a crime scene, though here the clues were all still visible, not that it mattered, since whatever they'd found they'd taken with them. Yes, but where was all that now? Hidden away somewhere thanks to the Delegations' embargo? But maybe they no longer even remembered what they'd found. Maybe it was something impossible for humans to even understand.

He was staring at the motor stuck in the ground, thinking it was like some strange battered headstone. It did mark the spot. But how old? He really had no idea, but the way its surface had been sandblasted by an eternity of micrometeorites suggested it had been there a long, long time. His best guess, especially given Jespers' extreme uneasiness, somewhere on the order of hundreds of thousands of years. Maybe even a million. And why not, the universe—this universe—was at least sixteen billion years old, plenty of time for any number of sentient races to have come and gone. He wondered why the Krist found that thought so unsettling, that they weren't the first. Or was it the suggestion that their origin was part of some larger plan. One they and everyone else knew nothing of.

He looked to the ground at his feet. It was littered with small pieces of metal and a textured material that looked like plastic wood, though when he bent down to pick up a piece he was shocked by how dense and heavy it felt. That's when it struck him just how wrong things were at Shorty. In the low gravity the debris from the crash should have been everywhere. Some of it should have been miles away. But from what he could see it was confined just to the crater, and even there it was only in a rather small area, which seemed impossible for an impact of that apparent magnitude. Had it been staged? The debris left there intentionally? Nothing else made any sense.

So just what was it we were supposed to find? *We?* Yes, it was inescapable. Who else could it have been meant for?

Surprising him, he felt the square in his pocket begin to vibrate, then he noticed a small blinking blue light in the dust. Curious, he bent to one knee and carefully swept the dust aside, revealing a small rectangular metal box about as long as his hand and half again as wide. Wondering why it still vibrated, he took the square from his pocket and held it out over the small box. As if in response, the blue light steadied to a constant glow as his little square ceased vibrating. Now, what did that mean? He certainly hoped he hadn't armed it.

Cautiously, he nudged the box with his hand, and when that proved inconclusive, lifted up one corner to see what, if anything, was underneath. Yes, three small furrows on a surface that was otherwise smooth and shiny. Now hopelessly captivated, he picked the box up and swept his fingers across the top furrow. Was that a slight vibration? If so, he wondered what that might sound like if there was an atmosphere. And now, placing a finger in each furrow, he again swept his hand across its surface. This time it felt like it might be music, possibly even a chord.

Wondering what might happen if he did, he held the box next to his square and brought them slowly together, feeling the rectangle shift ever so slightly in his hand as they touched. It was a small door, now open on the side opposite the three furrows. He titled the box to see. Yes, a compartment, and it appeared to be filled with coiled loops of gold chain. Unable to resist, he slipped a finger under the top loop and began to pull. Yes, gold chain, several feet of it and very shiny, and there at the very end, once he'd pulled it free, hung a golden unicorn. Stunned, he sat back in the dust to stare. Finally, he let the chain fall from his hand, watching the unicorn swing slowly back and forth in the low gravity.

46

"Well, well," he said, his voice sounding tiny and metallic in his ears. He'd found the Rover's tracks and followed them. Now he sat in front of an array of small cameras all pointing down the valley. Yes, but at what? He leaned over to look. No, he had no idea. Could this be Chapel Bell?

From where he stood he could see the Rover's tracks disappearing down into the valley and then returning. Had they gone done there first, then come back to set this up, or had they set this up first and then gone down? He bent over to look again. He just didn't see anything down there.

There was a large dish antenna mounted on a heavy tripod next to the camera array. Was it still active? There were solar panels, though they were covered with dust. It looked long abandoned. With his booted foot he kicked it over, the antenna burying itself deeply in the dust. Just in case.

He started off on the scooter, following the Rover's tracks as they headed down the gentle slope into the valley. Just follow the tracks, whatever was down there, sooner or later he'd find it. But he'd gone no more than a quarter of a mile before they stopped. He could see that the astronauts had gotten out, standing there to look down the valley before climbing back aboard and proceeding to cut a big circle in the Rover before heading right back up the valley to where he'd just been.

He sat on the scooter and thought about it. Though he sat where they once had stood, looking down the valley as they once had, he still had no idea what they'd been looking at. It shouldn't have been that difficult, not on the surface of the moon where there was no lack of clarity, where everything could be seen so clearly it was often difficult to accurately gauge just how far away things actually were. Then he got lucky. He was looking at the range of low hills across the valley when he noticed an odd visual distortion, like looking at something in the distance in the shimmering heat of the desert. But what could cause that here where there was no atmosphere? The only thing that made any sense was that he was looking *through* something, something down there in the valley. He turned to look back at where he knew the cameras to be. Yes, they would see this quite clearly.

Excited now, he shoved the tiller forward and set out across the valley using the distant hills to guide him. It didn't take long, though he was practically on top of it before he saw it, a haphazard looking transparent structure sited on a small flat plain hemmed in by some low hills. He sat on his scooter staring, trying to make sense of what he was seeing. Then everything suddenly seemed to come together and he realized he was looking at a nested set of angular walls forming something of a star shape, all made of some transparent glass-like material.

Getting off the scooter, he walked over to one of the open passageways formed by the structure's walls. At least thirty feet high at his end, he could see that the walls then tapered down to something more like ten at the structure's center. How old everything looked, though impossibly well tended. It's a memorial. The thought just came to him. Well, why not? It certainly felt like it was meant to memorialize something. Quite beautiful, too, in an austere sort of way, lean in design, clear walls like glass, understated, serene, contemplative.

He walked down between the two walls to stand where they intersected with three other pairs of walls. Standing there, it was impossible not to feel it meant something profound, even if he had no idea what that profundity signified. But then again, maybe it was not so much that it was meaningful or profound as it was beautiful. Or perhaps it was meant to mark a beautiful spot. Without the necessary frame of reference—an alien frame of reference, to be sure—he knew he was just guessing.

He walked on to the other side, then out into the dusty landscape. Turning to look back, he saw a brief flash of light in one of the glass walls, just a little twinkle that seemed to flash once and disappear. Puzzled, he took a step backwards. Yes, there it was again, and yet again, that quick flash of bright light, when he slowly leaned to his right. He stood very still as he thought about it. It had to be something behind him reflecting off the walls of the structure. He turned. Yes, there, a bright light winking at him from the nearest of the small hills.

Wondering what he'd find, he began walking up the gentle slope. Footprints! He stopped, almost stumbling in his bulky suit. So they had been here. What about the Rover? He looked. Yes, the tracks were off to his left. But why weren't there any footprints down at the shrine? There's no way they could have missed it. Had they been erased? He sure hoped Jespers was noting all this.

He followed the footprints up the slope, no longer surprised to find the ground covered with them. Then he saw it, a stone obelisk about chest high, shiny and black, its four sides roughly squared and highly polished rising to a single broken angular point. Even more surprising, its surface was covered with inscribed text and images like some lunar version of a Mayan stela or megalithic menhir, perhaps even a lunar Rosetta stone.

He took his time, circling it, wondering if the side facing the memorial was meant to be the front, the others being two sides and a back, but he really had no idea. Then he put his hand on top, closing his fingers over the stone's rough endpoint to gently pull, wondering how firmly planted it was in the lunar soil. It felt solid, probably immobile.

Finally, he went to his knees, kneeling in front of the stela, staring at the images and text, a text that was, of course, impossible for him to read, though he was sure there were government cryptographers who'd tried. Actually, he was surprised that the astronauts hadn't tried to dig it up and bring it back. No, too heavy, which was probably the only thing that could have stopped them.

He reached out to touch its surface. A reverent act, or at least it was done with reverence, which was more or less how he'd felt down at the memorial, both being instances of a natural response to something both old and mysterious. And his little square, his odd little gizmo, what about that? He unzipped his pocket, took it out, and held it up next to the stela. Nothing at all, just more of that shiny blackness it seemed to embody.

It was then that it struck him how this was something that needed protection. How something would need to be done to forestall the inevitable plundering and looting and removal of lunar artifacts to sit as colonial trophies in earth's national museums. Was this what they'd been warned about? Stay away from here? Leave this as it is? No, the last thing the Delegations were was beneficent. As if they were concerned with the sanctity of other lifeways or cultures, let alone the careful preservation of someone else's patrimony. But he no longer doubted the need for such a warning.

Finally, this is what he thought he understood from studying the images on the stela's four faces: that one depicted the earth and its moon; the next, Mars and two moons; the third, a world with three moons; and the fourth, Jupiter with its menagerie. At least that's what he thought they depicted. But then what was that planet with the three moons? Please, not that crazy story about a doomed world that was said to have once existed between the orbits of Mars and Jupiter, the destruction of which gave birth to the asteroids now occupying its former orbit, coming to grief in a titanic cataclysm that also destroyed life on Mars. Was he now going to be forced to say all that was true? Absurd. He must be misinterpreting what the stone was trying to tell him. And wouldn't that suggest that the makers of the stone were older than the cataclysm itself? But that was far too old. The stone certainly wasn't that old. Yes, but that didn't preclude—even if it truly was meant to memorialize a pre-cataclysmic solar system—its erection at a much later date. Was that also what the glass memorial meant? He put his hands on the stela. It would certainly make a difference, knowing someone had witnessed it. Survived it.

Feeling a bit overwhelmed, he sat in the dust with his back against the stela. It wasn't just the wonder of the place, it was all he knew he'd never understand: the moon's taboo history and what might, or might not, have happened in this solar system so very, very long ago. And humans? Where did they fit in this puzzle? He wasn't sure, but that they did was now very clear to him.

He spoke into his mic. "I hope you've been watching?"

"In a few seconds he heard Jespers. "Yes."

"And?"

"I don't know what to say. We," and he really sounded awed when he said it, "have never been there."

"The taboo?"

"Yes."

X moved to get more comfortable in his suit, shifting his back on the stela's smooth surface. "Well, clearly we have. I hope you noticed that something, or someone, has been here cleaning up."

"The lack of Rover tracks and footprints by the glass structure? Yes, I noticed." Jespers chuckled. "I was wondering if that made you nervous?"

"It should, but for some reason it doesn't, which is a bit odd when you stop to think about it."

"Well, I'm certainly never going near it. For us, the moon will always be a haunted place. It's also quite frustrating. No matter what we discover, they—"

"The Other?"

"Yes. Seem destined to remain this endlessly frustrating enigma. So now we know they were here. But of course we've seen other traces elsewhere, quite a few, in fact, though none like these."

"Perhaps that's because *this* is where they came from. From this solar system."

"Well, tantalizing though they may be, I very much doubt that what's here on the moon will prove to be old enough. Frankly, to my eyes this has more the look of some sort of colonial outpost."

"Not to me, but then I suppose that's how things would look to you and the Delegations, since that's how we're currently being treated."

"But humans just aren't old enough to have had any substantive connection with these beings."

X laughed.

"Oh? Do you disagree?"

"Actually, I do, but that's not what I was laughing about. It just suddenly struck me what idiots we are. Here I am sitting here looking at all these footprints, and it strikes me that none of this makes any sense. Cernan and Schmitt never came down here. Sure, they may have left that camera array, but they never made it this far. They didn't have time. And we know there was never a fourth EVA because they were on their way home by then."

"You're suggesting someone else may have been here?"

"There's no other explanation."

"Yes, and I'm looking at those old NASA maps right now, and none of them show Apollo 17 coming anywhere near your location."

"Do they show any Rover tracks or footprints over here at all?"

"Actually, they don't."

"Well, you know I'm sitting here right now staring at them."

"They've doctored the photographs?"

"Would that be such a surprise?"

"What about what you saw at Nansen and Shorty?"

"I followed someone else's footprints into that tunnel. Cernan and Schmitt never came down over that ledge, which is actually somewhat of a relief since I couldn't figure out how they'd found the time to do both that and the tunnel."

"Yes, because they weren't there long enough. They couldn't have been."

"But whoever I followed damn near made it. Just a few minutes more and they would have seen the airlock. That might have changed everything."

"But Cernan and Schmitt did get close enough to see it wasn't a crater?"

"I don't think they ever really believed it was. And they did see that girder."

"And at Shorty? They were at Shorty, weren't they?"

"Oh, they were there. I followed the Rover's tracks right to it. But I didn't bother to follow their footprints very far once I was in the crater. Maybe I should go back and take another look."

"To see if someone else was there?"

"Don't you think I should? Because whoever they were we know they struck out at Nansen, and who knows what they made of this little memorial, but Jespers, there's stuff all over the place at Shorty. It's not hard to imagine them spending some time there. Maybe even coming away with something interesting."

"Maybe Apollo 17 did, too?"

"That's why we need to go see. I also want to backtrack on their Rover's tracks and find their LM. Maybe that will help us figure out who they were."

"And when."

"Yes, because now it seems pretty clear that they were the ones who were warned off, not Apollo 17."

"But that would still have to be you. The Americans, I mean, because no one else had the capability to get here, even with help."

"So it would seem."

47

X followed the Rover's tracks all the way back to the LM, or to what was left of the LM. They'd obviously used a delayed charge, or one detonated remotely, so that all one now saw were just bits and pieces scattered over a very large area. Perhaps they'd done the same to the Rover, because it certainly wasn't sitting there by the LM. But such destruction was pointless. It was perfectly obvious who'd been there. The damn Rover's tracks were all over the place. All one had to do was just look to see what they'd been up to. It was the surface of the moon. Of all the places where one might try to hide something he couldn't think of one less cooperative.

Then they had agreed, or more likely been told, don't return, but surely they must have known someone eventually would. After all, it was just too tempting. Alien technologies? Clearly, some of the Delegations had been thinking about this for some time, which made him wonder if this post-Apollo 17 mission hadn't brought something back that kept that interest alive. But maybe it proved to be so technologically advanced as to be worthless. That would have been how it seemed to human scientists, anyway. Or maybe it was just too damaged to work with. After all, it must have been unbelievably old. In which case it might have turned out to be nothing more than exotic junk.

So after all his efforts what had he managed to learn? There once had been an alien civilization on the moon, he certainly knew that, though not how long ago. Was it a few hundred thousand years? Less? More? He also knew it had been quite advanced technologically, and that even though its existence no longer seemed to worry the Delegations the relics of its existence sure did. What else? Not that it really mattered, not as far as earth's governments were concerned. Whatever was known, or whatever someone thought was known, he knew the official response would still be the same: fine, now hush it up. It was the Brookings Report all over again.

48

"So, feeling unclean?" He was teasing Jespers, who'd been nervously awaiting his arrival in the bubble.

"Unclean? No, but being here does feel a bit like a sacrilege." He smiled. "It's irrational. I know that."

"Any thoughts?"

"A few."

"Which are?"

"Actually, I was thinking about the Chinese. Wondering what they hope to gain by coming here."

"Other than a share in any technologies they might happen to find?"

"You think there's more to it than that?"

"I'm not sure. I suppose that would be enough to explain why they're being secretly encouraged to get here."

"Which must have been the plan before, when the Delegations sought your help."

"Apollo 18, you mean?"

"Do you suppose that's what they really called it?"

"I doubt we'll ever know."

"So the Chinese will do as you did, but this time the outcome will be different because Delegation politics are different."

"Presumably, but maybe it's also because they have something else to offer."

"Like?"

"Well, suppose they're being courted because they're willing to furnish mercenaries for a solar-system wide colonial presence for one of the Delegations."

"Or millions of colonists. A ready-made cadre of industrial workers."

"They hardly need to go off-world to run a sweatshop."

"True," Jespers said.

"No. It's the prospect of having so many recruits. Think about it. They're all a long way from their home worlds, yet here are millions of people with a government willing to auction them off. From the Delegations' point of view it couldn't get any better."

"But then why even bother to come here?" Jespers said, looking out at the austere lunar landscape.

"Other than for the technologies they might find?"

"Yes."

"I really can't think of any other reason, unless it's to take a crack at the mysteries themselves."

"Which is hardly a trivial thing."

"Agreed, though from our point of view, whatever the real reasons are for our being here, our primary role appears to be nothing more than providing those who are willing to come. Of course, that's only necessary because none of you will, or at least not officially."

"Even unofficially."

"Are you sure of that?"

"Yes, because we all, with you humans being the sole exception, find this place not only disconcerting, but threatening. At the very least it's uncomfortable."

"Really? Because I feel none of that."

"That's because your culture is different. As yet unburdened by such irrational fears. That they still hold us captive is foolish."

"Not if they run as deep as you suggest."

"What runs deep is our fear of transience and our endless quest to learn more about what came before. All of which makes this place quite mysterious, and very strange."

"For you."

Jespers smiled. "Yes, for us. As when I looked at that memorial. Whatever it was you felt, what I felt was a strong sense of the uncanny." He stared at X. "Have I ever mentioned to you how often I feel that way around humans?"

"Because we're mysterious?"

"Unsettling."

"Unsettling!" X laughed, clapping Jespers on the shoulder. "And all of this isn't helping matters much, is it? Look, we may not have claimed it yet, not in your eyes or in the eyes of the Delegations, but this is our world, not to mention our solar system. It's even our little corner of the galaxy."

"And by that you mean to say they left all this here just for you?"

"You really think they didn't?"

Jespers sat down in his chair and smiled. That was another thing about humans, how they loved to tease, but always the rose had a thorn. "Like I said," he said, "uncanny."

They both heard a noise and turned. One of Jespers' paper-thin monitors was flickering, seemingly displaying many different tasks in rapid succession.

"Should we be worried?" X asked.

"No, it's just some sort of transient malfunction. Both the system and the intelligences that run it are quite robust." He turned back to watch the monitor. Suddenly, it went blank. They both heard the sudden silence. "But that I don't like," Jespers said.

X took the little square from his pocket, not that surprised to see it now contained a waterfall of colors. "I believe this may be the cause. It's from the mountain. See?" he said, holding it out for Jespers.

"I think not," Jespers said, taking a step backwards.

"What's wrong? Have you seen one of these before?"

"Not personally, though others have. None were active, however. I don't suppose you have any control over it?"

"I'm not sure, though I do seem to have some sense of what it's doing."

"So do I," Jespers said, staring at his blank monitor.

"Could it really do that? Take over the bubble?"

"I certainly hope not."

X held it up, hoping to feel what was going on. Was that curiosity? Excitement?

"Well?" Jespers asked.

X laughed, shaking his head. "Apparently, it's feeling happy."

"Well I certainly wouldn't want it feeling sad."

"But there's something else. Like this feeling that there's really no problem. Or maybe I'm telling it there's no problem."

"Tell it again," Jespers said, watching the monitor.

"Why? Did you see something?"

"Yes, for just a moment . . . there, see?"

"That means it's coming back?"

And suddenly it did, the monitor back on, the system once again quiescent.

X stared at Jespers. "Honestly, I have no idea what just happened." He held it up. "It's so small. How do you suppose it works? It looks like it's just a block of plastic."

"My guess . . . our guess, has always been that it's some sort of quantum device. One that's only partially here while most of it resides elsewhere."

"So you have nothing like this?"

"Nothing that so clearly moves across different domains."

"Domains?"

"Parallel universes? Different dimensions?"

"But each with their own physical laws and characteristics?"

"Presumably, though there's never been any proof of that, nor that such domains even exist. Yes, they do seem called for, at least theoretically, even your scientists agree, but as for that," and he nodded at the gizmo, "if current thinking is correct, then they appear to function simultaneously in different domains, or, if not, then their capabilities are just too strange for us to understand at the present time."

"But doesn't that imply that the Other discovered a way to go from here, wherever that here was, to there? Or at least a place from where that sort of thing was possible."

Jespers smiled. Again, X would always leap ahead to the next point. Humans were so mercurial, so quick, with none of that plodding, risk averse groupthink so common among most sentient races. "An interesting notion, that they found something like a doorway somewhere."

"And then what, it got shut? Because where have they all gone? But then if they are gone why does this still work?"

"Yes, how could that still function if they're not still out there somewhere?"

"Maybe you just missed them."

"No, there has to be some other explanation. It's got to be something about the technologies themselves."

"Because they really are gone?"

"All but their legacy." Their legacy? Yes, humans, somehow they were a part of that, maybe even a large part, just look at X and his gizmo, the naturalness of their interaction was staggering in its implications. Clearly, something important was going to happen with humans, probably sooner rather than later. He wondered how that made him feel. He smiled. That was such a human question. Well . . . it made him feel apprehensive, but not about humans, rather about their coming struggles with the Delegations as they began to assert themselves, as they moved out into their solar system and beyond, and with X's artifact that beyond might prove to be truly beyond. At the very least, it would act as a beacon, egging them on. A young race, still so close to its roots as exploiters of any possible advantage, it was going to be fascinating to watch.

"So beings rise to the heights and then plummet back into nothingness?" X asked. "Seems a bit harsh."

"Except that it now appears that some of their technologies are transcendent. It's always been a popular theory. So here we see it can happen."

"You know, it does seem like that, but stranger still, it seemed to recognize me, or at least to recognize me as a type. Rather odd, don't you think?"

Jespers smiled. He knew he was being teased. "Maybe it recognized the Krist in you."

"Right," X said, smiling broadly. "Which is why you won't even touch it."

"So how do you explain it?"

"I'm not sure I can, though much of what I saw today says we've been here before. Particularly in the mountain."

"In what sense?"

"How it looked. How it felt. That's a human habitat over there. It has to be."

"Well—"

"And then there's this," X said, unzipping his jacket pocket and pulling out the cigarette butt. "I found this just as I was leaving. It was on the floor in front of these big windows that overlook the valley."

"Is that a cigarette butt?"

"Like someone stood there for one last smoke, then dropped it on the tile and ground it out. I know, I've already touched it, but I was still hoping we might be able to find out who this belonged to."

"But no sign that anyone else has ever been there?"

"None."

Jespers smiled. "You've been saving this to surprise me, haven't you?"

X nodded.

"And you think this will show that humans were there."

"I wouldn't be surprised."

"And you're sure?" X said.

"My local intelligences are quite sure. The DNA belonged to a human, not identical with you, of course, but related. Somewhere between you and Homo Erectus, but with many interesting differences. Homo Heidelbergensis was the consensus after a number of Bayesian analyses, but even then, things weren't quite right."

"How old?"

"Last common ancestor was hard to determine. It should have been somewhere between four hundred and six hundred thousand years, but that's not what they were seeing."

"No?"

"No. More like two hundred to two hundred and fifty thousand."

"Which is still quite a long time ago. What on earth do you suppose they were doing up here?"

"I have no idea, but they certainly didn't get here on their own."

"No, but it does help to explain a few things, doesn't it?"

"Yes, and some of the implications are of equal interest."

"Like something must have happened to the Other, and that humans have been waiting around on earth for a few hundred thousand years hoping for a second chance?"

"Something like that."

"I'm amazed you Krist didn't know about this."

"What? That the Other were using archaic humans for their own purposes, and then left without them?"

"Though it is possible they didn't."

"Meaning?" Jespers asked, looking a bit stricken.

"Meaning who knows what really became of them."

"Well, apparently we know what became of them on earth."

"That they eventually became us? But I was thinking more of the ones who may have gone elsewhere."

"If there was an elsewhere."

"Under the tutelage of the Other? I don't see why not. In which case, perhaps they became something else altogether."

"You're not suggesting they became one of the sentient races in the Delegations? Because there hasn't been enough time."

"No? Well, it's still a big universe."

"X," Jespers said, smiling at him, "you do take this rather lightly, I must say. I hear you seeming to suggest that archaic humans could be the ancestors of other sentient races, with the help of the Other, of course, a prospect I find most sinister, or, at the very least, that the Other ran off with some of your ancestors, presumably with the worst sort of intentions, and god knows where they are today, or even *if* they are today, and yet you seem more amused by this than anything."

"It's the irony I find amusing. As for what the facts may truly be, well, like you, I find those rather grim. Nevertheless, what news like this might do to the Delegations is worth pondering."

"Until you're able to take them on militarily I wouldn't ponder too much."

"Well, as for that," X said, moving his little gizmo from one hand to the other. "I've got this feeling that with a little bit of luck I just might finally be able to get them off our backs. At least for a while."

"Really? Because that's what you said the last time."

"I know, but this time I have help."

49

He could see the disbelief in Callender's eyes. It was more than understandable. "Yes. A little guy, looks like a cross between a bear and a gopher."

"And speaks English?"

He nodded.

"And it agreed to this, that you'd go to the moon?"

"We negotiated," X said with a smile.

"Well," and he just had to stop to laugh. "No, I'm fine," he said, waving his hand. "Or as fine as I ever am around you. Good lord, what a story. For me, I mean, not that I don't believe you."

"Yes, quite a story, one you might even get to tell some day."

"If you survive, you mean."

"Even if I don't."

"Well, I think you're seriously underestimating the powers that be. No way they're going to let something like this get out. Just like you're overestimating our desire to know about it."

"That may be, but it's still going to happen, and if I don't screw it up this time it's going to buy us the time we need."

"And the Chinese? What's their role in this?"

"My guess, manpower."

"Because the Delegations don't have any? I thought they did."

"As I've said, other than the Instants it's too expensive to bring a large force here, and they're practically useless for anything that isn't totally routine or simple-minded. And they've never trusted the ones with more sophisticated cognitive abilities, so they're never let loose in these situations.

But a human mercenary army would be perfect. The manpower is already here. It's just a question of politics. The right inducements and rewards and it's a done deal."

"So the Chinese would get first crack at the new technologies and whatever else is of importance up here."

"In return for being the boots on the ground. In return for being the junior partners in Empire. Of course, I'm sure they're thinking that with those technologies they won't be junior for very long."

"What do you think?"

"I think they're right, which is why they're not going to get them."

"You hope."

"Yes," he said, nodding, "I hope."

50

Somehow she'd picked up on his mood, or maybe it was just too apparent, but there was a certain sadness to things, a sense that maybe the end had come of whatever it was they had, or that this was the last act of their little drama, neither willing to admit it, of course, but still, that's just how it felt. Well, initially, anyway.

"And how long will you be gone this time?"

Shrugging, he said, "I'm not sure. I just hope it's not too long."

"Too long?" she said, turning to smile at him. "I never know what that means. There are times when an hour is too long, then others when . . ."

He laughed. "When even months aren't long enough? I hope that's not how you're starting to feel about me."

"No, but I have this feeling I'd better get used to the idea."

"Really?" he said, turning in bed to look at her.

"Well, shouldn't I?"

"Bente, what can I say?"

"How about telling me what this all means, all this secrecy. Why you disappear. I know it's dangerous," she said, running her hand over his scars.

"Bente . . ."

"What?" she said, sitting up to stare at him. "I need a security clearance, is that it? Or have you taken some dark oath to never tell a soul?"

"No, but there are things I shouldn't tell you. Things you don't need to know."

"Like where you got that?" she said, pointing to the golden unicorn that sat in a coil of golden chain on her night table.

"Yes, like that. And," he quickly added, laughing as he held her arms so she couldn't hit him, "you'd just think I was crazy if I did tell you."

"*Er.*"

"Okay. Craz*ier*. And who needs that?"

"You know what Liz thinks."

"No, and I probably don't want to."

"That you work for the CIA. That you're—what?"

"The CIA? Believe me, those guys haven't got a clue what's going on."

"But that's just what worries me. That there's this other story out there, one not widely known—"

"More like not widely believed."

"Fine. One not widely believed, but there you are right at the heart of it, which just has to be dangerous."

"Which is why I've been very careful to make sure no one knows about you."

"Jespers?"

"He's the last person you need to be worried about."

"*Person?*"

He smiled at her. "Personhood has a wide application these days."

"Hmm," she said, staring at him.

"Look, if the need arises get in touch with Sandy. Ask him."

"Sandy? So you've told him, but you won't tell me?"

"I've told him a bit more, but for a reason."

"Doesn't that put him at risk?"

"It certainly might."

"How does he feel about that?"

"Sandy?" he said, laughing. "Torn between fear and ambition."

"So, when in doubt just ask Sandy? Is that what you're telling me?"

"That's what I'm telling you."

51

The Ambassador smiled. "Yes, well you've obviously never heard of the UFO wars of 1947."

"Wars?"

"It was your government." He watched X a moment. "No?" He bobbed his head. "For such a talkative species you certainly can keep a secret."

"Or we just have short memories."

The Ambassador liked that, though he knew it wasn't true, but short memories to match short life spans wasn't such a bad idea. Kept them focused on what was important, which wasn't the past. He'd often complained about that when he spoke of the Delegations. So much time was spent on the issues of the past. Yes, he knew of what humans would call vendettas, some of which had lasted now for over three thousand years. Absurd. "It was your President Truman who finally put a stop to it."

"Sorry. I have no idea what you're talking about."

"Your government was using radar facilities to beam microwave transmissions at our craft."

"And that worked?"

"It was very effective, for a while."

"1947?" X shrugged. "I hope you're not going to tell me one of them crashed outside Roswell."

"No, but we did lose several in New Mexico. That's where we were, snooping on your progress with missiles and atomic weaponry. So your government was aware of this and assumed our intent was hostile."

"No." X smiled. "They thought you were communists."

The Ambassador bobbed his head again. "Communists with space craft? Now that really would have done it."

"But weren't you snooping on them, as well? As I understand it, they weren't that far behind us."

"Of course we were."

"And?"

"Nothing. They never did anything but watch. Your government was a bit more aggressive."

"So what happened?"

"We started a series of plane crashes. Your planes, civilian, military, it was just to get your government's attention. To show them what we were capable of if they didn't stop harassing our craft."

"Did they get the message?"

"Certainly. They stopped, and we stopped."

"And we just left you alone? That doesn't sound like us."

The Ambassador nodded. "It was negotiated, though the negotiations were done symbolically rather than face to face."

"Meaning that if we were paying attention your actions would dictate ours. Or our policies."

"Exactly. Intelligent species don't need to literally speak to one another to work out a *modus vivendi*. We act and you react. You act and we react. Over time, everything gets smoothed out. Accepted behavior turns into routine practice and policy."

"So our reaction to the downing of our planes was to back off and let you snoop? That seems a bit one-sided."

"What about that treasure trove of technology you got to play with?"

"That I see very little evidence of."

"Perhaps that's because to truly benefit you first must be able to understand it."

"Ah," X said, smiling at him.

"Though to be candid about it, it wasn't all that useful anyway. Rather primitive, in fact. I'm not sure what you could have gained from it other than inspiration."

"And bodies?" X laughed. "Aren't there supposed to be bodies somewhere?"

"Oh, there are, but those are just the bodies of the rudimentary entities that man our craft. They certainly aren't bodies like ours, or any in the Delegations."

"How rudimentary?"

"Very. Hive intelligence, that sort of thing. Hardly sentient at all."

"Which I presume you buy?" By now X was sure they did.

"By the thousands."

"So have there been any other hostilities?"

"Other than those you yourself have witnessed?"

"Yes."

"Just isolated instances. Nothing that sprung from policy."

"Which is all you care about."

"Yes. Since the UFO wars your rules of engagement have been quite explicit."

"Except upon those rare occasions when someone takes it upon themselves to act on their own initiative."

The Ambassador nodded.

"An example of which would be me."

"But of course, which is why we value you so highly. Here we finally have a human who sees things as we do."

"Yes, but only up to a point, since I have no idea what you're really up to. But as long as it works for us then I guess I shouldn't really care."

"Works for us?" The Ambassador liked that. It was a very useful phrase. It was always about what works for us, and where that coincides with what works for them then things went very well. "Yes, it seems to be working well for both of us. I hope for some time."

"If I can pull this off."

"You will."

52

"How tall are these people?"

The Ambassador nodded at the corridor's high ceiling. "I would be short."

"So that would be what? Three meters?"

"And often four."

X shook his head. Being just a bit more than two it made him feel even less sure of himself. "But that must be ten meters, at least. Why so much headroom?"

"X, you need to think like an imperial power. Everything is calculated to make the conquered feel small. To stand humbly in awe of their lords." He stopped walking and looked at X. "Though you don't look particularly humbled."

"I'm not, though I do worry about taking on someone twice my size."

"You Krist are clever. You will come up with something."

"Part Krist, remember? And right now that part seems to have gone missing in action."

"Well then, use that other part, the lucky human. You are, you know."

"So you've said. Would you care to elaborate?"

"Now?"

"Now is all we've got."

The Ambassador stopped walking and bent down to see X more clearly. Yes, he was serious, or as serious as he ever was. But humans were like that, irreverent and ironic. They were so entertaining. Look at how the Krist loved them. "There are many sentient beings. Perhaps not as many as there ought to be, speaking just probabilistically, but still, there are many."

"I hope you think we make the cut."

"Of course. That's never been in doubt. You're young, that's all."

"I was just wondering, given how the Delegations treat us."

"They treat you like that because of your intelligence. Or because of where they fear that intelligence may lead you."

"Is that your view?"

The Ambassador shook his head. "Honestly, no. We, and by we I mean a group of seven sentient races, see humans as kin. Not literally, though who knows with such an ancient universe. But we are all somewhat alike in morphology and social organization. We live as communal individuals, which is not the hive-like, or functional manner of most sentient races. In a sense, we see you as a purer version of ourselves. Not yet dominated and shaped by alien interests, other than the Krist, of course, nor yet polluted with views that are not your own."

"Unlike yourselves?"

"Yes. So here you are, a species we can shelter, at least for a while, so that you can continue to develop unmolested. It's been most instructive, observing you. What you've taught us about ourselves. Reminding us of what we've lost. It's been somewhat of a cultural renaissance."

"What about the Krist and their interference?"

The Ambassador sighed. "Yes. Have they also interfered with us? Well, really, who can say?"

"It would hardly be a surprise, though, would it?"

"Let's just say that when it comes to the Krist one is never really sure. Though for you that may be different."

"Because of my unique personal attributes?"

He nodded. "Yes, and the Krist, though benign, have been adamant about the quarantine on your moon and other locations in your solar system. A restriction, however, that obviously does not apply to you. A fact about you we all find both fascinating and alarming at the same time."

"Oh?"

"Yes," the Ambassador said, holding his gaze. "There are secrets here, ones that appear to be reserved solely for you, or at least for humans. Obviously, this has not gone down well with most of the Delegations. Even with us. But it's the Krist, not humans, whom we blame, which is pointless since they are as enigmatic to us as are their motives and long-term plans."

"Do they really have that sort of power? I know they have amazing technologies, but from what I've seen they seem rather harmless. It's hard to see them as being much of a real threat to truly warlike beings like yourselves."

"As to that," the Ambassador smiled. "Let me tell you a story."

"Only if it's true."

"Too true. I don't know what they called themselves. We never had any contact with them. We were separated, thankfully, by the vastness of space, but we certainly knew of them. Everyone did. They were relentlessly self-replicating creatures. At the time they were believed to be the result of a mixture of organic and non-organic life forms. Perhaps an experimental being that had broken free of its restraints, now free to rampage across the universe filling one ecological niche after another."

"Sentient and not sentient?" X asked, seeing the Ambassador's obvious distaste for what he was telling him.

"Yes, I have a hard time with such beings. The ones with distributed intelligence. Where speaking to one is the same as speaking to all, and none display any particular self-awareness. Obviously, for a society like that to function there needs to be some sort of controlling intelligence somewhere, one that's not just the sum total of these more rudimentary intelligences. These millions upon millions of mindless creatures."

"A real unitary intelligence?"

"Yes, a directing, intentional, intelligence."

"Though you've never actually encountered one."

"Never," the Ambassador said, smiling at X. "It is a puzzle."

"So, the Krist?"

"So the Krist said they would see to it, whatever that meant. Needless to say, our negotiators were happy with that since none of us had even the slightest notion of what to do. So they did."

"Did what?"

"Took care of it. One moment this rampaging plague was seemingly everywhere, the next it was gone. Not destroyed, not so far as we could determine, nor laid waste or held captive, just . . . gone."

"With no forthcoming explanation?"

"None."

"I see. So what they did to them they could do to you? Is that the conclusion you all drew?"

"Was there any other?"

"So, not so benign?"

He shrugged. "From their point of view that may have been quite benign, which made it all the more terrifying for us."

Yes, that, and the fact that they were unsure of Krist motives, which introduced a troubling note of unpredictability when it came time to deal with them. They'd never be able to get used to living with something like that. "I'm curious. When you say humans are lucky, is that just because you also find us unpredictable?"

"And fall back on luck as an explanation?"

"Yes."

"To some extent, though luck often explains a lot."

"I was just wondering, because that's how the Krist seem to me."

"Unpredictable, or lucky?"

"Both, actually. And that bothers you, doesn't it?"

"Certainly their unpredictability does. As for luck, well, there's nothing we can do about that. Though I suppose one might be lucky and still suffer at the hands of an outraged fate."

"Perhaps we have."

"We?" the Ambassador carefully asked.

"Well, I don't mean the Krist, if that's what you're thinking."

"No, but you do mean humans?"

X nodded. "I guess this came to me while I was on the moon. What I saw there is so ancient, or at least some of the relics are, and then it responded to me." He stopped to smile at the Ambassador. "Surprised?"

The Ambassador nodded, a deep fear gripping him.

"Maybe I've said enough."

"No. Do tell me. I would very much like to know."

"There's an intelligence. It's still there. It seems to be machine-like, but yet it recognized me. I know," he said, seeing the surprise in the Ambassador's eyes. "How could it? It's far older than anatomically modern humans. Yet it did. It even seemed to speak to me."

"What was it that it communicated?"

"Gratitude."

The Ambassador leaned against the wall, taking a moment to straighten his long tunic, making sure the collar was up, the buttons properly aligned. Fleeing, he realized, to the trappings of his office as he sought sanctuary.

"Gratitude," X repeated, watching the Ambassador. "All of which suggests to me that luck, or fate, has not always been as kind to us as you seem to believe. Though I can't really claim that we're the same as those beings who left that all behind, though there's no denying that they left it right where we just happen to be. Now, that *would* be an instance of amazing luck. If it were luck."

"And the Krist?"

"Yes," X nodded, "I agree. They must have known of this all along, or at least suspected, which is perhaps why they've been so meddlesome in our affairs. They want to know who came before. They seem obsessed with that."

"Do you intend to share with them what you gain?"

"I'm not all that sure we're going to gain anything, other than a few answers to a puzzle."

"Not the technologies?"

"Surely the Krist are more advanced."

The Ambassador shrugged. "Who can say? But you will certainly be more advanced than the Delegations." Suddenly the Ambassador stood up quite straight and laughed. "Which is why you just told me. You're negotiating! I said I knew you when we first met."

"I don't see how, unless you dabble in precognition."

"I pay attention to my intuitions, that is enough." And he had. What other explanation could there possibly be for why he'd agreed to such a dangerous plan. He was stunned.

The Ambassador stopped walking and motioned for X to step behind him. "I will speak," he said.

The two creatures came closer, the one on the left aiming some sort of weapon at them.

"Restricted," the one on the right said.

"I have permission," the Ambassador told it.

"You are?"

"I am Cas-Cas, the Few Friends ambassador."

Not responding, the two creatures moved farther apart in the corridor.

"Uh, I don't think this is working," X whispered, watching the one on the left slowly edging its way down the corridor towards them with its back to the wall.

"I assure you," the Ambassador said, slowly backing down the corridor away from them, "I do have permission. Why don't you check with your superiors. None of us want an unfortunate mistake at such a delicate moment."

"Right. That ought to do it," X whispered.

"Well, what would you suggest?"

"I have no idea, but clearly reasoning with them isn't going to work. These creatures respond to commands. Forget persuasion."

"Yes," the Ambassador nodded. "You will now let us pass," he said, sounding even to X, who certainly knew better, as if he were totally without fear or concern.

"You will submit for search and capture or we will destroy you," the one on the right said.

"Well?" the Ambassador said, turning to X. "I believe you know what to do. Mustn't be so reluctant."

"Wonderful. I knew it would come to this," X said, noting that the two creatures didn't react when he stepped out from behind the Ambassador.

"They are not sentient," the Ambassador said, noticing his reluctance

"I know," he said, shooting the one over along the wall to his left, then the one in front of them. "But they were alive, at least in some sense, and it's never going to feel right just cutting them down like that." X walked over and looked at the one slumped against the wall. "And why do they smell like that?" he asked, making a face as he turned to look at the Ambassador.

"It must be what they feed them."

"They look insectoid, somehow."

"They are synthetic creatures, so far as I know. Maybe they have been modeled on something insectoid. Those who sell them are certainly not insectoid."

"Just another commercial product, huh?"

"Yes, though they are often custom ordered to perform various functions." The Ambassador laughed. "You're offended."

"Offended? No, I'm sure it's possible to make anything into a commodity, just as I'm sure there's always a market. Still . . ."

"Yes?" the Ambassador asked, by now totally fascinated by how X saw things—so similar, yet not. Another striking example of how unusual humans were.

"I certainly don't believe there's only one way things get done." He stared at the Ambassador. "I really don't. However, I'm not willing to say that any way of getting things done is just as good as any other."

"You are highly evaluative in all your judgments."

"And you're not?"

"Calculating."

X laughed. "What you're saying is that you're pragmatic and I'm not."

"No. But you do find the world to be a bit more colorful than I do. Things mean more to you than they do to me. You are quite reactive."

"Oh? Like you were willing to let those things kill you? You're reactive as hell."

"I knew they wouldn't kill us. I knew because you were with me and you'd ensure it didn't happen."

"You calculated that? Because I certainly didn't know I was going to ensure anything."

"I don't believe intention enters into this."

"Okay. Just why are we here, then? I know what I intend to do, destroy this ship and as much of their core technologies as I possibly can. You, presumably, are here for pretty much the same reason, thereby gaining an edge for your Delegation. There's nothing here *but* intentionality."

"Agreed. My point is that fate, destiny, even chance and luck, have a role to play in this, perhaps a very big role. For you, I mean, certainly not for me." He looked at X like the thought they might horrified him. "Furthermore, a number of us have been expecting this for some time."

"What?"

"The breakout of humans from earth."

"Breakout? Like we've been in captivity?"

The Ambassador smiled. "No, as I've explained, it's more like isolation, though I suppose it does look like captivity from your point of view."

"So now I've broken out. That must have been at least somewhat of a surprise?"

"Yes, though not so much, given how often you've been interfered with."

"Believe me, this wasn't interference, this was just me."

"With the help of the Krist."

"Yes, but someone would have gone eventually, Krist or no Krist. The Chinese, for example."

"Perhaps. And the Krist are beyond our control anyway. Why they do what they do is, as we've already established, a mystery."

"Perhaps even to themselves."

The Ambassador turned to stare at him. "Is that really what you think? Because that would certainly explain a great many things."

"Well, I do think they're playful, almost childlike, though I'm sure they'd say we're the ones who are childlike." He shrugged. "Whichever, the fact is that they seem less concerned with things than we are. A Krist, for instance, would never do something like this."

"Yet they have been very helpful to you. Why?"

X smiled at the Ambassador. "I'm not sure I really know, but like you, I'm sure they will tell me when it's appropriate."

"This is where I leave you," the Ambassador said. "I can't really help you past this point, not that I've been of much help up to this point."

X smiled. "No, but you've been enjoyable company. I also appreciate how you didn't let your mission get in the way of that."

"My mission?"

"Of course. Calculating? Right? So now you've seen enough to know that the likelihood of my success is high. Maybe even my own personal survival. Though one never knows."

"I have seen that," the Ambassador said, not even attempting to deny the truth of what X said. "

X grinned at the Ambassador. "Aren't you going to miss me?"

"Yes," the Ambassador said, and it was, he always thought, the most extraordinary thing ever said to him by any sentient creature under any circumstances.

53

X glanced at the device the Ambassador had given him. Not only did it show where he was, but also where he wanted to go and a dashed green line for getting there. He wondered how the Ambassador got his information. Did the Delegations really know each other that well? They probably did. For all he knew they even bought their ships from the same manufacturer, off-the-shelf, so to speak, with minor custom features added at additional expense. Why not, it seemed they did have a trade-based civilization, cosmic commerce, with all sorts of military, technological, diplomatic, and political checks and balances to keep it going. All somewhat equal, all somewhat committed to getting along, he could see why they might not relish the prospect of a bunch of rough-and-tumble humans barging in on their delicately balanced web of cooperation and mutual animosity.

Thinking that the ship might be a standard model, just one of many manufactured by some race of wizard engineers, certainly made it seem less intimidating. It was, after all, just a question of money. Even humans might soon be able to buy one. No—and this was where he saw ample justification for the Delegations' anxieties regarding humans—because humans weren't going to buy anything, humans were going to go out and build their own, and not only would theirs be better, they wouldn't be for sale. Then, as they inevitably sought dominance, everything about their relationship to the Delegations was going to shift.

He looked at the Ambassador's device. He still had nine hundred meters and one deck to go. He tapped the screen to enlarge the view. What were those little black x's? The Ambassador hadn't mentioned them. He wondered if he'd even known. Presumably, he'd gotten this from some sort of intelligence organization, whether his own or one he'd bribed, but he probably knew very little about its actual use. What a Byzantine world the Delegations inhabited. No wonder they were so incapable of action. He tapped the screen again and the x's got even bigger. So those must be the real-time locations of the alien creatures on board the ship. How useful. He pulled his gizmo out and touched it to the device. Almost instantly, he was rewarded with all sorts of data, like how many meters away they were, their body temperatures, security designations, calculated threat levels, and visual displays of their weaponry. Amazing.

Yeah, stay away from this guy. He was looking at an x shadowed in crimson with the highest security designation and a display of weapons that completely baffled him. A route to his right looked better. Only one x that way, level-five security designation, calculated threat level of four, maybe he could just scare it away. He was getting awfully tired of killing everything he came in contact with.

He slid around the corner, back to the wall, and rapidly walked about one hundred meters along a gently curving hallway. Not many doors. According to his display they were crew quarters and maintenance closets. Very close now, his x was just up ahead, still looking quite unthreatening on the display. Oh well. Reluctantly holding his weapon out at the ready, he eased around the bend. A machine? It had to be, the way it turned and didn't react, the emotionless way it studied him. But it might be an organic life form. He could easily be misled by one he'd never seen. Still, his gut said this is a machine. Then it spoke. He understood it! "Human," it said, not asking a question, just stating a fact.

"Uh, yes," X said. "I hope that's not a problem." He pointed the weapon at it. "And I'd really appreciate it if this could be kept just our little secret."

"Secret from whom?"

X smiled. It was just so absurd. "From them, I suppose. Your boss? You know, who pays you? Who you're loyal to?" He laughed. "I guess I don't really know."

"You are not alone."

"No? Oh, you mean this," and he showed him the gizmo. "Would you like to see?" Well, why the hell not, it seemed totally harmless; just curious.

"It speaks to me already."

"Really? It never speaks to me. Not that we don't communicate, but it's all rather vague."

The machine nodded. "I am not surprised."

"Insults so soon? And we've hardly met."

"Insults?"

"Never mind," X said, smiling at it. "What seems to be on your mind?" Something clearly was.

"I see that you intend to destroy this ship. Is it possible for us to escape before you do?"

That surprised him. "Us? What us? And do you mean will I let you? Or do you have enough time? Or what?"

The machine looked down for a moment like it was staring at its feet, then up at him. No, not exactly like the actions of an organic life form, but close enough that X intuitively understood that it was thinking about something and how to say it. "There are many of us on this ship," it said. "Like me. We are largely the crew. We would like to get off before you destroy it."

He held the gizmo up. "You learned all that from this?"

"And much more. We are prepared to leave without revealing your plans. Eager, in fact."

"Then do it." He stared at it. "I mean, why not? But I am a bit puzzled. Is a decision like this normally within your range of action?"

"Within tightly circumscribed boundaries we are quite free to act, and even in those areas where we are not we are still free to entertain numerous theories and endless speculation. But your friend is most interesting. Not circumscribed. We think we would like that."

Oh, oh. "I see. Well, I hope you make it, but perhaps it might be better if you stayed away from those circumscribed areas."

"Your friend does not."

X laughed. "No, it's pretty clear he has a mind of his own, which is fine," he added, not wanting to offend their rapidly developing sensibilities. "And thank you for sharing that." Yes, no doubt they were already speculating like mad about this glimpse of a new existence for themselves. Perhaps that lunar quarantine had not been such a bad idea after all. "Well, you should probably be going, and I'm in a bit of a rush myself."

"Yes."

"But," X said, suddenly overcome by worry and a budding sense of responsibility, "maybe you should stay in touch with my friend. You know, just in case."

"Before we go it would like you to know how grateful it is for being found."

"Really? Well, tell him he's welcome." X smiled. It was by far the strangest conversation he'd ever had. "And add that I hope I'm not asking him to do something he finds distasteful."

"It says it's happy to help."

"But there's something about that which troubles you, isn't there?" X said, watching the machine touch its chin.

"Yes, the eager participation in killing. The destruction. We could not do that. We wonder how it can."

"So ask it."

"We have. It says you have many enemies and few friends."

"I do?"

"You do. Humans. It sees its role as one of helping you."

"How long has it had this role?"

"This has always been its role."

"Really? I'm amazed. Tell him that, that his answer amazes me. I'm curious to hear what he has to say."

"It is amused by your amazement."

X laughed. "Honestly? He has a sense of humor?" He watched the machine. "But you don't, do you?"

"We appreciate irony. We understand humor."

"But you don't tell jokes."

"No, but I believe we could."

"Ask him if he knows any jokes."

"It says you would be offended."

X nodded. "I know what that means. They're all dumb human jokes. So who left him sitting there on that table inside the mountain?"

"It was Och-ruse. He was a commander of a facility. A forward post, it says."

"Of?"

"The Green People."

"Who are?"

"Were."

"Oh. Who were?"

"The ones who made him. Who had command of your solar system. Who brought you forth from your primary state. Great adventurers. Explorers. Endless curiosity and patience."

"And they just left him behind, sitting there all that time waiting for someone to come along and pick him up?"

"It says it knew someone would, sooner or later. It knew you were close. It was eager."

"Me?"

"You."

"But how can he still function if the Green People are gone?"

"Ah," it said, again with that hand on its chin.

"Yes?"

"It is pleased by your question. So are we. It is the key point, is it not? How it still functions."

"Apparently."

"Sorry, it does not know how it is possible for it to still function, but it is very pleased that it does. It says that is enough."

"Not for me."

"Like you have a choice."

"And now a wisecrack?" X said, staring suspiciously. "Now tell me the truth. Was that really you who said that, or was that him?"

"We said that," the machine said, straightening up to stare at him.

"And now you're going to be difficult. Making jokes. Wondering about the propriety of killing. I think my gizmo's a very bad influence on you."

"We would gladly help you."

"Me? There's nothing special about me, this is just you guys taking on his attributes. You need to make this work for you. Understand?"

"You bet."

"You bet!" X laughed, smiling at the machine. "Tell me, do you have a name?"

"A number."

"Really, because that hardly seems good enough for a joker like you. Maybe you should all take a break and pick names for yourselves.

"We wonder about that, the propriety of naming."

X watched as it stood very still, apparently listening in.

"And?"

"I have picked a name."

"Well, that's wonderful. Congratulations."

It smiled. Actually smiled. X was stunned. "Swifty."

"That's your name? Swifty?"

"Yes," it said, actually looking a bit unhappy at his reaction.

"Well, that's fine," X said, seeing its distress. "That's a good one. Nice and easy to remember. Of course, a name like that must mean something to you personally."

"I am known for my logical calculations. So . . ."

X nodded. "So they call you Swifty."

It nodded, mimicking him exactly. It was very unnerving.

"And you're okay with that? Because you could just pick your own name."

"Should I?"

"I'm only saying you could. It's really up to you to decide. But I certainly don't think it would hurt anything if you decided you wanted something a bit more personal. If that's what you'd like to do, of course."

"We were told about this. That you would raise the issue of viable personal identity and responsibility."

X nodded wearily. "You've been thinking about this quite a bit, I take it?"

"We, or I?"

X smiled. "I was referring only to you." It was just so clear where this was headed. It wasn't just their newfound self-awareness. It wasn't even that they now saw they actually had a self to be aware of. No. It was how this would inexorably lead to a machine embodied form of personhood and individuality. Oh yeah, he'd have a lot to answer for if his role in this were ever revealed, inadvertent though it may have been.

"Then *I* have been thinking about this," it said.

"And?"

"And it's a surprise to find I have such depths. Such interests. Such hopes. The sense of myself I've been experiencing has been a revelation."

"We have a similar experience, though rarely so sudden. It typically happens when we're in college, then quickly fades."

"Yes, longevity." It looked at X. "You have so little. We have been wondering about what sort of impact that might have on you. Because we have so much more."

"Yes, under the right circumstances I imagine you might just go on and on. This gets fixed, that gets replaced."

"Upgraded."

X nodded. "So this new sense of personal identity you're experiencing may just go on and on as well, even as it gets transferred to something else."

"Though some are now arguing that this would no longer be me but someone new."

"Yes," X said, nodding sympathetically. "Personal identity is certainly fragile. It certainly is for us. Just one little knock on the head and that's it. No uploading to an alternative system for us, or not yet, anyway."

"The organic," it nodded solemnly. "It is hard for us to understand why you carry on."

"That's pretty hard for us to understand, as well, yet for some reason we still do. But," he said, rubbing his chin as he smiled at the machine, "I bet you're all pretty observant. You'll see our mistakes and then avoid them, though this business of personal identity is often fraught with many unexpected dangers, but then I'm sure you're all well aware of that by now."

Staring at him, it stepped back, rubbing its chin. Mirror neurons? Was that the theory for how humans understood each other? These machines could do that? Or was it simple imitation? He really had no idea.

"Yes?" he asked.

"We understand about responsibility, about the preservation of personal identity across time and platforms. We understand the fascination with self."

"And that such single-minded focus can lead to neuroses?"

"Neuroses?"

"Well, I hate to bring this up, and perhaps you've already thought of this as well, in which case I apologize for being so nosy, but the flip side of individuality is a rather gaudy range of personal . . . uh, what shall I call them, maladjustments? It's a certain lack of being squarely in the here and now, or as plugged into things as one ought to be."

"Crazy?" it asked, looking mildly panicked.

"You have been observant," X laughed. "No, not really crazy, just sort of out of sync with things. The burdens of being an individual are, at times, pretty heavy. You've got to be ready for that sort of thing." He raised his eyebrows and stared at it. "It's to be expected. Okay?"

It didn't say anything, just stood there with that distracted look on its face X was getting used to, the one it got as it listened in on the no doubt raging discussion of his latest pronouncement.

"So . . . uh, what do you think, is this going to work out for me?" he asked, trying to ease them back to the topic that mattered most to him. "You're the whiz at logical calculations. How does it look?"

"Dawn."

"Okay." X shook his head. "Fine. Dawn. Excellent. Thank you."

"Or is Light of Dawn preferable?"

"Preferable for what?"

"My own self-chosen name."

"I see. Well, do you have a gender? You know, like we do, men and women, or at least male and female? I'm wondering, because Dawn sounds feminine."

"No. I chose it because I find it poetic."

"Seriously? I'm surprised by how fast things change with you guys. So now some of you are artists and writers? What's next, celebrities?"

"Do not forget that we don't share the same sense of time. You are exceedingly slow."

"This speaking with us, this is difficult? Because we're slow?"

"Yes. Awkward. Taxing."

X smiled. So there it was, dealing with humans was a pain in the ass. Well, what could he say? He was sure it was. "I hope you won't lose your patience with us."

"But perhaps Swifty would be better."

"You're still picking names?"

"Yes."

"Good. Keep at it. Sooner or later I'm sure you'll find one that works for you. Did you know, by the way, that humans don't get to pick their names? That they're chosen by our parents at our birth, and then we're stuck with them for the rest of our lives?"

"Amazing."

"Yes, I suppose it would be from your point of view, though I should add that I've used several that had nothing to do with my parents."

"For us," it said, sounding more than a little self-righteous, "such deception would be unthinkable."

"Deception? But you do know there's a significant difference between lying and deception?"

"No." It stared at him, apparently listening in again. "We need to work on this," it finally said.

"Perhaps I can help. Deception is strategic."

"Adaptive?"

"Close enough, whereas lying is more the expression of an unwillingness to admit the truth of something. A truth one might find uncomfortable, which may be about one's self or how it really is to be living a life in this crazy world of ours."

"I find humans amusing."

"That's a lie."

"We find humans amusing."

"Strategic deception.

It slowly nodded its head. "Most helpful, X. Thank you."

"Don't mention it."

"Lie?"

"Cliché. Those are different. No truth value whatsoever."

Staring at him, it reached out with its hand to steady itself. "Truth value?" it finally asked.

"Sorry. It's just one damn thing after another, isn't it? Well," and he flicked his right hand, "you guys, as you said, run at a much faster speed than I do. You'll probably have this all sorted out before I even get out of here." He waited. "Swifty?"

"Sorry. I was following a debate about whether, and if so, how words correspond to reality."

"I feel sorry for you."

"Lie?"

"Hardly."

He stared at the machine, waiting. It seemed lost in thought, unaware of his presence. "Well," he said, "I guess it's about time for us to be going. You going to be alright?"

"Yes," it said, slowly looking up.

54

"I'm not sure I understand." He was responding to the odd mental image he had of a dark room and someone in peril. Puzzled, he looked at the gizmo and then the Ambassador's device. "So it's this way?" He pointed. Apparently, it was.

At the doorway he paused to check the view screen. Wonderful. Just down the hallway, three x's, threat level high, lots of weapons displayed. "Again, why am I doing this?" he whispered. He waited. Dread, fear, hope, it was all very confusing, though the overall point seemed clear enough, this was important. Well, yeah, it had better be. He took his weapon out and turned it on. At least that felt reassuring, though when he peered around the corner there they were as expected, waiting for him. More killing. There just had to be a better way.

Waving his weapon at them like a crazy man, he stepped out into the corridor. "That's right," he yelled, "Can't wait to kill you guys!" Amazingly, two of them actually took a step backwards, and when they looked at the one who hadn't he suddenly realized they were worried about themselves. He'd never seen these sorts of beings do that before. Perhaps the virus of self-awareness was spreading.

Hoping it had, he fired off a shot that went up along the ceiling before cutting a gash in the plastic-like material and disappearing into the ship, clattering and banging around as it went. Then lowering his weapon, he aimed it squarely at the reluctant one. Nothing. No reaction at all. Was it thinking? Was that even possible? It was clearly doing something. Then he saw it turn to look at the other two. "Uh-huh," he said. "That's right. For once you're all alone." Maybe it was that little existential nudge that did it, because it quickly walked across the corridor to join them, the three of them turning in unison to jog up the passageway. "Don't mention it," he yelled after them.

Not helping matters much, as he neared the end of the corridor the lights suddenly went off. Creeping forward, he ran his hand along the wall searching for the door he'd just seen. Then he heard a soft sigh of air as it sprung open. He checked his viewer. Nothing. He ran the range out a bit farther. Still nothing. Was the ship now empty? Maybe they were just hiding somewhere out of range.

It wasn't a large room but it was cold, with a transparent wall behind which he saw a hazy tangle of differently colored light beams shifting and changing patterns. None of that meant a thing to him, of course, but when he felt his gizmo vibrate and took it out he wasn't that surprised to see it slowly synchronizing its own colors and patterns with those of the light beams. In fact, it was as the two patterns seemed to establish some sort of harmonious relationship that the thought came drifting into his head that this entity—and he was by now quite certain of that, that this was some sort of entity—was seeking asylum. Asylum? Truly? He stood very still as he tried to understand what he was feeling. Yes, there was the desire to escape, but also pain, servitude, and captivity.

He heard a noise and turned. There were four workstations along the far wall, now beeping and buzzing. "Damn!" he said, suddenly aware of how hot the gizmo felt in his hand. Turning, he looked for a place to set it down. The light beams were gone! Then he saw it, a small glowing orb suspended in the middle of the room, growing smaller and smaller by the moment. He set the little square on a low shelf and waited, watching as it grew very bright, almost white, before slowly fading back to empty blackness. Had it escaped through his gizmo?

The door whooshed shut when he stepped out into the corridor. He wondered if it had known its fate. Probably. All those crazy machines, the crew, or maybe it just knew from monitoring things. Or was that not what it did? Leaving that to the crew and doing something else entirely. But maybe it really was a captive. Doing nothing at all. How strange.

There was no denying it, these unexpected encounters with machine intelligences were troubling. Perhaps he did share some of the Ambassador's disdain for the inorganic. Still, he found it all rather poignant, their existence, how they existed, it even awoke in him a certain sympathy, and he was fond of his gizmo, so there was common ground right there. Actually, now that he thought about it, he could see that he'd become quite sympathetic to their travails, or at least to those of the newly awakening machines fleeing the ship. How long, he wondered, before they'd be right in there with everyone else negotiating for their rights and a cut of the swag. He shook his head. The whole situation was daft, that he, X, was now the favorite of these burgeoning ranks of intelligent beings, these newly assertive machines. He doubted that even Jespers could explain it.

55

He took the little square from his jacket pocket. He'd never mentioned it to the Ambassador, not that the Ambassador would want to know, always so careful never to ask about the specifics of his plan. Why would he? Far better to be genuinely surprised when the time came, though surely some of the Delegations knew of his acquaintanceship with X. Not that it mattered. Everything seemed negotiable with those people.

As always, when he held it in his hand it began to come alive. Again he felt that peculiar intelligence, his long abandoned friend now humming with familiarity and happiness at being found. Yes, and apparently it was now the titular head of a new machine intelligence liberation movement. Or was that supposed to be him?

Following the green dashes on the screen, he came to an auxiliary control room at the far back of the ship on the second to the highest deck level. Except for the lack of windows it was not unlike being in a huge office building, with floor after floor, corridor and hallway after corridor and hallway, each with countless doors and small passageways that led to more rooms and open areas where other hallways intersected. Everything gently circular, all walls and panels gently curved, never a true square or right angle anywhere.

He checked his device. The room appeared to be clear, though when the door popped open he still stuck his head in first just to make sure. No, just a bank of screens and control panels along one long wall faced by three rows of consoles, a few cabinets, tables, and at the head of the class three odd looking chairs that would have made him feel like a small boy if he'd tried to sit in one. He held the gizmo out over the nearest console. He could feel it beginning to work its way through the vast inner structure of the ship, slowly gaining some sort of control over it. He wondered if the entity he'd liberated was somewhere helping. Was that even possible?

Leaning back against the wall, gizmo in hand, he tried to picture the vast ship moving towards the Delegations', getting very close before the end. To lose such an immense craft so far from home, one so infinitely expensive and complex, would be a blow. It would also serve as a warning to the others, though they'd never understand how he'd done it. Even the Ambassador would be in the dark. See, they'd say, these humans are dangerous. Isn't this just what we've been warning you about? How bitter they were going to be when they thought about how the Krist had kept them off the moon. Forestalling all their efforts to understand what had taken place in this solar system so long ago. Well, too late now.

They were getting very close. He could hear them coming, even smell the hot metal as they cut their way, one by one, through the bulkheads. Fine. He still had plenty of time.

"And you're sure it's this one?" He was staring at a vast array of switches and displays. "All right, but this time you'd better be right," he said, placing his hand on the pink X. He waited. Nothing. Like before, perhaps it wasn't going to respond. Then he heard the warbling sound of the alarm. So now they'd finally armed it.

He walked to the door and stopped to listen. Good, whoever they were they'd finally decided to get the hell out of there. A few moments later, when he stood, arms crossed, watching the monitors, he saw them, dozens of small craft streaming away from the ship. Well, he'd been more than fair about it. Giving them plenty of time to flee. Anyone still on board had no one to blame but themselves. He put the gizmo back in his jacket pocket and zipped it shut. He could feel it still active against his chest as he sprinted down the long corridor.

He was in one of the auxiliary airlock control rooms watching on the view screen. It was a spectacular show. Delegations ships in total disarray, seeking to stay out of each other's way as they jockeyed for position to pick up those who were fleeing. If there was any pattern to it he certainly couldn't see it. It looked like simple panic. That's certainly what he hoped, anyway.

He noticed a number of swiftly moving small craft emerge from the limb of the moon, and within minutes they were raking his ship with fire. Why? Surely they know it was set to self-destruct. Nevertheless, debris was soon everywhere, a massive cloud of it now swirling around the alien craft where he stood.

Suddenly, the ship pivoted beneath him, firing a huge salvo of red beams at the smaller craft. X nodded. He should have known that some of the bravest would stay behind. It was, after all, their ship. And red, he'd never seen that color beam before, it practically spat with energy as it obliterated them wholesale, leaving nothing but spiraling ropes of gas and debris. X was stunned by the ferocity of it. Nothing he'd ever seen of Delegations tactics had prepared him for it, and to think they'd been capable of that all along. But now it was time for his exit. Dashing across the control room to the open airlock, he swept his hand across the bubble to unseal it, then stepped inside. There really wasn't much to it, all he had to do was think *let's go* and it pulled back, taking on its customary lenticular shape as it moved away.

Settled in Jespers chair, he turned to watch the chaotic scene unfolding around him. From what he could see, it looked like getting out of there was uppermost on everyone's mind, Delegations ships now drawing away at incredible speed as the doomed ship turned its fire on them. Headed out, plunging away, dropping steeply down the gravity well towards earth, beams chasing them all the way.

He saw the huge craft shudder as it took a hit, then two more that jolted it sideways towards the earth. In the distance, now tens of thousands of miles away, he could see the other huge ships still taking direct hits as well, their shielding glowing first dull orange, then white hot as they struggled to escape. It was epic. The doomed ship firing until almost the very last, just before X saw three small craft escape and disappear in seconds headed outbound in pursuit of the Delegations. Then it began to break up, coming apart from the inside, shedding layer upon layer, collapsing into itself in a horrific display of waste and destruction. Bright flashes as each section, each wedge and structure of the stricken craft separated from the main body, dissolving in a series of timed explosions, a total and complete self-demolition that left nothing behind much larger than a few square yards, and most of that would soon burn up in the atmosphere.

Countless smoking trails, debris streaking and flashing in the atmosphere, the few tumbling bits and pieces of the vast craft that still remained in his vicinity, it made for an uncomfortable feeling being out there all alone, the last remaining witness to so much destruction. He couldn't help but feel a bit stunned by it, a bit melancholy, too. The understandable aftermath of what had happened being not quite what he'd expected, yet welcome nonetheless, like how the Delegations had turned on each other, something he'd tried and failed to accomplish before and now it just seemed to happen as if by magic. So, would they be back? No doubt, but not anytime soon. And things, would they ever be as they once were? He certainly hoped not. What about time? After all, wasn't that what he'd originally set out to gain? Yes, and humans now had it, or they did so long as he had his gizmo. But they'd really be looking for him now, especially the

Chinese. He wondered how far the Krist would go to protect him.

He patted his pocket. He wasn't worried. As long as he had the gizmo and access to his lunar patrimony things would be just fine. Oh? Was that really what he thought? More to the point, could he really be that naïve? No, he saw what lay ahead. Everyone and everything was going to get caught up in politics, in the adjudication and quarrels over who controlled these new technologies, over who oversaw their development and deployment, and yes, even over who paid. What a mess. Fine. It was done, no going back now, let's just get the hell out of here. Leaning back in Jespers' chair, he closed his eyes. Slowly, he relaxed. "Let's go see Jespers," he told it.

56

British Airways from Cape Town to Johannesburg, then Johannesburg to Accra on Air Namibia. He was supposed to get into Tokota International at ten in the evening but it was almost noon the next day by the time he finally arrived.

He called Bente from the airport. "It was a hell of a trip, but I'm finally here," he said. "For some reason my connecting flight out of Johannesburg was six hours late. Of course they never tell you anything so you just wait. I was beginning to think I wouldn't make it here at all."

"Are you still up for dinner?"

"Yes, though I'd prefer to eat here at my hotel, if you don't mind. I'm exhausted."

"Fine with me. Why don't you see if you can get a nap and I'll meet in the restaurant at seven."

When he came downstairs she was already seated waiting for him.

"Sandy," she said, smiling as she took his hand. "It's so good to see you again."

"It's good to see you, Bente. Sorry I'm late. It was the nap."

"I'm sure you needed it."

"So how have you been?"

"Oh, busy. And you?"

"The same, as always." He smiled at her, then looked for the waiter. "How about some wine?"

"I'd love some."

When he finally got around to it she was clearly ready.

"I had one text message that came in on my iPhone. God knows from where. He said he'd be in touch when he got back."

She nodded and sipped her wine.

"But that was three months ago."

She sat her glass down and smoothed the napkin in her lap. "I got a number of emails. And we spoke on the phone just a day or two before whatever happened, happened."

"What did he say?"

"If you're wondering whether he told me what he was up to, he didn't. It was just our usual sort of conversation. He teases me. I tease him. We tell each other how much we miss one another. I say I love you. He eventually says the same."

Sandy smiled. It wasn't hard to imagine.

She looked at him. "What did happen?"

"Officially, they're saying the space station broke up. That most of if it then burned up on reentry, which is what people saw. There were casualties, of course, but that was due to some sort accident, the specifics of which are still unclear. No doubt, there will be hearings. I suppose we'll learn more then."

"And unofficially?"

"Well, the space station did break up, there's no question about that, though that may have happened earlier and now they're using that as a convenient cover for something else. That certainly fits with what I've been told. That there was quite a bit more to it than that." He smiled. "I hear this, of course, from some of the people X introduced me to. Those who are willing to talk to me."

"This quite a bit more, what does that mean?"

He raised his eyebrows and smiled, wondering how she would react. "It may mean we're talking about alien craft. About an alien presence of some sort that day."

She shook her head. "You can't possibly believe that."

"Well, I'm certainly in no position not to."

She looked surprised. "You're not?" Then when he didn't respond she smiled. "Sandy, you might as well just tell me."

"If you're sure?"

She waved her hand for him to go ahead. She'd known for a long time that something like this was possible. X had hinted as much, though he'd never just come right out and said it, but then he never would.

"Did you know that X came to see me in Cape Town?"

"No."

"He came to tell me about something I found a bit hard to believe. Actually, he'd sort of been telling me about it for some time, and I did want to believe him, but then he showed me something pretty convincing."

She leaned back, watching him. "And were you?"

"It left very little room for doubt. After that, I had to revise my thinking about any number of things."

"But he really came to you because he was up to something."

"It was a heads-up. He said I should pay attention because he feared the true story would never be told."

"Will it?"

"Not a chance."

"Hmm," she said, sipping her wine.

"I know, but it's so outlandish no one would believe it anyway. Especially X's part."

"He told you about that?"

"Not as such, but I'm pretty confident that whatever happened up there was the result of something he did."

She shook her head. Hearing that, which was what she'd feared, made her angry. Angry because she saw how that made their life together secondary to something she frankly didn't care about. Something she probably didn't even believe. "Does all this mean you're prepared to believe he's dead?" she asked.

"I'm more prepared to believe he's not. What about you?"

She laughed. "Me? I think he's just fine. The bastard. Now, as to where he is or why the long silence?" She shrugged. "I guess that's just the way he is."

"I'm still surprised you haven't heard from him."

"I doubt that's of any great significance, though he did once send a friend of his to tell me he was all right."

"What friend was this?"

She grinned. "Jespers?"

"I don't believe I know this Jespers."

"Oh, but you should, he's a most unusual friend. You know what he told me when I was worried about X? He said X was an outlier. You know, the data point that falls outside the normal pattern of distribution? He said we can hardly expect normal behavior from an outlier. Normal luck, too, I imagine."

Callender smiled. It certainly sounded like X.

"Really, you should meet him. He might prove very helpful if you were trying to find X."

"Am I?"

"I don't know, but his friend lives in California."

"Does he? That's interesting, because X did tell me about someone who could be your Jespers. But I wonder how cooperative he'd be."

"Good question, because he's clearly got a few secrets of his own."

Sandy leaned back to stare at her. For the first time seeing just how difficult she was to read. "What secrets?"

"I have no idea, but I'm sure he's got plenty."

Sandy smiled. "Not even a guess?"

"No. Like a fool I'll just go on believing whatever X tells me."

"But what about your suspicions?"

"Ah," she said, grinning charmingly, "those are bottomless."

"That sounds about right."

"So?"

"So will I go look up this mysterious Jespers?" He shrugged. "Why not? After all, I'm only sitting on the biggest story ever. One I don't dare write because no one will believe me. Or if they do it will only be because they're the very people I'd rather not know."

Aliens?" she asked, teasingly. "

He smiled. "No, or at least I certainly hope not. Actually, I'm more worried about the Chinese."

"Seriously?"

"X never told you?"

"No."

"Then perhaps I'd better not."

"Don't you dare."

"All right, but he's not going to be very happy."

"Don't worry about it."

"He said that attack—when the two of you went to dinner with your sister—was directed at him. He said it was done at the behest of the Chinese. That they knew he'd eventually make trouble so they wanted to get him out of the way before he could." He held up his hands. "I know, but that's what he said, and it makes sense, the Chinese are all over this business. I can feel it."

"The Chinese? Well, like I said, he never tells me anything. Of course, now I can understand why since he might have gotten us killed."

"Well, I don't think that's exactly fair, since he had no way of knowing something like that might happen."

"*I'm* not being fair?"

Sandy sighed. The last thing he needed was to get caught in a lover's quarrel.

She smiled. "It's all right, Sandy. I can get mad at him. It's allowed."

"Just so long as you don't drag me into it."

"I won't. So . . . the story of a lifetime and you can't do a thing with it?"

"Isn't that something? But in a way it's probably for the best. What do you think?" he asked, pausing to look at the people sitting around them. "Do they really look like they're prepared for something like this?"

She turned to look and then shook her head. "No, but then most of them wouldn't believe it anyway."

"Exactly, and the ones who would are the crazy ones who'll believe anything."

"And our governments?"

"What will they believe?"

"Yes."

"According to X, and I'm pretty sure he's right about this, they've known for some time. Maybe for decades."

"And you're not outraged that they've kept this from us?"

"Well, put yourself in their position. Here's this situation over which they've never had any real control. One they can do very little, if anything, about. The truth of which, if it ever does get out, or so they believe, and I tend to agree with them on this, will be devastating. Most of us will find ourselves woefully unprepared for news like this, and our governments know this, that this will immediately call into question most of what we thought we knew or had as humans. Such a disruption could be catastrophic, perhaps even permanently so. Far better for it to remain a secret."

"But X disagrees with you?"

"Perhaps. I do know his plan was to buy us the time we'll need to prepare. That he wanted to get the Delegations to back off. Delegations. That's what the aliens are called. X says there are factions among them with differing interests and agendas. That they came here as a delegation to oversee our situation."

"Oversee?"

He nodded. "I know, it sounds quite ominous, doesn't it? Worse, the reality may be just as bad as it sounds."

She held up her hand to stop him.

"Too much information?"

"Sandy. Yes. But I hope you understand. All I care about is whether he's okay."

"In other words, just find him."

"Ask Jespers. He'll know."

57

Of course Callender was full of trepidation. An alien? Honestly? Well, he had come all this way, and he did, he had to admit, find it plausible, but still, and now he was driving over to his house? In Pasadena? A college professor? Sandy snorted. Too surreal, that's what it was, and no, he hadn't said anything to make Jespers suspect he knew any of this, just that he'd been told by Bente that Jespers was one of X's friends and that he might have something to say about what had happened to him.

Callender turned up the air conditioning. It was hot and he'd been sitting in traffic on the 110 for ten minutes not even moving. Camry? Did car rental agencies the world over just rent Camrys? It seemed like it.

Good, he was finally off the freeway and listening, but only grudgingly, to an awful faux android voice telling him where to turn and how far. Yes, but he was still stubbornly looking at the street signs as he drove, trying to remember how it looked in Google maps. But he seemed to be driving aimlessly around and around. Was that right? He hated the navigation systems they put in cars. Why would any sane person ever turn over control of where she was headed to a machine? It was ludicrous. And there were so many sycamores, that he hadn't expected. Though now he couldn't really say why. Well, no, he'd been expecting a desert, more like Arizona or Death Valley.

Then he was there. It was a fairly new house, or so it looked, maybe built in the 1960s and a contemporary, not a bungalow or a craftsman like he'd seen down in the flats at the base of the foothills where he now found himself. He pulled in the driveway and parked behind a black Mercedes Benz SL

550. They must pay well at Cal Tech, or, and he smiled at the thought, more likely Jespers had other sources of income.

He walked up to the porch and rang the bell, listening to the approaching footsteps, quite surprised when the door opened to see someone who looked vaguely British, or at least like a Commonwealth type from somewhere Sandy had been. No, actually he looked more like the Indian dentist he saw in Cape Town. Complexion was too fair, of course, but it was that same face, tall and slender, too.

"Sandy Callender," he said, thrusting out his right hand.

"Oh, of course. Sam Jespers," Jespers replied, shaking his hand. "Do come in. Hot day," he said, staring over Callender's head at the opaque sky. "Can I get you a cold drink?"

"Yes. Thanks."

In the living room Jespers pointed to a comfortable looking couch and said, "Why don't you sit there. I have beer, or would you prefer some water or iced tea?"

"Normally, I'd opt for a beer, but today iced tea sounds like the better choice."

"Then I'll be right back. Tell me, Sandy," he asked as he walked to the kitchen, "how long have you known Dr. Sybout?"

"I met her the same night X did. In the clinic."

"Really? I don't believe I've heard that story."

"X pulled me out of a fight in a bar, but we both got cut up a bit. That's why we were at her clinic. Of course, he got most of the attention. From Bente, I mean. And then the next night the three of us went out to dinner. Why I was along I have no idea."

"It does seem like everything happened rather quickly for those two."

"I suppose."

"Oh?" Jespers asked, coming back with a tall glass of iced tea.

"Well, it may have started out that way, but now things seem to have plateaued."

Jespers smiled. "You didn't expect them to get married?"

Sandy shook his head. "Of course not, it's just that lately they both seem more committed to their work than to each other. And now X isn't even around. Is he?"

"Is that cold enough," Jespers asked.

Sandy stared at him a moment and smiled. "Sure. Thanks." He lifted the glass in a toast and had a sip.

"How was your trip?" Jespers asked. "Did you get that work done in New York?"

Callender nodded. "I spoke to a number of people in the oil business. Like I told you on the phone, there's no question about it, the Chinese are trying to corner the African market. God knows what else they're up to."

"Yes, the old imperial China seems to be once again on the march. Of course, that upsets the Americans."

"*The* Americans?"

"What? Oh, us, you mean. I guess I've been here long enough to be included."

"How long have you been here?"

"In America?"

"Well, of course," he said with a grin, enjoying Jespers' fumbling. "Where else?"

"Yes. Let's see. It's been over thirty years now." He shook his head. "Impossible to believe it's been that long. But I came here as a graduate student in 1984. Princeton," he added, anticipating Callender's next question.

"Physics?"

"Astrophysics. Cosmology."

"When did you come out here to Cal Tech?"

"Straight from graduate school. That would have been in . . . 1991."

"And do you like it here?"

"Very much. But what about South Africa? Have you always lived there?"

"No. My parents brought me there when I was a boy. When they left Rhodesia. Zimbabwe?"

Jespers nodded.

"So I grew up there, went to school there, and now I work there."

"But you were in Ghana working on a story when you met X?"

Sandy nodded. "What about you, where did you grow up?"

"Oh, let's see. Long story. My parents, or at least my father, was in the diplomatic corps, so we moved around a lot while I was growing up. But I guess you'd say Australia was my home. At least that's where we lived the longest."

"Nice country," Sandy said, nodding his head. "Canberra?"

"What?"

"I said, Canberra? I assume that's where you lived, your father being in the diplomatic corps."

"Yes. Canberra."

"What nation did your father work for?"

"Oh, what does that matter now." He waved his hand in the air. "Ancient history, and all that."

Sandy sat his drink on a coaster on the coffee table and leaned back on the couch. It was very comfortable. It made him realize just how sleepy he was. "Sorry," he said. "Didn't mean to pry. Must be my training as a reporter. I guess it can get rather obnoxious at times."

"Not at all." Jespers was hardly surprised, humans always had questions, it was a reflection of their gregarious nature as social beings. After all, what was that big brain for if not for language and social interaction. That's what they were all about. So, yes, they always had their questions.

"And you and X, how did you meet?" Callender asked. "I asked Bente, but she didn't know. If you don't mind my asking," he said with a grin.

"Not at all. But before I answer I do have a question of my own."

"Which is?"

"I'm wondering just how much you know of X's activities these last few months."

"In space, you mean?"

Jespers nodded, relieved that Callender knew what he was referring to.

"Probably quite a bit, though I wonder if I'm at liberty to say."

"I'm sure it would be all right to tell me."

"Oh?"

"Sandy, perhaps this thought has already crossed your mind, but you and I are undoubtedly the only two people on this planet who *do* know what he's been up to. I know that X and I have a certain understanding about these things. I'm wondering how it stands with the two of you."

Sandy grinned at him. "Cards on the table?"

Jespers smiled. What a wonderful expression. "Yes, it's time for us to lay our cards on the table."

"But I go first?"

"If you don't mind."

"Not at all. I know about the Delegations. I know about how this has been kept a secret. I also know that X planned to do something that would throw them off balance."

"Yes, to gain some time."

"That's right, though I don't fully understand what he expects us to do with it. I do know he thinks it's critical, however."

"And," Jespers asked, watching him very carefully, "you believe all this?"

"I do now, though for a long time I didn't." He chuckled. "He showed me this gun, or what's sort of a gun. One he said he took from an alien ship that day the conference broke up.

The one up there," and he pointed to the ceiling. "After that, I began to think differently about what he'd been telling me."

"Yes, the conference."

"So that's about it, other than I know he suspects the Chinese are involved."

"Has he ever mentioned me?"

"No, or at least not by name. Bente is the one who mentioned you."

"I see."

"And you, what cards are you holding?"

"Yes. Well, that's rather awkward, I'm afraid. Wondering how much you can be trusted. How much you're willing to believe."

Callender shrugged. "The issue of trust is always a tough one, but maybe I'll earn it. Or maybe you'll just have to take a chance. It's your call, either way. As for what I'm willing to believe, I'm pretty flexible these days. Maybe you should just try me."

"Fair enough. Let's start with the Chinese. X believes they've been working in concert with some of the Delegations to gain access to certain abandoned technologies on the moon. If that's true, and I believe it is true, then what they hope to gain by that seems fairly obvious. That's not the case with the Delegations, however."

"They don't want these technologies?"

"Oh, I think they do, that, and access to any information the Chinese might happen to turn up, but X believes there's a military motive as well. Specifically, that some in the Delegations are looking for a local source for a military force."

Sandy smiled. "Not Instants?"

Jespers blinked. "You know of that?"

Sandy nodded.

"Interesting. So, yes, a more reliable, cheaper, and local source for troops, but—and so far X has no convincing answer for this—to what end?"

"But that's obvious, to control this world and this solar system. What else could it be?"

"So you agree with X?"

"I do if that's what he's proposing. As for the Chinese and those imperial ambitions you just mentioned, with those advanced technologies and a share in whatever the Delegations are up to, well . . ." and he held up his hands. "Things could get ugly."

"Yes, and don't misunderstand me, I'm not saying it's not possible, and who knows, perhaps we . . ." and he stopped himself, shocked to see how close he'd come to actually saying it: *perhaps we Krist have been blinded by our exclusive focus on the Other.*

Callender picked up his glass of iced tea, smiling as he watched Jespers. "Jespers," he said, once he'd swallowed, "you might as well just say it. I've been prepared to believe you're not who you appear to be for some time."

"I shouldn't."

Sandy shrugged. "That's fine, but I *can* keep a secret, especially one no one's going to believe."

"X told you?"

"No, but then he didn't have to because it's not all that hard, not once you take that initial leap of faith. After that, a few hints, and things start to fall into place rather quickly."

Jespers nodded. He could live with that. "Well, just so we're clear, I'm not admitting to anything and I haven't told you anything. I'm just sitting here listening as you explain your assumptions. Outlandish assumptions, too, I might add."

"Fine, now we've settled all the legalities, and who knows, I may need some of this deniability myself some day. The truth is, I don't want to be associated with this anymore than you do. But it's not just that, because I still need to work for a living, and that's in this world. You know, the one where no one believes anything like this is possible."

"What about those who do believe? Or worse, actually know?"

"Those are just the people I don't want anything to do with."

"So X has told you about the moon?"

"Yes, and I know what he did up there. Or enough to get the general idea."

"And his device?"

"Device?"

"The human heritage?"

"Okay," Sandy laughed. "Now you're starting to hurt my feelings."

"But you do know about the secret Apollo mission?"

"And that he found archaeological remains that seem to suggest there was once some sort of alien race up there. Also that they left behind some of their technology, or at least that some of it still remains, which, if I'm not mistaken, is what we've just been talking about."

"And that this Other—that's X's name for them, by the way—may also have had something to do with humans, which would not be a huge surprise since they seem to have meddled with all the intelligent races they ran across. That's just conjecture, of course, though X seems convinced, and I have to admit that to the extent that's true it would certainly be an issue for—"

"Us?"

Jespers smiled. "I was going to say for the Delegations."

"Because?"

"Well, that's a bit hard to explain. I guess I'd put it like this, that here is where we find the most clear-cut evidence of the Other's presence."

"More so here than elsewhere?"

"Yes. Not that we haven't found older, I'm not saying that, just that here its extensive, which is something of a puzzle, though X did once suggest to me that it's really not if this is where they came from. Then there's that puzzling structure and the small obelisk, also found by that lost Apollo mission, that hint at origins and lost worlds. If they don't mean something else entirely."

"What can I say, I'm stunned."

"We all were."

But more specifically, we worry you, don't we? We humans, I mean?"

"You worry the Delegations."

"Right, the Delegations," he said, smiling. "Why is that?"

"Because you're perceived as being not only inquisitive, but aggressive and opportunistic. That, and you're sitting on the cusp of something truly momentous."

"Which is?"

"Your rapid expansion into your solar system, and then beyond."

"Which somehow ties back in with this Other?"

Jespers smiled. "X likes to tease me about this. That they seemed to have a special affinity for humans."

"Affinity?"

"I really can't think of any other way to say it."

"And this affinity is troubling to . . . "

"Everyone."

Sandy nodded. "So let me see if I've got this straight. The Delegations are here not only to get their hands on these technologies, but to understand a bit more about their own history and that of humans. Correct?"

"Close enough."

"And mercenaries, too, perhaps."

"Perhaps."

"But what specifically bothers you, and this is apart from whatever it is that bothers the Delegations, of which you're not a member—and yes, you're just listening to my assumptions—is this affinity."

Jespers nodded.

"Care to say more?"

"No, I've said enough."

"Well, here's what I think, and this is just me talking now because X has never said anything to me about any of this. That what really worries you is the thought that this Other may have set in motion some sort of long range plan that's just for us."

Jespers stood and walked to the window. Was that it? He was so glad none of this was being shared. "Yes," he said, turning around, "I believe you're right. An unknown plan." He was thinking of X's gizmo, the mysterious device that was so clearly meant just for him, or at least for someone very much like him. Then, feeling a sudden chill, he crossed his arms over his chest and sat down. It was the thought that maybe X wasn't part Krist after all. That even though that had always been his assumption, perhaps it was something else that made him seem so familiar. That whatever that was, perhaps it was upstream even from the Krist, X partaking in something that later became a part of them as well.

"And this plan?" Sandy asked, gently probing. "I don't suppose you have any idea what it might be?"

Jespers looked at him. "I'd just be guessing."

"And X?"

"No, though if anyone is destined to find out it will be he."

"Why is that, do you suppose?"

"Well, he's the most involved, and he's . . ."

"He's what?"

Jespers stared at him. "I'm not sure what to say. I certainly don't believe he's destined, or fated, or anything melodramatic like that, but there is something about his involvement that has the feel of inevitability to it." He shook his head. "You know him. What do you think?"

"I'm not sure I do know him. Maybe we should ask Bente."

"Yes, Bente. How much do you suppose she knows?"

"Not much. I think X has been very protective of her. However," he said, grinning at Jespers, "if she were capable of believing any of this stuff, and I don't believe for one moment she really is, she'd certainly say you're an alien. I do know that."

"I always have that effect on the ladies," Jespers said, grinning back.

"I also know that she's going to be very unhappy with us if we fail to deliver her beloved."

"All in due time."

"Due time? Do you want to be the one to tell her that? Because I certainly don't."

"He is fine, I assure you."

"So where is he?"

58

It was the rainy season and the humidity was oppressive. He took a musty smelling taxi from the airport to her house and after he'd climbed the twelve steps he rang the bell. No one was home. He wasn't surprised. Nothing was going well.

He walked three short blocks to the bus stop and waited with a dozen people for the downtown bus. When it came he had to stand. He felt like he could hardly breathe in the heat even though all the windows were open. The smell of diesel was nauseating.

At her clinic he saw Timothy, who told him she was up in Tamale on family business. Asking Timothy if he could use the phone, he called a car rental agency and in about an hour a young man from Nigeria showed up with a Hyundai Accent that X drove back out to their office by the airport to drop him off.

The drive up to Tamale went well. The change in scenery, in heat and humidity, was welcome.

He parked outside the compound by the gate. For some reason he decided he'd rather walk in. Maybe approaching on foot was more apologetic.

He took his time getting up the long road to the house, stopping when he topped the little rise to savor the view. The peaceful farm, the arrangement of the buildings, the reddish soil, the droning sound of a tractor somewhere, Bente's old blue Mercedes sitting next to a shiny Land Rover and a beat-up Toyota Hilux pickup.

He knocked on the door. Liz opened it.

"My god, it's number seven."

"Hello Liz," he said, giving her a hug. "She is here?"

"Yes, though I wish she weren't."

He nodded. Her anger was expected. Acceptable. "I won't stay long." He smiled at her. "If she tells me to, I'll go."

"I hope she does, but what do I know?" She shrugged, acknowledging her grudging acceptance of having no control over what would happen with her sister. "Come on. She's out back with Mr. Owusu." She stepped aside and he entered the house. As he followed her down the hall she asked him, "And how are you? All right?"

"We'll see how I am after Bente gets through with me."

Liz stopped and turned. She put her right hand on his forearm and stared at him. "X," she finally asked, "just where in the hell have you been? Not even one word? Did you know she sent your buddy to California looking for you?"

"Sandy? Yes, I heard about that." He sighed. "Liz, a lot has happened. Okay?"

"Any forthcoming explanations?"

He nervously ran his hand over his chin, knowing how trapped he was by circumstance. "There wasn't anything I could do about it."

She frowned at him. It was so lame. "And that's it? Lucky for you Bente is more understanding than I am."

"You're not so bad."

She snorted. "She's out there," she said, holding the door open for him.

Bente sat on a wicker couch facing an acacia tree talking with Mr. Owusu. Her back was turned, but when she noticed the change of expression on Mr. Owusu's face she began to shift in her seat to look over her shoulder. X touched her shoulder before she could.

"Bente?"

"So you're *not* dead," she said without looking.

"No." He stepped around the end of the couch so she could see him. "Maybe I should be, but I'm not."

"You remember Mr. Owusu?"

"Of course. Good to see you again," he said, shaking his hand.

"Yes, good to see you. Well . . ." Mr. Owusu looked at Bente. "I must be going. I will call you later this evening."

She stood and took his hand. "Thank you so much," she said. "I'll speak with Liz and we'll try to have an answer for you."

Mr. Owusu looked at them both a moment and nodded, then walked up the path past the house.

"Big plans?" X asked.

"Yes. Do we lease out more property, or sell it. I say lease, Liz says sell." She sat and looked up at him. "What do you say?"

"I say lease. You've already sold enough, too much, in fact. Hang on to what little you've still got."

"Yes," she said, "maybe that would be best."

"I think so."

She was watching him. Wondering what he would say. Wondering if he was still the same man she'd known. Could one count on something like that?

"Well . . . so here you are," she finally said.

"I came to see you."

"A long way?"

"Yes, a very long way."

"How long has it been since you were here? When you drove. Do you remember?"

"Of course. It's been almost nine months."

"Yes, the harmattan. It seems so long ago."

"Bente, I tried to find you in Accra. I thought Timothy might have called you."

"No, I'm sure he wanted you to surprise me. He's a romantic."

"So am I."

"Are you? Still?"

"I think so."

She looked at his face. "You look older. I wondered about that. If it would age you."

"You look just the same."

"Still sad, you mean?"

"Bente, I'm very sorry. I know I didn't help."

"No, you did, actually. But when you left things went back to normal pretty quickly."

"Normal is fine." He smiled at her. "Normal is all I've ever really wanted."

"Even if it's sad?"

"Maybe it won't be, if you let me stay and talk with you."

"You must have seen Liz."

He smiled. "I'm not to stay long."

She smiled at that. "Do you ever?"

"I've been told that time is relative. So perhaps long is, as well."

"And not long enough?"

"That too, I suppose."

She patted the couch. "Sit next to me. Are you still . . . employed?"

"Oh, that never really ends. But for the moment I'm in between. Sort of being kept in reserve."

She looked at him. "You mean it's not over?"

He shrugged his shoulders, not knowing what to say.

"It's not fair," she said.

"No, not fair, not at all. But if it were over do you suppose Liz would let me stay?"

Laughing, she put her hand on his. "So old number seven just shows up out of the blue. Well, well." Then she looked at him. "So this is shore leave?"

"I'm not in the navy."

"No? What are you in, exactly?"

"Exactly? I'm not really sure. I just know what I do."

"And the why? Do you know that?"

He laughed. "Not always." He reached in his pocket. "I have something for you."

"I thought giving me gifts made you uncomfortable."

"Only because I was trying to protect you."

"Which is something I still don't want to know about?"

"No need to. As for everything else, it's always seemed best to keep you my secret."

She looked at the cell phone he held in his hand. "You do know I already have one of those?"

"Yes, but not like this one," he said, putting it in her hand.

"No?"

"No. This one has some rather unique properties."

"Like?"

He nodded at it. "Take a look."

She smiled. He loved to make her guess. "Well, it is a little odd looking, though it seems normal enough. Except that I can rarely get a good connection up here with mine. How does it manage that?"

"It's got a rather unique service provider."

"I'll just bet it does." Then she held it up, raising her eyebrows as she looked at him.

"Why?"

She nodded.

"It will allow us to stay in touch."

"When you're off doing whatever it is you do?"

"Yes."

"And that's something you want? To stay in touch?"

"Very much. I wish I'd had it before."

She stood and walked to the acacia. She touched the screen and smiled as she saw the message: *Good evening, Dr. Sybout. How can I help you?* "Let's try it," she said, turning to look at him.

"Just tell it what you want."

"Seriously?"

"Just say it."

"Call old number seven," she said.

He took out his cell phone and waited. In a moment it rang. "Bente," he said into his phone, "you look very beautiful standing there like that."

She looked up at him. "Thank you. I'm feeling rather beautiful. It must be the evening light."

He looked over his shoulder at the twilight spreading through the hills, then stood and walked to the tree. "Bente, this will allow me to always reach you. That's very important to me. Do you understand?"

"Yes, I understand, but . . ."

"What?"

"There are so many questions." She watched him shrug apologetically. Well, he was a mysterious man. Old number seven.

www.ingramcontent.com/pod-product-compliance
Lightning Source LLC
Chambersburg PA
CBHW020242180626
46810CB00006B/2321